THE DYING SEASON

A DETECTIVE KAY HUNTER CRIME THRILLER

RACHEL AMPHLETT

The Dying Season © 2022 by Rachel Amphlett

The moral rights of the author have been asserted.

This is a work of fiction. While the locations in this book are a mixture of real and imagined, the characters are totally fictitious. Any resemblance to actual people living or dead is entirely coincidental.

ONE

Martin Terry took a sip of Heineken, smacked his lips, and cast his gaze around the cramped battered interior of the remote pub.

Half past ten, a Wednesday night and – apart from a handful of people he didn't know by sight – the rest of the clientele comprised the usual suspects. That was normal for the time of year – summer brought the grockles, the tourists who swarmed through the Kentish villages and clogged the narrow lanes, leaving discordance and litter in their wake.

Here, now, in the cooler aftermath of late September that cloaked the North Downs, a more sedate atmosphere had descended on the hamlet and surrounding houses.

Martin leaned his elbow on the pockmarked wooden bar, then wrinkled his nose and tugged his shirt sleeve away from the sticky patch of spilt drink that pooled across the surface.

The drip trays under the lager taps in front of him stank, a tangy bitter stench of stale beer mixing with the aroma of someone's cheese and onion crisps from the table behind him turning his stomach.

In the background, a slot machine pinged and brayed while a pair of women in their twenties cackled and poked coins into it, the loose change clattering over the low voices around him.

Conversations were muted, a respectful distance being kept between the different groups gathered within the cramped space.

Talk here could mean anything from asking a favour to covering up for someone, and as Martin casually eyed the group of four elderly pensioners dressed in muted colours at the far end of the bar, he reckoned at least one of them was the poacher rumoured to have wrecked the barbed wire fencing over at the Parrys' property last week.

It had taken two days to locate their daughter's Shetland pony, and all because someone decided to drag a deer carcass across a field to avoid getting caught.

Nothing had been said in the pub, though.

The regulars were used to turning a blind eye, and the strangers who did venture inside on occasion rarely returned, such was the closed atmosphere that clung to the place.

The landlord, Len, nodded to him in passing, and Martin raised his half-empty glass in salute before watching the other man wrench open a low door behind the bar and disappear down the cellar steps in a hurry.

The sixty-year-old was adept at keeping his customers happy and the local police at bay, a skillset honed by the army.

So the rumour went, anyway.

Martin knew better than to ask.

A rush of cool air swept across his ankles as the solid oak door swung outwards. As always, the regulars paused their conversations to see who entered, then relaxed as a familiar pair of smokers ambled towards the bar reeking of nicotine, their habit satiated for the moment.

Lydia brushed past him, her dark hair tied into a top knot and her face flushed while she dashed towards a waiting middle-aged couple with two pints of ale.

'Why does everything run out at the same time?' she hissed under her breath.

'Stops you getting bored,' he replied, grinning when his wife rolled her eyes.

'That's what I tell her, but she don't listen,' Len grumbled, emerging from the cellar and wiping his hands on the tea-towel slung over his shoulder.

'About time, Len,' said one of the pensioners at the far end of the bar, an empty pint glass held out in hope. 'I'm dying of thirst here.'

'I should be so lucky, Geoff,' the landlord shot back, smirking as the old man's friends berated him. 'I'm almost done. Just let me check it first.'

Martin watched as the man reached up to the shelving suspended above the fifteenth-century bar and selected a half pint glass, wrapped his hand around the pump and eased it back.

The familiar golden hue of locally brewed ale flowed into the glass, sloshing against the sides and forming a thin foam.

Holding it to the light, he then took a sip, savouring the flavours.

When he turned around, Geoff Abbott and his three friends were staring at him, almost salivating.

'I'm not sure,' Len said, lowering the glass and frowning. 'Barrel might be off.'

'What?' Geoff's mouth dropped open, his bushy eyebrows flying upwards. 'You're joking.'

Len grinned. 'Four pints, is it?'

'You bastard. Get on and pour them before you ring the bell for last orders.'

Martin smiled at the familiar banter, thankful that for once the place was calm.

Too many times, Lydia had returned home telling him stories of punch-ups in the car park, threats that may or may not have been carried out, and more.

The one thing Len wouldn't stand for was drugs, so at least there was that.

It was why, for the most part, the police were never called – or better yet, didn't show up unannounced and uninvited.

There wasn't much that the landlord couldn't sort out himself, despite his age.

The scars that criss-crossed his sun-damaged features stood testament to the number of times Len had thrown himself into the middle of a brawl, often welcoming the same people back into the pub after only a week of being banned.

It was the way it was in here.

As far as Len was concerned, said Lydia, if people didn't like it then they could drink at the posh place down the road and pay more for their drinks.

Which was why this place stayed popular amongst the

stalwarts. It was cheap, and the tourists took one look at the ramshackle exterior as they drove by, then kept going.

Martin shook his head and turned in his seat to stretch his legs out, grateful for the chance to relax after a nine-hour shift stacking shelves.

There were about twelve people dotted around the tables spread throughout the pub, plus the four pensioners who sat anchored at the bar.

Two separate tables were taken by couples, heads bowed over their drinks as they spoke in low voices, the occasional giggle from one of the women carrying across to where he stood.

He ran his eyes over two men sitting beside the stone hearth, the grate filled with a dried flower arrangement Lydia had put together as a focal point during the summer months, most of it now scattered around the base of the vase, remnant twigs poking upwards in defiance.

He frowned.

Whatever it was the two men were discussing was proving problematic, the younger jabbing his finger at the other. His face was in shadow, and the other man had his back to Martin so he couldn't make out whether he knew him.

He looked away, checked the rest of the room for any trouble and then caught Lydia's eye and waved her over from where she had been standing by the till sipping a lemonade.

'Do you know the two blokes over by the fireplace?' he murmured.

She drained her drink, crossed to the dishwasher under the bar to his left and then returned, shaking her head.

'Never seen either of them before,' she said. 'Trouble?'

He wrinkled his nose. 'Heated conversation.'

'I'll give Len a heads-up.' She glanced over her shoulder towards the clock on the wall. 'Time's up, anyway. They won't be our problem for much longer.'

The clang of the large brass bell above the till was followed moments later by Len's baritone soaring across the heads of those at the bar calling for last orders, and Martin watched as a steady stream of drinkers made their way towards Lydia for a final pint.

It wasn't quite a Friday night stampede, but it was busy enough and the next ten minutes were filled with the sound of last minute arrangements, muttered agreements that would never be spoken of beyond the four walls of the bar, and underneath it all the sound of the till ringing in the cash that passed across Len's fingers.

Twenty-first century or not, the landlord still refused to accept plastic and the associated paperwork trail that came with it.

Eventually, chairs scraped back, and the front door swung on its hinges as the pub emptied and people made their way home.

At the other end of the bar, Geoff drained the last of his pint, slapped the empty glass on a sodden cardboard coaster and pulled a navy wool hat over his thinning hair, despite the warm night outside. He grinned at Len, aimed his thumb towards one of his companions, and removed a pipe from his jacket pocket.

'I've got a lift home, so I'll see you tomorrow night.'

'Cheers, Geoff.' Len lowered the front of the

dishwasher and wafted the air with a tea-towel as steam rose into the air. 'Watch how you go.'

He reached in for the first of the glasses, moving to one side as Lydia joined him, and swore loudly as the hot surface scalded his fingers.

While the pair of them worked, Martin scanned the room, noting the two men who had been arguing were now making their way towards the exit.

'Thanks, gents. Have a safe trip home,' Len called.

Neither acknowledged his words.

The older of the two gave the front door a shove, not waiting to hold it open for the younger man who hurried after him, his voice raised.

'I wonder what that was all about?' Lydia said, reaching up to hang wine glasses by their stems as she dried them.

'No idea,' said Len, unruffled. 'What time did they come in?'

'Just after you went upstairs to get more change for the till. They ordered a couple of pints of IPA, didn't say much, and then moved across to that table.'

Len shrugged. 'Probably wanted somewhere private to talk, rather than their local. You know how it is.'

He draped the tea-towel over his shoulder then turned his attention to the till, programming in the closing sequence for the day and removing the coin tray to take upstairs to the office after he locked up. 'Do you want to do the Sunday lunchtime shift? Rose has got her daughter and family visiting so she's asked for the day off.'

'That all right?' Lydia turned and cocked an eyebrow at Martin. 'We could do with the money, after all.'

'Go on then. Just the lunchtime, mind. We promised your mum we'd—'

When the first shot echoed through the walls, Lydia's eyes widened like a fox caught in headlights.

'What the fuck?' Martin spun to face the door, the bar stool tumbling to the floor.

'What's going on?' said Lydia, edging to his side, shaking.

Len spun away from the bar. 'Gunfire. Get down.'

Taking one look at the other man's face, Martin did as he was told, dragging Lydia with him.

'Martin…' she whimpered.

'Stay still.'

A second shot exploded out of the night, the report filling his ears and turning his stomach. He cringed lower to the floor, wondering if he could reach the door to lock it before the gunman turned his attention to those remaining inside, then saw Len shake his head, features pale.

'Stay where you are,' he hissed, before holding up a hand.

Martin strained his ears, willing his heartbeat to cease its pounding so he could hear if someone was approaching, but there was nothing.

Nothing but a stunned silence.

TWO

Detective Inspector Kay Hunter eased her car to a standstill behind a faded grey panel van, eyes widening at the scene beyond her windscreen.

Flashing blue lights strobed across the night sky from three Kent Police vehicles splayed across the gravel, their rooftop LEDs reflecting off the branches of a horse chestnut tree that leaned at a precarious angle in one corner of the car park and then filtered across the façade of the downtrodden pub.

Shadows merged as one between the lights – lumbering figures in protective coveralls with heads bowed at the perimeter of the property, and taller silhouettes that weaved between them while gripping assault rifles.

The radio clipped to the plastic dashboard holder beside Kay squawked with activity as commands were issued back and forth, devoid of all emotion, while her superiors coordinated the manhunt from their Northfleet headquarters.

Access along the lane behind her had been blocked by uniformed constables and as she climbed from her car, a tactical officer in full body armour crossed to where a liveried armed response vehicle had been abandoned in haste.

His colleagues moved out of the shadows and towards an inner cordon, the blue and white tape stretched across the car park separating the vehicles from the pub's weather-beaten front door.

Light pooled out from the opening, the people milling about inside visible through the grime-laden windowpanes.

The tactical officer's gloved hands cradled his semi-automatic rifle with a casualness belying the uniformed presence around her, and he nodded in recognition as she loosened a cotton elastic over her wristwatch and tied back her hair.

'Evening, guv.'

'Are you okay for me to proceed?'

'We declared the scene safe twenty minutes ago, and we've allowed forensics access to the body. We're all done here. The shooter made a run for it, and the bloke who copped it isn't going anywhere. Not now.'

She bit back a grimace. 'How bad is it?'

'Put it this way, he ain't going to be winning any beauty contests.'

'What's the latest on the shooter?'

'There are roadblocks being established on all major routes, but that's all I know at the moment. We've checked the immediate area and confirmed he's nowhere to be found. All of the outbuildings and nearby houses are clear.'

'Who's in charge of the scene here?'

He jerked his head towards the cordon. 'Paul Disher. He's the tall bloke standing over there next to the pathologist.'

'Thanks.'

Raising her hand to shield her eyes from the glare of the strobing lights, Kay hurried across the uneven gravel, unwilling to waste another second.

She paused when she reached the first cordon.

A crumpled form lay beyond the plastic tape, a man's body splayed out across the dirt and stones on his stomach with his face turned away from her, his arms outstretched as if trying to break his fall.

As the emergency lights ebbed around him, his dark-coloured clothing alternating in hue, the questions already started to form in her mind.

'Detective Inspector Hunter?'

Kay turned her attention away from the victim to see a tall sergeant in his forties heading towards her. 'You must be Paul Disher.'

He nodded in response, the bulk of his armoured vest hiding his uniform. 'I'm leading the tactical team. Your colleague got here a moment ago – he headed straight inside the pub.'

'Sounds like Barnes to me.' Kay gave a faint smile, then jerked her chin towards the broken man on the floor. 'What can you tell me so far?'

Disher took a set of protective coveralls from a junior officer before passing them to Kay, reaching out to steady her with his hand while she tugged on the matching booties.

'The landlord, Len Simpson, said this bloke and an older one were in the pub before the shooting,' he explained, lifting the cordon while she ducked underneath. 'He says he's never seen either of them before, and that they were arguing. Not loudly, but enough that anyone close by could see it wasn't a friendly conversation.'

'Was there a fight?' Kay fell into step beside Disher and followed him across to where the man's body lay.

'Not inside the pub. Simpson says the two men were among the last to leave, along with a group of four of his regulars and a local couple. With Simpson at the time was Lydia Terry, who works for him, and her husband Martin. The first shot was fired between five and ten minutes after all the customers had left.'

Kay circled the dead man, her gaze sweeping over the fingernails, bitten to the quick and crusted with dirt, the worn shoe soles, and then—

'Jesus.'

She blinked, then forced herself to move closer.

What was left of the man's face was little more than a pair of eyebrows that seemed surprised to find the rest of his features missing.

A bloody mass replaced what had been eyes, a mouth and nose, and when she lowered her gaze to his chest, another gaping wound glistened in the poor light.

'Don't ask which one was first, I won't know for sure until I get him back to mine.'

She straightened at the voice to see the Home Office pathologist Lucas Anderson returning to the cordon, his face grim.

'Suffice to say, he was trying to run away when he was

shot – those are the exit wounds you're looking at,' he added.

A pair of younger men unfolded a gurney and rolled it to one side out of the way, awaiting further orders.

'One in his spine to stop him, the head shot next?' she suggested.

Lucas waggled a gloved finger at her. 'Possibly, but that's all you're getting out of me at the moment. I'll get the post mortem done within the next forty-eight hours for you.'

She gave him a curt nod, then turned back to the sergeant.

'Any identification?'

'There wasn't anything in his pockets, but there's a cheap-looking watch on his left wrist. He isn't wearing a wedding ring, either.'

'There's no sign of any rings having been removed from his fingers,' said Lucas, crouching beside the dead man and sweeping his torch over his hands.

'What about the clothing?' said Kay. 'Does that match what the younger bloke was wearing who Len Simpson saw earlier?'

'Barnes showed him some photos on his phone, and he reckons it's the same bloke,' said Disher.

Kay straightened, patted Lucas on the back before he turned to his two assistants, then walked with the sergeant back to the cordon.

'All right, thanks Paul. Good work getting this under control tonight. I'll take over the scene now so you can catch up with the rest of your team in case the shooter's located. Do you think you could attend the briefing tomorrow? I'd like you to be on hand to help me coordinate any arrest once we've identified who the shooter is.'

'Will do, guv.'

'Thanks.'

Stripping off the protective suit, gasping for fresh air as she tore away the hood from her hair, Kay scrunched the whole lot up and shoved it into a biohazard bin set up by the CSIs at the perimeter, then turned at a familiar shout.

Detective Sergeant Ian Barnes hurried towards her, suit jacket flapping under his arms as he side-stepped a pair of constables to reach her.

'Evening, guv.' He wrinkled his nose when he peered over her shoulder. 'Did you take a look?'

'I did, yes. Not pretty, is it?'

'I can't remember the last time we had a shooting incident to deal with.'

'It's been a while.' Turning her attention to the pub, she saw three pale faces at one of the lower windows, their features blurred by the grime across the panes. 'And I suppose nobody saw anything?'

Her sergeant managed a wan smile. 'Even so, I'm sure you'll want a word.'

Kay set her shoulders, then nodded. 'Damn right I do.'

THREE

Kay's first impression of Len Simpson was that he was only a handful of cigarettes away from a heart attack.

The man buffered himself against the smooth worn surface of the bar by way of a sizeable belly, layers of skin under his eyes riffling while he watched what was happening beyond his windows.

He picked absently at a ragged fingernail as her officers hurried back and forth from the bar, his thick lips downturned in perpetual disappointment, his brow furrowed as if he were trying to fathom how he was going to salvage his reputation after the night's events.

His pub seemed to be hanging on to trade with the same grim determination as its owner.

All around her were the telltale signs of a business in decline, no doubt aided and abetted by a clientele who appreciated the privacy rather than the latest culinary trends.

Dust covered the surface of every shelf, cobwebs hugging the knick-knacks that cluttered the spaces between flickering light fittings, and a dirty hearth to Kay's right looked as if it hadn't been cleaned since the previous winter.

'Mr Simpson, this is Detective Inspector Kay Hunter,' said Barnes.

Simpson removed a toothpick from between his lips and leered at her, a limp hand outstretched in greeting. 'Well, you're an improvement at least.'

Kay ignored his hand, and kept her gaze passive as she swept her eyes over the middle-aged couple huddled at the far end of the bar. 'Can we have a chat in private, Mr Simpson?'

'I've already given matey boy here my statement.'

Barnes raised an eyebrow at the man's turn of phrase, but said nothing.

'I'm sure you have,' Kay said, then beckoned to him. 'Come on. It won't take long.'

She led the way over the dusty parquet flooring to a rectangular oak table with four chairs around it, and dragged one of them around to the end for Simpson, settling into another as far away from the landlord as was feasible. She leaned her elbow on the table, then grimaced and lifted it once more, her sleeve departing with a faint sucking noise as old drink stains relinquished their hold.

To her left, a pair of CSIs were processing a round oak table set for two people, and she nodded towards it as Simpson settled into his seat with an ill-disguised sigh.

'Is that where the two men were earlier tonight?' she said. 'Including the victim?'

'Yeah. We'd only just started clearing the tables after last orders when the first gunshot went off.'

'What about the glasses they were using? Did you hang on to those?'

He grimaced. 'Sorry – they went through the washer just before it all kicked off.'

Kay bit back the first word that threatened to slip from her lips, and sighed. 'Okay. Take me back to when they first arrived. What time was that?'

'I dunno.' Simpson tugged his earlobe. 'About half nine, quarter to ten perhaps. Late. They weren't here long before closing.'

'Who ordered the drinks?'

'The older of the two. Didn't talk much.'

'Did you serve him, or…?'

'Lydia served him. Two pints of bitter.'

'Just the one round?'

'Yeah.' His top lip curled. 'Glad they ain't regulars. Took 'em over an hour to drink that one.'

'Have you seen either of them before?'

'No.'

'What about accents? Did they sound local?'

He shrugged. 'Anywhere south of the estuary.'

'You told my colleague that they were arguing. Did you hear what that was about?'

'No. Too busy serving.'

'What happened when they left?'

'They got up and walked out after I rang the bell for last orders. I told them to have a good night, but neither of them took any notice.' Simpson ran a fat hand over his chins. 'A group of regulars walked out a couple of minutes later and I heard one or two car engines start. Me and Lydia were about to start wiping down tables when we heard the first shot. We all got down on the floor.'

Kay leaned back and peered past Simpson to where Barnes waited beside the bar, his head bowed while he listened to one of the CSIs at his shoulder. She waved him over.

'Mr Simpson, what time would you estimate you heard the first shot?'

'I dunno. Pub was empty, so maybe ten past eleven, something like that?'

'And the next?'

'Within seconds of the first.'

Kay glanced up at Barnes. 'What time was the triple nine call received?'

'Eleven forty, guv.'

When she turned her attention back to the landlord, he was chewing his lip, his eyes darting back and forth over the surface of the table.

'Anything you're not telling me, Mr Simpson?'

His gaze snapped to hers. 'No.'

'Are you sure? You seem nervous.'

'Some bloke's just had his brains blown out in me car park.' He glared at her. 'So, excuse me if I seem out of sorts.'

'I understand that. What I don't understand is why you waited so long to dial triple nine.' She pointed to where Lydia Terry was standing next to her husband, pecking at her mobile phone. 'What were you all doing?'

'Keeping our bloody heads down. What do you think we were doing?'

'We'll need a list of everyone who was in here tonight,

both before those two men arrived and after. Names, phone numbers…'

'Yeah, figured you might.' He jerked his thumb over his shoulder. 'Me and Lydia started writing them down before you turned up.'

'Good.' Kay pushed back her chair. 'Please give that to my colleague when you're finished.'

She ignored the bitter snort that emanated from the man and led Barnes over to an internal doorway leading from the bar to a box-like kitchen.

Turning her back to the grease-slicked stainless steel surfaces of the worktops and gas hob, she folded her arms.

'What do you think, Ian?'

'He's worried about something.' Her colleague tucked his notebook into his jacket pocket. 'I thought that when I first got here and spoke to him.'

'What did Lydia and her husband have to say for themselves?'

'Martin – he's the husband – confirms what you just heard from Simpson. Lydia's obviously shaken up, so I couldn't get much out of her. I was going to suggest we talk to them both again tomorrow morning. At home, rather than here.'

'Away from Simpson, you mean?'

'Exactly.'

'What about that list of people who were in earlier?'

'She's got phone numbers for some of them, so I'll have Laura go through those.' He checked over his shoulder before lowering his voice. 'I recognised a couple of the names, but we'll need to run the others through the system too.'

'They've got previous convictions, you mean?'

He nodded. 'Sounds like this place is living up to its reputation.'

'I thought I recognised the name when I got the call earlier.' Kay moved back towards the bar. 'It's not exactly going to win a Pub of the Year award any time soon, is it?'

'Not this year, that's for sure.'

FOUR

After making arrangements to visit Lydia Terry and her husband the following morning, Kay allowed the couple to leave the pub and turned her attention to a group of CSIs working within the taped-off area of the car park.

Heads bowed, their protective suits stark against the temporary lights that had been erected around them, they moved methodically from one side to the other, their gait unhurried.

She glanced down as her mobile phone started to ring, a familiar name displayed across the screen.

Gavin Piper had been a regular member of her tight-knit team for a number of years now, and possessed a sixth sense when it came to anticipating her requirements.

'Gav – any more news about the gunman?' she said while she watched the forensics team.

'Nothing yet, guv,' came the reply. 'No one driving erratically has been spotted on any CCTV in the immediate area, and there haven't been any reports of unusual activity around houses or farms yet.'

'Okay, well the tactical firearms team have handed over the scene to us here now, so I'll let you know if we find anything to help you. Have you got arrest teams on standby?'

'Yes, and your request for additional manpower has been escalated. I'll keep you posted about that, guv.'

She ended the call and turned to Barnes. 'This isn't going to be easy, is it?'

'Lydia and Martin say they can't recall hearing a car drive off so although we've got roadblocks in place, there's also the possibility the gunman escaped on foot.' He scrolled through a new text message, his phone screen illuminating his clenched jaw. 'Uniform are making house-to-house calls at the moment to warn people in the immediate vicinity, but we're screwed without a better description of the older bloke they say was with the victim earlier.'

'Christ.' Kay frowned and eyed three vehicles parked at the fringes of the gravelled area. 'Whose are those, then?'

'The old four-by-four belongs to Len Simpson, the green hatchback is Martin Terry's, and the other two belong to locals who had too much to drink tonight and decided to walk home.'

'Have you got a note of their names?'

'Yes, and addresses. I'll pass them on to uniform when I leave here so they can interview them and make sure they're not still over the limit when they come back for their cars tomorrow.'

'Did you find anything on the system about Len Simpson?'

'He's been a licensee since being dishonourably discharged from the army almost thirty years ago. I can't find anything that says why he left – I was going to suggest you might like a word with Sharp to see if he can find anything out for us.'

DCI Devon Sharp had been in the military police for a number of years prior to joining the civilian police force in Kent, and still kept in contact with many of his old colleagues.

'I'll make a note to speak to him after the briefing tomorrow. As soon as the call came in earlier, he went over to headquarters to coordinate at that end. With any luck, we'll have some more manpower by the morning too,' she said, then watched as Lucas's assistants rolled their now-laden gurney towards the grey van, the dead man's body encased within a body bag.

Barnes raised his hand to shield his eyes from a set of headlights as one of the patrol cars exited the car park in the van's wake. 'There have been plenty of complaints about this place over the years, not to mention rumours about what goes on here, but there's never been enough to bring Simpson in front of a magistrates' court. Somehow, he's always managed to avoid that.'

'How long has he been the licensee here?'

'Six years now. It's a free house, so that's probably why he's been here so long – he doesn't have to worry about what a head office might think about the way he runs the place like he would if a pub company owned it.'

'It'll be interesting to hear what Lydia Terry has to say about it all when we speak to her tomorrow, out of earshot of him.' She turned away from the pub, her attention returning to the painstaking search being undertaken by the gathered CSIs. 'Let's find out if they can tell us anything yet, so at least we can bring the team up to speed at the briefing.'

A familiar figure lowered a mask from her face and hurried towards them as they reached the cordon, pushing away her hood, her green eyes keen.

Kay lifted the tape for her. 'Harriet – I didn't know you were back from holiday.'

The other woman gave a grim smile, her protective suit crackling as she shifted a tablet computer in her grip. 'We got back from Cancún yesterday. I have to admit, I already wish I was back on the beach…'

'Has your team managed to find anything to give us a head start with this one?'

'There wasn't a wallet or mobile phone on him, and I've currently got some of my team searching the area with the help of uniform to try to find those. We've taken fingerprints and those have been sent for processing,' said Harriet. 'And we've got the two shell casings that were discharged.'

She beckoned to one of her assistants, who hurried over and held out an evidence bag. The lead CSI opened it, and Barnes shone his phone screen over the contents.

Inside, nestled within a plastic swab container and packed with polythene to stop it moving around during transit, Kay saw a gleaming brass casing and gave an involuntary shudder. 'It's bigger than I thought it would be.'

'I'll get my ballistics expert to confirm the calibre.' Harriet closed the bag and handed it back. 'I'm not promising anything, but we'll obviously test both for traces of DNA. We're currently trying to find the remains of the rounds that went through the victim, which is proving to be bloody difficult in this light.'

'So a rifle, rather than a shotgun?'

'Exactly.'

'Those didn't lodge inside him?' said Barnes.

'We can't assume anything until Lucas has done the post mortem,' Harriet explained. 'Given the state of him, you'd think they went straight through but we have to process the area anyway. I'll warn you now, though – we'll be here well until daybreak.'

Kay bit her lip. 'The second shot at the victim – why do that? I mean, that shot in his back was enough to kill him.'

'Spite, perhaps?'

'Or he didn't want us to be able to identify him easily.' Harriet glanced over her shoulder as one of her team members approached the cordon and beckoned to her. 'I'm needed. I'll let you two work out why this happened. In the meantime, I'll make sure you get my report as to *how* it happened as soon as possible.'

'Thanks,' said Kay, and sighed as she watched the CSI manager walk away.

'Okay, Ian – I'll take it from here. Get yourself home and I'll see you at seven tomorrow.'

'Are you sure, guv? I don't mind staying if you are.'

She managed a smile. 'Thanks, but you're going to have enough to do as it is. You'd better get your head down for a few hours.'

'What are you going to do?'

Kay ran her eyes over the scene before her, then checked her wristwatch.

Almost one o'clock.

'I'm going to make sure Gavin's got someone processing those fingerprints from the victim, and then I think I'd better risk finding out what Len Simpson's coffee is like.'

FIVE

Bleary-eyed, hair still damp from a hurried shower prior to running up the stairs to the incident room, Kay surveyed the crowd of officers milling about the space.

The morning commute was already underway beyond the windows overlooking Palace Avenue, the honk and shove of nose-to-tail traffic a constant white noise under the fraught conversations that filled the room while she turned her attention to the agenda in her hand.

A cacophony of telephones ringing swarmed around them while Kay logged into her computer and glared at the stack of files already overflowing from the in-tray on the corner of her desk.

She raised her voice over the throng.

'Debbie? Which ones of these are urgent, and what can wait a day or so?'

A uniformed constable elbowed her way past two sergeants who towered over her and ran a practised eye over the folders. 'Those three on top are the authorisations I need for overtime, cross-departmental agreements and budget schedules,' she said, handing them over. 'The rest of these you can ignore, but only until Monday. After that, I'm going to be chasing you.'

'Deal, thanks.' Kay signed the documentation where indicated with a flourish, and handed everything back before making her way over to where Gavin Piper stood at the far end of the room. 'Gavin? What admin support have we been given?'

The detective constable stepped away from the whiteboard, eyeing the notes he'd been writing for the imminent meeting, his normally spiky hair subdued after a recent cut and dark circles under his eyes from working overnight.

'Ten,' he said, and pointed the end of the pen towards the back of the room. 'Plus we've been told to expect four more probationary constables to help with the legwork from tomorrow. We're putting those in the conference room next door. Sharp arrived twenty minutes ago – I put him in his old office. I think he's talking to headquarters at the moment, but he's taken over the search and arrest side of things so I can support you here.'

'Okay, good.' Kay ran her thumb down the list of items generated from the HOLMES2 database, relieved that her old mentor was on hand.

Detective Chief Inspector Sharp had been based at Northfleet these past two years and she only now realised how much she had missed his guidance and support.

With a press release emailed to all local journalists in the past half an hour, her team had swelled to accommodate additional help from other stations in the division and now all of those faces turned to her as she called for their attention.

'Those phones behind you are going to start ringing within the next thirty minutes, so let's make a start,' she said, gesturing to the whiteboard as Gavin moved to a spare seat at the front of the group. 'Given the nature of last night's murder, you can expect that we're going to be receiving a lot of attention from both headquarters and the public, who will all want a fast result. Most of you have worked a major incident before, so I won't waste time this morning on procedure. I'll give you your points of contact and you can liaise with them rather than me for the duration of this investigation. Ian? Can you start us off with a review of where we're up to with regard to our victim?'

She stepped aside as Barnes joined her, his face grim.

'Okay, so for those who haven't yet had a chance to read the briefing notes, we have a Caucasian male victim estimated to be in his twenties who was shot in the chest and head while trying to outrun his killer. The pub where the incident occurred, the White Hart, has a reputation for unsavoury characters but to date we've had no major crimes there.' Barnes crossed his arms as he peered at the crime scene photographs that Gavin had pinned to the board. 'The killer escaped, and the landlord and the only member of staff there last night tell us they'd never seen either man before. Prior to the shooting, both men had been seen having an argument in the pub, but no one could hear what was being said. This morning, Traffic division reported finding a twelve-year-old silver hatchback burnt out in a stretch of woodland four miles away from the

White Hart. Forensics are currently over there trying to ascertain if there's any evidence to suggest it belonged to the killer.'

'At the present time, we're keeping an open mind on whether the killer escaped by car or on foot,' Kay added, nodding her thanks to Barnes as he retook his seat. 'No one in the pub at the time can recall hearing a vehicle driving away, and the landlord doesn't have CCTV. Gavin, how are you getting on identifying the victim's fingerprints?'

'The results came through just now, guv,' said the detective constable, scrolling through an email on his phone. 'We haven't got him in the system for anything. He's as clean as a whistle.'

Kay narrowed her eyes. 'No one's that clean. So, we still have no identification for either man. We'd better hope Lucas has more luck with dental records when he does the post mortem. I'm guessing by now you've all heard that Len Simpson destroyed the only evidence we had in relation to the killer by washing the glass he used?'

'I had a word with Harriet before I left the scene last night, guv,' said Barnes. 'They lifted fourteen different partial prints from the table the two men were at, and uniform are currently processing those to see if that helps.'

'Okay, thanks. I guess we should be pleased that cleaning the pub isn't a high priority for Simpson, even if the glasses are. Debbie, can you give me that list of task leads?'

The uniformed constable edged past the gathered officers crowding one side of the room and handed over a roster. 'That includes the personnel expected to turn up tomorrow, guv.'

'Thanks. Okay, Ian will be my deputy SIO and I don't want anyone speaking to the media except me, is that understood?'

A murmur of agreement met her words, and she craned her neck to see over the assembled crowd. 'Is Daniel here?'

'Guv.'

She waited while a sandy-haired sergeant in his thirties weaved his way towards the whiteboard, and then turned to face the rest of the team.

'For those of you who haven't met him, Daniel Westland is one of our firearms enquiry officers,' she said. 'Daniel's been seconded to the investigation to assist with accessing the National Firearms Licensing Management database in order that we can identify and interview certificate holders within the divisional area.'

A hand was raised from the back of the room, and Kay paused as Detective Constable Laura Hanway cleared her throat. 'Yes?'

'What about shotgun certificate holders, guv?'

'Early indications from the CSIs working the scene last night indicate that the injury was caused by a semi-automatic firearm or similar, rather than a shotgun given the nature of the wounds and witness statements regarding the closeness of the two shots,' she explained. 'However, we won't rule out shotguns entirely. Keep an open mind, as always. Daniel – I'd like you to work with Laura to develop an interview strategy for those certificate holders and make a start on researching who those people are this morning.'

She paused as a tall figure emerged from the office at the other end of the incident room and Sharp hurried to join her.

Despite being called in at midnight on his rostered day off, the DCI's expression bore no indication that he might be ruffled by the events unfolding since the shooting.

Instead, a grim determination emanated from him, one that provided a balm to the tense atmosphere around her.

'Good to see you, guv,' she said, unable to disguise the relief in her voice. 'Would you like to update the team about the latest on the search for our suspect?'

'Thanks, Kay.' Sharp turned his keen grey eyes on the officers. 'I've just spoken with headquarters and there have been no further reported incidents involving firearms in the divisional area since last night's murder. We're conducting interviews with all 24-7 stores and petrol stations within a four-mile radius of the pub and reviewing CCTV cameras belonging to private properties and businesses on minor routes near the pub's location in case we can spot our man passing by on foot. The media release that has just gone live across all networks is telling the public not to approach anyone seen carrying a firearm or acting suspiciously but to phone our hotline immediately. Trained administrative staff at headquarters will process those calls to eliminate any time-wasters before passing on the rest to you here to follow up. I'll be dividing my time between here and headquarters until such time as the suspect is arrested.'

He nodded his thanks to her, and moved to one side.

Kay peered around him until she saw an imposing uniformed sergeant at the fringes of the group. Aaron Stewart had proven to be a lucrative asset within her team in the past, and she had no doubt he was capable of the task she was about to hand over.

'Aaron, I need you to work up a background profile for the victim as we receive information from all the interviews that were conducted last night and tie that in with new details over the course of the day. Once we know who he is, I'd like you to take on the family liaison role please, given your expertise in that area. Call me if you find out something that needs addressing immediately.'

The sergeant nodded, lowering his gaze to his notebook as he continued to copy the notes from the whiteboard.

'Ian, I'd like you to work with me to follow up with the regulars from the pub this morning, as well as speaking with Lydia and Martin Terry. Harry – I'd like you to lead the house-to-house enquiries today,' Kay continued. 'Uniform patrols spoke to residents in the immediate area last night but the focus was on their safety at the time rather than gleaning knowledge about the shooting. We need to ascertain whether our killer dumped his weapon in someone's garden, so make sure outbuildings are checked, too.'

'Will do, guv.' Sergeant Harry Davis stood a little straighter. 'I'll also liaise with Laura and Gavin in case we hear about anyone who was in the pub who wasn't on the list of names we were given.'

'Actually,' said Sharp, glancing at Kay, 'I'd like Gavin to come back to Northfleet with me and act as liaison between the two investigations – the search and arrest, and your efforts to identify the victim. That all right with you?'

'If you think we can spare the manpower, guv. However, we've only just made a start, and we're going to have a lot of new information to sift through once any media statements are released.'

'I'm sure the officers here will manage, and you've got more administrative staff turning up in the morning. It'll be prudent to have someone able to coordinate between us with the authority to action any urgent matters that need addressing.'

Kay's heart sank. 'Okay, guv. Gavin – you heard. You're with DCI Sharp so I suggest you make arrangements with Debbie and Laura to hand over any outstanding matters before you leave for Northfleet.'

'Thanks, guv.' Gavin tried and failed spectacularly at keeping a wide grin from forming. 'I'll make sure I let you have regular updates.'

'Make sure you do. Okay, finally – Lucas Anderson has scheduled the post mortem for nine o'clock tomorrow morning, and he's arranged for a ballistics expert to be in attendance to assist. I intend to go to that, and I'll report back with anything that can clarify what Harriet's team start processing with the forensics laboratory.'

She glanced up as one by one, telephones started braying across the incident room.

'And on that note, you'd best answer those. We'll reconvene again at four o'clock this afternoon unless we have a substantial breakthrough. Dismissed.'

34

SIX

'Daniel, thanks for getting here in time for the briefing,' said Kay, following Laura and the firearms enquiry officer into the conference room. 'We're going to need all the help we can get with this one.'

'No problem. I'm waiting to hear from two of my team to see if we can bolster the numbers you've got here,' he said, untangling cables that dangled over the back of a worn laminated desk near the far end of the room and plugging in his laptop. 'I don't doubt the capabilities your officers have, but mine are more familiar with the firearms licensing database. In the circumstances, we need to move as fast as possible on this.'

Laura hauled an overhead projector from an oak-effect cupboard under a window, placed it on the table beside Daniel and then aimed a remote control at a screen that emerged from its housing among the ceiling tiles.

'I suggest we split our team into two,' he continued. 'Then Laura can pass on any solid leads through to you as we go.'

'That sounds like a good plan.' Kay crossed to the door as the assigned personnel began to appear, and directed them towards the screen.

Moments later, a semi-circle of twelve officers were staring at the projected images, faces grim while they listened to the firearms officer.

'The National Firearms Licensing Management System is what we use every time we receive an enquiry from someone wishing to apply for a shotgun or firearms certificate,' Daniel began. 'In theory, no one should be in possession of a shotgun, firearm or ammunition without a valid certificate. And before you ask, 3D printed guns also fall under the legislation.'

As he spoke, he flicked through the database's different sections. 'Most of the information you're going to need for this initial review process can be found here. Every person who applies must be able to present a good reason to need a firearm or shotgun. That means a legitimate reason for work, such as being a gamekeeper or Forestry Commission worker, sport or something like museum collections. Good reason might also include historical re-enactment, antiques collectors or target shooting clubs.'

Kay leaned against a spare desk as she listened, as rapt as her colleagues.

'The system also captures the names of people whose certificates have been revoked, as well as refused applications – so those are elements you'll be looking at alongside legitimate owners,' said Daniel.

'What sort of reasons would cause a certificate to be revoked?'

Kay turned to see Phillip Parker frowning, pen poised above his notebook, and gave a slight nod.

It was a good question.

'Any claim involving domestic abuse, a drink driving charge, medical issues, reports of a certificate holder losing their temper – basically anything that gives us cause for concern and gives us a fair reason to suspect that person shouldn't be in charge of a firearm of any sort,' said Daniel. He jabbed his finger to the laptop keyboard and the image changed. 'You'll all be given temporary access to the database and when you get to your desks, IT should've emailed your login details to you so you can set it up on your computers and get started. Guv, how do you want to split the workload?'

'I think if we split it alphabetically into groups of letters, that gives us a better chance of getting through all of this,' Kay said after a moment's consideration. 'Does your database reflect recent deaths and instances where people have told you they've sold their firearms?'

'It does, yes. We ran a complete purge of the system earlier this morning so we know we've captured everything up to yesterday's intel.'

'Right, well if you could make sure each person knows how to filter out those people from their search, that'd save wasting time. How many firearms certificate holders are there in Kent?'

'From memory, over 17,000 people are holders,' said Daniel, acknowledging the surprised whistles that filtered through the group. 'And that doesn't include shotgun certificates. If we were looking at those as well, it's closer to 70,000.'

A shocked silence greeted his words, and Kay's shoulders slumped at the realisation that there wouldn't be a quick result.

She ran her gaze over the team. 'I know some of you will be wondering why you've been allocated to this task and some of you will be feeling left out from the other enquiries we're managing as part of this murder investigation. Let me tell you now that the information we need from this database is imperative to finding out who our killer is, so don't underestimate the importance of what's expected of you. However long it takes, we need this information cross-checked. Is that clear?'

A few of the older constables near the back stood a little straighter as a murmur of acquiescence swept over her, and then she nodded to Laura.

'They're all yours.'

She stepped out into the corridor when her phone started to ring, and answered it as soon as she saw the name displayed on the screen.

'Harriet? How're you getting on?'

'We're just packing up at the pub,' said the forensics manager. 'I've had two of my team acting as couriers throughout the night getting evidence across to the laboratory, and thanks to Sharp calling in a favour or two and given the nature of this one, they're already working on what they've got.'

'Thank God for that,' said Kay, running a hand through her hair as she stared out the window at the street below.

Down there, pedestrians moved back and forth along the pavement oblivious to the frenetic activity within the police station, and she watched as a woman stopped to talk with another, their faces animated as they gossiped.

It was all so normal, so far removed from the scene that had confronted her last night, that she could imagine two separate worlds passing by each other without knowing the other was there.

'Kay?'

'Sorry, Harriet – I've got a million tasks running through my head at the moment, and I've lost a key member of the team to headquarters. What did you say?'

'I've managed to borrow a ballistics expert from the Metropolitan Police – he's someone I used to go to university with and one of the best experts within a fifty-mile radius of here.'

'That's great news – how soon can he—'

'He'll be here by three o'clock this afternoon, as soon as he's finished giving testimony at the Old Bailey.' Harriet's voice grew muffled, and Kay heard someone else talking in the background before the CSI lead returned. 'I'll give you another call as soon as we've got more news, but I've got to go – we've got the last swabs to record into evidence, and I need to make a start on my initial report for you.'

'Thanks, Harriet. I owe you.'

Kay lowered the phone, then leaned forward and rested her forehead against the coolness of the window's privacy glass.

'I am so out of my depth with this one,' she murmured.

SEVEN

Ian Barnes tucked his reading glasses into his jacket pocket, reached across the central console and opened the passenger door ready for Kay as she emerged from the back door of the police station and hurried towards the car.

She tossed a manila folder and her bag into the footwell and climbed in, fastening her seatbelt while he edged into the dual lane traffic.

He risked a sideways glance.

She looked tired, which was understandable given the night they'd all had, but there was an underlying weariness to her posture, as if the strain of the shooting incident and unparalleled workload was already taking its toll.

Especially now that Gavin was on his way to Northfleet with Sharp.

Negotiating the twisting one-way system, doubling back around the ring road, the car finally shot along the A20 towards Bearsted behind an empty single-decker bus hellbent on beating every red light out of town.

He wound the window down a crack, letting the warm

air tickle his neck and losing some of the staleness from within the vehicle, which he was sure had been used for covert surveillance at some point within the past week if the underlying stench of fast food was any indication.

'Laura all set up, then?' he ventured, his eyes travelling to the dashboard GPS.

'Yes.'

The single word came out in a sigh, and then his colleague chuckled.

'Sorry – I've been a bit preoccupied this morning. How are you doing after last night? All right?'

He shrugged, then took a left-hand turn after passing a paddock filled with gymkhana paraphernalia. 'It's a lot to take in, guv. Biggest case we've worked on together so far, isn't it? And the fact we have an armed man still on the loose is a worry.'

'It is. Thank god Sharp was available to take on the gold commander role. I wouldn't fancy managing this with someone I didn't know. I mean, we've got all the procedures to follow but it makes such a difference working with a familiar team.' She peered at the GPS as the soft voice of the computer directed him to take the next right. 'Whereabouts do Lydia Terry and her husband live in relation to the pub's location?'

'About three miles east of it. It's so small, it hasn't even got a place name, just the name of the lane their house is on. We should be there in five minutes.'

'Given that you interviewed them both last night before I got there, do you want to lead this one? At least then it'll provide some continuity.'

'No problem.' He tapped his fingers on the steering

wheel. 'I know they were both in shock last night, Lydia in particular, but I'm interested to find out how much more forthcoming she might be.'

Kay snorted. 'I'm sure Len Simpson has got mixed up in plenty of dodgy dealings in his lifetime. I suppose it depends on whether Lydia and Martin have ever benefited from some of that.'

'It's a big leap from bagging a few pheasants here and there to murdering some poor bloke though, isn't it?' He slowed, anticipating the Terrys' cottage within the next few hundred metres. 'And given Lydia's had a few hours to think about it, and time to talk it over with her husband, maybe they'll decide it's time to say something.'

'Perhaps.' Kay straightened and pointed through the windscreen. 'Is that the place?'

Barnes eased to a standstill beside a terrace of five farmworkers' cottages, the rough stonework battered and bruised by the elements.

Slate tiles covered the roof, and each property had a wooden porch in various states of disrepair that provided a modicum of protection from the elements in inclement weather.

'Nice view,' he said.

Opposite the houses, the roadside verge gave way to a panorama of tumbling hillsides, golden barley bobbing and swaying as a breeze rippled across the landscape in gentle waves. Half a mile away, a dark green tractor dragged a trailer across a field behind a combine harvester, a cloud of dust rising into the air as the machines worked.

'Wait until the winter, when that wind whips straight

up here and into your front room,' Kay said. 'Hope these are well insulated.'

'We've been spotted.' Barnes watched as a curtain twitched at the downstairs window to Weavers Cottage. 'Shall we?'

By the time they'd reached the front door, Martin Terry was standing on the threshold, brow furrowed.

'You haven't caught him yet, then?' he said.

'Only a matter of time,' said Barnes, his voice neutral. 'How are you both?'

Terry shrugged. 'As well as can be expected. Lydia's in the living room. She's insisting on watching the news coverage, although I keep telling her it's not a good idea.'

'I need to know.' A voice carried through from a doorway to the left of the hallway, and then Lydia appeared.

With her make-up removed since the previous night, her pale face was almost translucent against her dark hair, and Barnes could sense the stress emanating from her.

'We won't take up too much of your time,' he said. 'We just need to ask a few more questions.'

'Come on through.' Lydia turned on her heel, picked up the television remote from a low table beside an armchair and muted the newsreader's commentary.

Barnes noticed the same repeating footage on the screen that had been playing across the local and national networks since the media release had been issued, and battened down the rising frustration at the amount of speculation being forced upon an already worried local population.

'Would you like to sit down?'

He looked away from the television at Martin's voice to see the man gesturing to a mushroom-coloured sofa under the front window, and waited until Kay was seated before perching on the arm and unbuttoning his jacket.

Flicking through his notes while the couple settled into matching armchairs, he glanced around the room.

Compared to the White Hart, their home was clean and tidy, with bookshelves each side of the television and an eclectic collection of trinkets and mementoes wedged in between the paperbacks.

The walls appeared to have been recently painted, a bright colour that offset the north-facing aspect and accentuated the framed prints above a stone mantelpiece.

When he turned his attention to Lydia, she was watching him closely.

'What do you want to know, detective? I gave you my statement last night.'

'And I appreciate that,' he replied. 'What I'd like to do now is go back over what happened, simply because I'm sure you were shocked by the events in the pub. It's often the case that once we've had a chance to decompress after a stressful encounter that we remember extra details, and those details could be critical to our investigation.'

Lydia nodded, folding her hands in her lap. 'Okay. That makes sense.'

'Before we start, how are you both doing today?'

'All right, I suppose.' Lydia glanced at her husband, who gave a slight nod. 'We didn't get to bed until nearly three o'clock this morning...'

She paused as a helicopter clattered overhead, the windows shaking. After it had passed, she shot him a rueful smile. 'Needless to say, it was near impossible to sleep.'

'I can imagine. Apart from that?'

'Like she said, we're okay,' said Martin, reaching out for his wife's hand and giving it a squeeze. 'We were talking about it this morning, and as long as you catch whoever did it, then it'll be all right, won't it?'

'Good.' Barnes smiled. 'But do speak to your GP surgery if you need to. They can put you in touch with the right people if you find it does get overwhelming. So, back to last night. Lydia, what time did the two men come into the pub?'

The woman pursed her lips. 'I was busy serving at the other end of the bar and had my back to the front door so I didn't really see them at first. They only had one drink each. I poured those, but after that I didn't take much notice of them again until Martin mentioned that they were arguing about something.'

'Did you manage to overhear anything they were saying, Martin?'

The other man paused for a moment, staring at the carpet. Then, 'I've been trying to remember. They were doing their best to keep their voices down but I think I heard snatches of the conversation. The odd word here and there, you know? I got the impression they only came to the pub to have that talk.'

'What makes you say that?'

'One of them said something along the lines of "no one knows us", something like that.' He lifted his gaze, a sheepish expression crossing his face. 'I tried to listen after that. It piqued my interest for some reason.'

'Why was that?'

'I'm not sure. Perhaps because I hadn't seen them before, and – well, it's no secret that Len's place has a reputation for trouble, is it?' Martin turned his attention to his wife. 'I've never liked Lydia working there. I'm always worried she's going to get caught up in the middle of something and get hurt. It's why I try to call in on my way home from work when she's there, just to keep an eye on her.'

'Oh, love…' Lydia wiped away tears and forced a smile before facing Barnes. 'I've never had any bother with the locals before, and Len always keeps an eye on me…'

'But you said the two men who were there last night weren't locals?' said Kay, leaning forward.

'No. Well, not local to the pub.' Lydia shrugged. 'I mean, they might be from around here, but I haven't seen them drinking in the Hart before.'

'Given that one of the men was murdered last night, would either of you recognise the other if you saw him again?' Barnes asked.

The couple looked at each other for a moment, then Lydia spoke.

'I don't think so,'

'I might,' said Martin. 'I mean, I was trying not to be obvious about it, but because I got the impression an argument might be about to start I did have a look when I thought I could get away with it.'

'Did either of them notice you?'

The man shook his head. 'Whatever it was they were discussing, they weren't interested in anyone else in there.

Every now and again one of them would look over his shoulder just to make sure no one was listening but I made sure they didn't notice me.'

'The gunshots you heard. What can you recall about those?'

'When I heard the first one, I wasn't sure what I was hearing,' said Lydia, her voice trembling. 'I mean, you hear shotguns around here all the time, people out shooting rabbits or pheasants. It just sounded so different coming from the car park, and so close by.'

'Len was the first one to react,' Martin added. 'It's almost like he knew straight away what was going on. He told us to get down on the floor, and a split second later we heard the second shot.'

'How far apart were the two shots?'

'They were close together,' said Lydia. 'Last night, it seemed like it slowed down after I heard the first shot, but I suppose that was just the shock at hearing it.'

'Yeah, they were definitely close together,' Martin said. 'Maybe a second or two between them.'

'What happened after you heard the second shot?'

'We stayed on the floor.' Lydia shuddered. 'I was so scared he'd come back inside and kill us.'

'What was Len doing during that time?'

'He crawled around to the back of the bar and disappeared out the back for a bit,' said Martin.

'What was he doing?'

'I'm not sure – I assumed he was locking the kitchen door so no one could come in through there.'

'The thing is, we're at a loss to understand why he left it so long to call triple nine,' said Kay. 'Given that there was an armed man in his car park, two shots fired and a likely injured or dying man out there too, he didn't phone it in for another thirty minutes. Nor did you. Why was that?'

'Len told us to stay still and not move, so we didn't,' said Martin. He jutted out his chin. 'My phone was in my jacket, which was hanging on a peg under the bar and Lydia's was in her handbag tucked behind the till. We couldn't get to those without raising our heads—'

'And there was no way I was doing that while I thought there was a man with a gun still wandering around out there,' said Lydia.

'When did Len come back to the bar?'

'I don't know, it seemed like a while. I couldn't hear what he was doing.'

'Was he still in the kitchen?'

'I thought I heard him go upstairs,' said Martin. 'I figured he might be having a look out the window up there to see what was going on. I suppose it was about twenty minutes later he walked back in—'

'Not crouching this time?'

'No, which is why I figured whoever it was out there was gone. Len picked up his mobile from where he'd left it on the bar and called your lot.'

'He didn't take his phone with him when he went out to the kitchen?'

'I suppose he was more concerned about making sure the back door was locked.'

'Okay, fair enough.' Barnes rose to his feet. 'We'll arrange to have one of our sketch artists come over later today while your memory is still fresh. I'd be grateful if you'd work with them to describe both men as best you can – it would be very helpful to our investigation.'

'Of course.' Martin gave his wife's hand another squeeze, then showed the two detectives out of the room, easing the door shut behind him. Reaching the front door, he lowered his voice as he turned to Barnes.

'I haven't said anything to Lydia yet, but I'm going to ask around and see if I can find her a job somewhere else,' he murmured. 'I don't know what I'd have done if anything had happened to her last night. It keeps going around in my head...'

'Try not to worry yourself, Mr Terry,' said Barnes. 'She's safe now, and here with you.'

He shook the man's outstretched hand, the grip firm.

'Just you make sure you catch whoever killed that man,' said Martin. 'That's when I'll know we're safe.'

EIGHT

Despite only being four storeys tall, the concrete and darkened privacy glass structure of Kent Police's headquarters at Gravesend cast a long shadow over Gavin as he walked across the concourse from the car park beside Sharp.

Behind them, a steady stream of liveried vehicles roared towards the dual carriageway, sirens blaring as soon as they met the traffic leading past the industrial park.

The steel bollards on either side of the baked paving slabs created a guard of honour, gleaming in the sun's glare and making him squint against the harsh light.

His black canvas backpack bumped against his right shoulder, the bag laden with several manila folders containing briefing documents and his laptop. He unzipped a side pocket on it when they drew closer, pulled out his Northfleet security card and clipped it to his belt while Sharp swiped his own across a security panel to the right of the door.

As soon as he followed the DCI into the atrium, he exhaled.

Cool air conditioning wicked away the moisture at the nape of his neck, and he straightened his tie.

'Which floor are we on, guv?' he said, following Sharp to the two lifts beside a vending machine and trying to ignore the taunting cans of soft drink behind the glass.

'Third.' Sharp stepped into the empty lift and jabbed the button. 'Chief Superintendent Greensmith will be in attendance, as well as the area commander for East Division.'

Gavin swallowed, the thought of so many superior officers in one room causing his heart to palpitate. He glanced sideways at Sharp, who was eyeing him closely.

The DCI winked. 'Don't worry. If anyone's arse is going to get kicked on this one, it'll be mine. Just make sure you can lay your hands on the information I need when I'm asked, and you'll be all right. This will be good experience for you, if anything.'

Managing a faint smile, Gavin watched the numbers above the lift doors blink from left to right as they ascended. 'I'll try to remember that, guv.'

There was a slight bump as the lift came to a standstill, and then he was following the DCI past rows of partitioned desks, every one taken by a harried-looking officer.

Phones rang, voices called across the room to one another, and as they approached the last row before a suite of private offices, he saw that the enormous screen on the wall nearest to him displayed a live aerial view of the pub.

The volume had been muted, but it appeared that the police helicopter was flying a circular route encompassing the countryside north of the M20 between Maidstone and Lenham, its progress methodical.

'Oof... Watch where you're going.'

He stumbled, turning his attention back to where he was walking. 'I'm so sorry.'

Crouching to pick up the paperwork that now covered the carpet tiles like cheap confetti, his cheeks burning, he looked up at the woman he'd collided with.

She wore a uniform that looked as if it had been pressed to within an inch of its life, and when he rose to his feet his heart sank at the sight of the pips on her shoulder epaulettes.

'Detective Constable Piper, meet Assistant Chief Constable Tess Bainbridge,' said Sharp. 'The ACC is acting as our firearms commander on this one, given her experience in anti-terrorism operations.'

Gavin handed over the paperwork, sure that the volume of conversations in the room had ebbed around him while everyone stared. 'Sorry, ma'am.'

She cocked a perfectly tweaked eyebrow in response. 'In a hurry to get to our meeting, Detective Piper?'

'I... yes, I am.' He nodded towards the screen. 'Is that a live feed?'

'It is. We've had the helicopter up at regular intervals using thermal imaging equipment since the call came in last night.' Bainbridge's lips thinned. 'No luck yet, but the chief constable's approved the budget so we'll keep looking.'

He glanced over his shoulder as the hubbub in the room increased. 'Are all of these people taking calls from the public, or...?'

'No. This is our tactical command centre, purely for managing the search and arrest. We've got another team downstairs fielding phone calls from the public and media, specially trained for the role.' Her eyes softened. 'Maybe another time I'll give you the grand tour, but given the current situation...'

'Please, lead the way,' said Sharp.

Gavin's heart sank as the DCI aimed a slight shake of his head at him before falling into step beside Bainbridge.

The two senior officers hurried away, heads lowered in conversation.

'Nice one, Piper,' he muttered. 'At this rate, Laura will make sergeant before you.'

Three doors along from the open-plan space, he walked into a large conference room full of senior officers.

An ash-coloured oval table filled the centre of the room, with twelve chairs placed around it at intervals and a smaller screen on the wall beside the door displaying the same aerial footage he'd seen a moment before.

This time, however, the sound was turned up and after taking a seat beside Sharp with his back to the window, his attention wandered back to the running commentary.

'The pilot's with the National Police Air Service. He and the crew are talking to another team downstairs,' the DCI murmured. 'They'll stay in the air for three to four hours, stop to refuel and return to the site.'

'Do they alternate crew members, guv?'

'Yes.' Sharp checked his watch. 'I would think this is the second crew up now if the aircraft has been used all night.'

Tess Bainbridge turned away from the group of senior

officers she'd been talking to, and raised her voice. 'Right, if you could all take your seats please, we'll make a start. The chief constable wants to release a statement by noon providing an update so we'd best make sure he has something to say. Can someone mute the screen?'

Moments later, the door was closed and a silence fell amongst the gathered officers.

'If I could please start with an update from you, Devon?' said Bainbridge, flipping open a leather-bound notepad. 'We'll work our way up the chain of command first, and then proceed with what needs to be done to bring in this suspect.'

Sharp cleared his throat. 'At the present time, we have officers conducting house-to-house enquiries in the immediate vicinity of the White Hart. That includes all properties within a two-mile radius, including any that are holiday homes. We're working on the basis that although we spoke to many homeowners last night, it was impossible to conduct thorough searches of outbuildings and private land until daylight. Paul Disher is managing our local tactical firearms team, and is on standby if we uncover suspicious activity.'

'Paul's an excellent officer,' said Bainbridge, nodding to herself as she jotted notes. 'I've worked with him on a couple of operations before and he's the right man to have around you when the shit hits the fan.'

'Good to know, ma'am. From what DI Hunter told me last night about his handling of the situation, I have no doubt he's an asset to our investigation.'

'Kay Hunter is silver commander on this one?'

'She is, and DS Ian Barnes is her deputy SIO.'

'What's their current remit?'

'They're working with their team to interview everyone who was in the pub last night prior to the shooting, and I've been informed that a sketch artist will be working with the husband of the woman who works there to provide images of both the victim and the suspect by this afternoon. We've also made progress with drawing up a list of firearms certificate holders in the divisional area and will start those interviews this afternoon.'

'That's good progress within the time you've had, Devon. Thanks.' Bainbridge turned to Susan Greensmith. 'That's going to be a significant number of people to get to within a short amount of time. How are we managing manpower?'

'The initial visits will be kept shorter for those who live farthest away from the crime scene,' explained the chief superintendent. 'It'll be the case that certificate holders will be asked about their movements last night, and a brief check in relation to the security of their firearms will be carried out while officers are at the premises. For those firearms holders closer to the pub, the same checks will take place but we'll be speaking to alibis as well.'

'Good, thanks.' Bainbridge peered at the large screen on the wall and leaned closer to the conference phone in the middle of the table. 'Constable Woods, can you let us have an update airside, please?'

Sharp leaned closer and murmured in Gavin's ear. 'That's Erin Woods, one of the tactical flight officers on board. She's based with the NPAS at their Redhill base.'

He nodded in response, then listened as the woman's voice carried over the speakers.

'Ma'am, we're continuing a watching brief on all major routes leading past the crime scene and coordinating with Traffic division on minor roads,' she said. 'Infrared hasn't picked up anything suspicious within wooded areas around the White Hart, and one instance we had this morning of someone crossing a field was confirmed by on-ground officers as being a local out on a run.'

'Any abandoned vehicles or suspicious activity within the five-mile radius of the pub?'

Watching the live feed as the TFO provided her update, Gavin's stomach lurched as the helicopter banked and began its next circuit of the area.

'Negative, ma'am,' said Erin, raising her voice over the clatter of the helicopter's rotors. 'The burned-out car that was spotted earlier this morning has been eliminated from enquiries and its owner located. We'll continue to provide regular updates throughout the day.'

'Thank you, constable.'

Gavin listened as the ACC continued to work her way around the table, providing suggestions to her officers and listening without interruption as each person spoke.

Finally, after the last update was provided by an older DCI from East Division confirming no suspicious activity at that end of the county, Bainbridge shuffled the papers in front of her and eyed the people gathered around the table.

'I have to agree with what I've heard this morning, in that the general consensus is that this shooting incident wasn't a random attack but that the victim was the only person the killer had in mind. Given that no shots were fired at or inside the pub, and there have been no reports of threatening behaviour in the area, we should assume that the general public are not in as much danger as was first thought.' The ACC slipped the paperwork into the leather folder and zipped it closed. 'I would therefore like to lower the current threat level, issue an updated media release informing the public that we believe this to be an isolated incident, and then concentrate our efforts on the immediate area around the White Hart pub.'

She pushed back her chair, focusing her attention on Sharp. 'Devon, I'd like you to continue to act as gold commander for the search and arrest of the killer. I expect regular updates, and remind your team not to take any risks. One death this week is enough.'

Gavin rose to his feet beside the DCI as Bainbridge left the room without another word, his hands trembling while he gathered his notes.

When he turned to Sharp, the man's face was grim.

'You heard her, Piper,' he murmured. 'Let's make sure everyone back at the incident room goes home safe once this is over.'

NINE

Compared to the Terry's tidy home, Geoff Abbott's tumbledown cottage resembled a moth-eaten shack.

Placed squarely in the middle of a plot of earth that might have once been turf but was now a tangled and twisted knot of overgrown weeds, the tiny dwelling looked as if it might fall down at any moment.

Oak and beech trees crowded the air above it, an eerie white noise filling the glade that eliminated all sound from the lane beyond.

Moss covered the roof tiles that weren't missing, and a strip of dark green tarpaulin covered one end above a gutter that constantly dripped onto the dirt below, despite there being no rain for over a week.

Plaster was peeling from the anaemic stonework on each side of the battered front door, and as Kay walked up a cracked and uneven brickwork path, she tried to work out what colour had once graced the walls between the dark timber work that criss-crossed the building.

'Bloody hell, guv,' Barnes muttered. 'We should've brought hard hats with us.'

Kay eyed the rotting hatchback car that was propped up on bricks to the right of the path, the driver's window smashed and a bright green mould visible across the steering wheel and upholstery, then turned and rapped her knuckles against the door.

A fug of fetid cigarette smoke belched through the gap as it opened, and then Geoff Abbott emerged, squinting against the bright sunlight that penetrated the tree boughs.

Nicotine stains coloured his grey hair a dingy yellow, and lesions peppered his nose and cheeks.

'You the police?' he said, arthritic fingers dangling the remains of a butt.

Kay held up her warrant card, and introduced Barnes. 'We'd like to speak to you about the incident at the White Hart last night. Can we come in?'

'S'pose so.' Abbott shuffled backwards, opening the door wider so they could pass, and gestured towards the back of the house. 'Best go in the kitchen. Living room's a bit of a state.'

As she eyed up the bales of newspapers stacked against the hallway wall and the damp patches seeping through the faded wallpaper, Kay suppressed a shudder.

The kitchen wasn't much better, but at least a large window above a cluttered sink let in ample light to offset the gloom from the trees.

An elderly Golden Retriever staggered to its feet from a well-worn bed beside a stove, wobbled across to where Kay stood beside a chipped and pitted formica table, then promptly leaned against her.

As its dark brown eyes stared up at her, she groaned, ruing the choice of black trousers that morning as its hair moulted over the fabric. Then she reached down and rubbed the soft fur between the dog's ears.

'What's his name?' she asked.

'Bernard.' Abbott's voice softened. 'He's thirteen now, so doesn't get about as much as he used to. Misses going to the pub, too.'

The dog's ears pricked up, and Kay chuckled.

'He still recognises the word though, doesn't he?'

'That he does.' The old man gestured to four rickety chairs surrounding the table. 'I'd offer you a hot drink, but I'm out of milk and—'

'Not a problem, Mr Abbott. We just have a few questions to follow up with you, and then we'll be on our way.'

Mollified, the man nodded and took a seat beside Barnes while the detective removed his notebook from his jacket.

'Talk us through what happened in the White Hart last night,' said Kay. 'Who were you with?'

'Three friends.' Abbott shrugged. 'All locals. We tend to go in four or five times a week. I s'pose you'll want their names?'

'We will.'

'Trevor Shadwell, Barry Peters, and Malcolm Cross.'

'Have you got their phone numbers and addresses?'

Kay waited while Abbott recited them for Barnes, noting the way the old man dabbed and poked at the screen of his ancient mobile phone, his brow puckered in concentration.

She recognised the names from the list that Len Simpson had given them the night before, but having the details cross-checked and clarified was essential.

'How long have you known them?' she asked when he'd put the phone away.

'Me and Barry go back thirty years or more. Used to work on the railway together out at Sittingbourne. Trevor's local – lived down the road there about twelve years. He didn't used to drink in the Hart, but his wife died four years ago. It was Malcolm who introduced me to him – I can't remember where they know each other from, but it's been a while.'

'Did you spot the two men who were arguing last night?'

'If they were arguing, I couldn't hear it from where I was sat.' Abbott sniffed. 'Deaf in one ear, me, so I has to concentrate when I'm in the pub to hear what the lads are saying, even when it is quieter. I did see 'em get up to leave though.'

'Did you get a good look at them?'

Abbott scratched at his earlobe. 'One were taller than the other. The older one. The younger one looked a bit rat-like.'

'Oh? In what way?'

'Shifty. His eyes were all over the place. He had his hands in his coat pockets and didn't look like he'd slept for a few days.'

'What about their ages?'

'I don't know. Gets harder to guess someone's age the older you get.' Abbott shot her a shy smile. 'Everyone looks about twenty to me these days.'

'Best guess, then.'

'I suppose the youngster might've been mid to late twenties. No older than that. The older chap… late forties, fifties perhaps. Only a bit of grey in his hair, see.'

Barnes flipped through his notes. 'When you left the pub, did you notice anything out of the ordinary about either of them?'

'No – I left before them, see. Like I said, Trevor lives down the road from here so he offered to give me a lift. That lane's got too many twists and turns in it to risk walking along it at night.' Abbott shrugged. 'I don't mind it in the summer, but not now the nights are starting to draw in.'

'Did you hear them leaving the pub after you?' Kay prompted. 'Or did you see them when you were in the car park?'

'Not really. Me and Trev were talking all the way over to the car, and then once we were in we were still at it, making arrangements for tonight.' He paused, his brow puckering. 'I think I might've seen them walk out the door – you know, seeing the light come out through it as they left. But I didn't see nothing after that – Trevor don't hang about, see?'

'Any trouble amongst gun owners around here?'

'Not like that, no. I mean, you hear people taking pot shots at stuff in the woods around here but nothing big like that. Shotguns, mostly.'

Kay bit back a sigh, signalled to Barnes that the interview was over and gently moved the dog out of the way so she could stand.

'Thanks for your time,' she said, handing over a

business card. 'We'll be in touch if we have any further questions, but if you think of anything in the meantime that might help us, or if you overhear something, perhaps you could give me a call?'

'Will do, lass.' He took the card and held it close to his face, peering at the text. 'The sooner you find out who's behind that murder, the better I'll sleep at night.'

'You and me both, Mr Abbott.'

TEN

A frantic energy permeated the incident room later that day, a purple and gold sunset smudging the sky beyond the windows as Kay's team took their seats.

The sweet stench from cans of energy drinks filled the space around the whiteboard, and she eyed the latecomers as she took a slurp of strong coffee, noticing the dark circles under their eyes.

If she wasn't careful, they would be exhausted before the investigation had properly got underway, something she could ill afford at such a critical time.

She straightened as the last officer took his seat at the back of the small crowd, placing her mug on the table beside her.

'Thanks, everyone. Let's get through this and then those of you who are rostered to be back here in the morning can head home and get some rest.' She paused to scan the action list at the top of the latest report she'd printed from the HOLMES2 database, and checked her watch. 'Okay, first of all I can confirm the ACC and gold commander have advised that the immediate threat to the general public has diminished, and that this shooting is being treated as an isolated incident rather than terrorism or otherwise. Right now, local media will be broadcasting that information following a press conference that was held at headquarters earlier this afternoon. That should mean the phone calls die down a bit, and hopefully any we receive from now on will be more useful. Lucas Anderson has confirmed he's doing the post mortem for the victim first thing tomorrow morning, and if we're lucky we'll have some answers about who he is before the weekend. Can I have an update on the house-to-house enquiries?'

Harry Davis joined her by the board, and raised his voice so his colleagues at the back of the group could hear.

'We spoke to all but six households within a two-mile radius of the White Hart,' he said. 'Two of those properties are holiday homes, and we've subsequently conducted searches of those with the help of the agencies that manage them. The other four homeowners are currently overseas or away on business, and permission was obtained from all of them to search the gardens and any outbuildings in their absence. In summary, there was no sign of any firearms being hidden at the properties, nor any reports of anyone acting suspiciously last night following the shooting at the pub. The four properties currently empty hadn't been broken into, either.'

'Makes you wonder if our killer just went straight home afterwards,' said Barnes, tapping his pen against his notebook. 'If he didn't look like he was panicking, he wouldn't have drawn attention to himself.'

'Jesus, that's coldblooded.' Kay exhaled. 'But it's

possible. Which means it's entirely plausible one of us spoke to the killer today, and didn't realise.'

A shocked silence followed her words, and she gave a slight shake of her head to refocus.

'I'm still not happy with Len Simpson's statement about why he took so long to call triple nine either,' she continued, pacing the thin carpet tiles. 'Let alone the fact he washed the pint glass used by our suspect. What else do we know about Simpson? Anyone?'

Laura stepped forward, pulling out a page from the stack of folders in her arms. 'Guv, I've managed to find out a bit more about the discharge from the army. It was given to me off the record, but according to the retired corporal I spoke to, Simpson had a temper on him and belted someone round the head so hard during a fight that the bloke ended up in hospital with a serious concussion. He nearly didn't make it.'

'What was the fight about? Did your contact know?'

'Just some drunken disagreement that got out of hand, according to him. Simpson did six months in the glasshouse at Colchester, then got booted out.' Laura frowned. 'I got the impression there was more to the story than what I was told though, especially given that the corporal told me that it wasn't so much a discharge, more like a persuasive argument that convinced Simpson he wasn't welcome back in his old regiment, or anywhere else in the army.'

'All right, good work. Thanks.' Kay turned to the whiteboard and updated the notes under Len Simpson's photograph. 'I'll have a word with Sharp and see if he can find out anything else from his old military police sources.

It still doesn't answer the question about what he was up to in the thirty minutes between the last shot and the phone call to us, though.'

'Do you think he was hiding something, guv?' Gavin asked.

'That's the first thing that came to mind, yes. I mean as soon as he made that call, he'd have known we'd be crawling over that place for the next twenty-four hours.' Kay turned back to the gathered officers, her expression pensive. 'But suspicion isn't enough to get a search warrant, especially when we don't know what we're even looking for, or whether it has any connection to what went on there last night. Have we got the results from Harriet's lot about the fingerprints taken from the table the victim and his killer were using last night?'

Phillip Parker raised his hand. 'Patrick phoned from the lab just before we started the briefing, guv. We've worked through what they had, and we've come up with two names already in the system. The other prints were too smudged to be of any use.'

'Who are the two names?' Kay said, her heart rate lifting a beat.

'The first one is Clive Workman, who lives near Thurnham – he was arrested for assault four years ago but was given a suspended sentence...' Phillip paused for the collective groans to die down '...and then there's Mark Redding. Got caught drink driving two years ago and lost his licence. Neither of them were included on the list of names given to us by Simpson last night.'

Daniel Westland raised his hand to catch her attention. 'When I cross-referenced them against the firearms licensing database, both are shown as having licences revoked some time ago.'

Kay folded up the agenda. 'Right, that's good work both of you, thanks. Can you email me both of their records, Phillip?'

'Will do, guv.'

'Thanks. Myself and Barnes will interview Mark Redding. Laura and Phillip, I want you to speak to Clive Workman. The rest of you, I know it's been a long day already but keep going. I'm willing to bet that whoever did this didn't plan to kill our victim. Something went wrong when they left the pub and that argument got out of hand. Whoever he is, he'll be panicking, and he'll make a mistake.' Kay eyed each of her officers in turn as she spoke. 'We just have to make sure we're there when he does so we can arrest him.'

ELEVEN

Laura took a sip of lukewarm energy drink and grimaced before sliding the half-empty can into a holder under the dashboard vents.

'I don't know how you can drink that stuff,' she grumbled. 'It's disgusting.'

'And yet you always steal mine.' Phillip smiled, steering the car expertly through a chicane designed as a traffic-calming measure by the local council, the headlights illuminating a sleek cat before it dived underneath a parked van. 'Anyway, it's better when it's straight out the fridge.'

Running her tongue over her teeth, wondering how much enamel had just been slicked away by the sweet drink, Laura checked her notebook for the address Phillip had found.

'Clive Workman's house should be on the next street up from this bus stop on the left,' she said. 'According to his social media, he works for a local picture framing company. Single, never married as far as I can tell, and hasn't posted anything since March. Apart from the suspended sentence four years ago, there's been nothing since.'

'Anything in the record about why he attacked the other man?'

'Drunk, by the look of it. Got into a fight outside one of the nightclubs in Maidstone, and it turned nasty. The other guy ended up in hospital and Workman needed twelve stitches to his head.'

'How old was he when he was charged with assault?'

She waited while Phillip negotiated the turning and found a parking space a few metres past Workman's rented accommodation, then peered at her notes again in the light from her phone. 'Almost thirty-three. He was thirty-seven last month.'

'Maybe he's matured since that incident, then?'

Laura chuckled as she loosened her seatbelt and opened the door. 'One way to find out.'

She followed her colleague along a cracked and uneven footpath, careful to keep to the middle for fear of treading in the dog shit she could smell near the overhanging garden hedges and lamp posts.

Clive Workman's house was a narrow red-brick terrace squashed between four of its neighbours, the lawn turned over to concrete and a scuffed uPVC door perched above a slab of stone for a doorstep.

She ran her eyes over the handwritten sign that had been pinned to the letterbox warding off junk mail and unwanted callers, and when Phillip reached up to press the grubby doorbell she noticed he used the knuckle of his forefinger.

A feeble chime sounded from somewhere within the property, followed moments later by a dim hallway light being switched on and a shadow falling across the frosted glass panel at the top of the door.

'Jesus, how tall is this bloke?' she murmured, then craned her neck as it swung inwards.

The man who glared out at them towered over her, his wide shoulders breaching the gap in the doorframe as he crossed his arms over his chest, biceps bulging.

'What do you want?'

'A word,' said Laura, holding up her warrant card, her demeanour unflustered. 'I take it you're Clive Workman.'

'I've done nothing wrong.'

Laura saw a flicker of confusion graze the man's eyes, his jaw jutting out in indignation.

'If we could step inside, Mr Workman,' she said breezily. 'I'm sure this won't take long.'

He rolled his eyes, but stepped back to let them pass. 'I'm up early. Couldn't this have waited until tomorrow?'

'Where were you between eight thirty and eleven last night?' Laura said as the door slammed against the frame.

Workman turned to face them, a snarl on his lips before he remembered who he was talking to.

Laura watched as he forced himself to adopt a relaxed position, leaning against the scuffed hallway plasterwork and tucking his hands under his armpits.

'I was down the pub with a couple of workmates. There was a pool match on.'

'Which pub?'

Workman told him, and she watched Phillip write it down before glancing at the stack of bills piled up on one of the carpeted stair treads.

There was nothing untoward amongst the logos she could see sticking out, only one belonging to a national bank and the other from an insurance company.

When she turned back, the man was watching her with interest.

He dropped his arms to his sides. 'Is this about that shooting out north of Bearsted?'

'Do you own a firearm, Mr Workman?' she asked.

'No I bloody don't.'

'Do you know anyone who owns a firearm?'

'Look, what's going on?' Workman's eyes shifted from Phillip to Laura, then back. 'I just told you, I don't own a gun. I sold mine after I lost my licence.'

'But you have been to the White Hart recently.' She took a step forward. 'When was that, exactly?'

Workman blinked. 'A few weeks ago. Just to have a drink.'

'With whom?' said Phillip, pen poised.

'Matty Oakland. I used to kick about with him at school.' A slight smile appeared. 'Not that either of us has aged well since then.'

'We'll need a name and phone number,' said Laura.

'Yeah, 'course you do.' Workman fished his phone from his pocket, dabbed at the screen and then turned it around and held it up to Phillip. 'There you go. He lives over Folkestone way these days.'

'And the date you were at the White Hart?' he said. 'You didn't say.'

The man frowned. 'Christ, I dunno – it's not like I put it in my diary or anything. Matty called me out of the blue and said he was in the area, and did I fancy a drink.'

Phillip said nothing, taking his cue from Laura, who waited patiently while the seconds ticked by.

'It must've been three weeks ago,' said Workman eventually. 'Yeah. A Tuesday night, so I only had a couple of light beers. Driving, see?' His smiled widened. 'I've changed my ways.'

Phillip snapped shut his notebook as Laura turned for the door.

'Thanks for your time, Mr Workman. We'll be in touch if we have further questions.'

The man hovered on the doorstep a moment, then called out before they reached the far edge of the concreted garden.

'Hey, you won't say anything to my boss about coming here, will you?'

Laura peered over her shoulder, her face cast in shadow from the streetlight above. 'Not unless we suspect you of being involved, Mr Workman.'

'Right.'

She glanced at her colleague as the sound of Workman's door slamming shut echoed off the surrounding cars. 'I'll give this Matty Oakland bloke a call, but I didn't get the impression that Clive's our killer, did you?'

Wrinkling his nose, Phillip aimed his key fob at their car.

'To be honest, I'm still getting over the fact that Len Simpson hadn't cleaned those tables for over three weeks.'

She laughed, and pulled out her mobile phone.

'I guess we'll cross off the White Hart for potential locations for our Christmas party, then.'

TWELVE

Kay peered up as the gabled roof of Mark Redding's late Georgian house came into view, and then cursed as the last bar of signal reception disappeared from her mobile phone screen.

The entire property was surrounded by thick vegetation. Mature conifers filled the boundary alongside the lane that led them here, giving way to ancient horse chestnut and ash trees that cast a darkness over their car as Barnes steered it along the twisting driveway towards the house.

The gravel widened into a large parking area circling an ornate fountain in the middle, the water feature illuminated by spotlights that cast shadows over the frolicking stone-hewn nymphs in the centre.

She saw a manicured lawn beyond the car's headlights as Barnes braked to a standstill at the farthest end of the building, then spotted the gleaming front grille of a top-of-the-range sports car at the far end of a second driveway running down the side of the house.

'How the hell does he run a business from home if he can't get a bloody phone signal?' she muttered.

Barnes pulled the keys from the ignition. He pointed beyond the spotlights fixed artfully to the lime mortar walls between dark ivy that curled around the windows.

A junction box protruded from under the eaves, connecting to a telephone cable that swayed between the house and a wooden pylon farther along the driveway.

'God knows. Maybe he has to rely on the landline out here.'

Shoving her phone back into her bag before slinging it over her shoulder, Kay got out and followed him towards the front door, her shoes sinking into thick gravel.

A blinding security light blinked to life above the door when they were still a few metres away, and she cupped her hand over her eyes to shield them from the glare before looking over her shoulder.

'If I lived here, I'd have security lights too,' Barnes said under his breath as they drew closer.

He reached for a button underneath a security panel beside the door, and a loud buzzing noise emanated from the speaker above.

A split second later, a dog started barking, the noise growing louder until Kay could hear the scrabbling of claws on a wooden floor and heavy breathing on the other side of the door.

'Bloody hell, it's the hound of the Baskervilles,' said Barnes.

Then there was a rattle at the other end, and a woman's voice filtered out.

'Who is it?'

'Detective Sergeant Ian Barnes and Detective Inspector Kay Hunter. We'd like a word with Mark Redding.'

'Do you have an appointment?'

'No. We're currently undertaking an urgent investigation and his name has been given to us as a person of interest.'

'One moment.'

A clatter followed her words, then she was gone.

The dog continued to bark.

Kay cocked an eyebrow at her colleague. 'Reckon she'll let us in?'

'How could she resist my charm and wit?' He winked.

'Very funny. What does Redding do for a living, anyway?'

'Phillip says he's the director of an online training course business. From what he could work out, Redding farms out the work to different freelancers to write and deliver the video courses but does all the marketing and networking himself from home. There was no record of any other premises.'

Kay nodded, then turned her attention to the house as the door was inched open.

'Shush, Benji.' A woman in her fifties peered over a brass security chain. 'Have you got some identification?'

Recognising her voice from the security system, Kay held out her warrant card and waited while they were scrutinised.

Finally, the woman handed them back, loosened the chain and stepped to one side.

'Come in. My apologies for the security precautions.' She gave them an apologetic smile, her fingers wrapped around the collar of a black Labrador. 'Living out in the sticks, we can't afford to be too careful.'

'Have you had problems in the past?' Kay asked, automatically wiping her shoes on the coir doormat before walking on the oak timber flooring.

The dog sniffed at her outstretched hand, then pressed his nose against Barnes's trouser leg before trotting away, evidently satisfied that they posed no danger.

'We haven't, but the previous owners were burgled twice.' The woman slammed shut the door and fastened the chain once more. 'I'm Patricia Redding, Mark's wife.'

'We're sorry to disturb you at such a late hour, Mrs Redding,' Kay continued. 'But we have some urgent questions we'd like to ask your husband, and they couldn't wait until morning. Is he in?'

'He should be finishing a telephone conference with New York any moment. Come this way.'

An aroma of garlic and rosemary wafted in the air, and a pang of guilt rose in Kay's chest at the thought they were interrupting a normal family weekday routine.

She pushed the thought away, recalling the sight of the dead man in the White Hart car park the night before.

They followed Patricia Redding across the wide hallway and through heavy double doors into an anteroom, the plaster walls on either side of the shuttered front window painted off-white to accentuate the artwork displayed at intervals.

Thick carpet covered the floor, muffling their footsteps as they walked towards a closed door.

'One moment, and I'll see if he's finished.'

Patricia disappeared, and Kay held her breath, listening

to the confused tones of a man's voice and his wife's soothing response.

The woman returned moments later, and threw open the door. 'In you come. I explained to Mark that it's urgent and can't wait. Would you like some tea while you're talking?'

'That won't be necessary, thanks, Mrs Redding.'

Kay turned her attention to the man rising from a chair behind a large desk.

He paused to draw thick curtains across floor to ceiling windows that she guessed overlooked the parked sports car, then crossed the room to where they stood.

Several inches taller than her, he wore casual khaki trousers and a checked shirt open at the collar.

'Trish tells me this is important,' he said, 'and if she says that, I'm trained to do as I'm told.'

The skin around his eyes crinkled as he waved them across to a cluster of four armchairs beside an empty fireplace. 'Shall we sit over here? It'll be more comfortable.'

'Call me if you need me.' Patricia threw a cheery wave at them, and closed the door.

Kay looked around the office. Apart from a filing cabinet off to one side, another cupboard beside it in a matching ash finish and the computer set up on the desk, the rest of the room resembled a living room with its comfortable chairs and stone hearth.

A highly polished brass fireplace tool set stood beside a matching empty log cradle, and her shoes sank into the thick rug when she crossed to the chair nearest the desk.

Redding dropped into the one opposite Barnes with an

ill-disguised sigh and ran a hand over tired eyes. 'Sorry. I've been awake since five. It's all very well having a successful international business, but my contractors work in different time zones and sometimes a face-to-face conversation is better than an email.'

'We're sorry to interrupt your evening,' Kay began. 'However, we're investigating the murder of a man at the White Hart pub last night.'

'What?' Redding's eyes widened. 'Really? I wondered what the helicopter was about – it's been clattering overhead all day.'

'We still have a suspect at large.'

Redding's eyes flickered between Kay and Barnes, a frown appearing. 'Why do you need to speak to me about it?'

'We're speaking to everyone who visited the pub in the past few weeks leading up to the incident,' she said. 'Your name came up because your fingerprints were found on a table in the bar, which matched those taken when you were charged with drink driving two years ago.'

Redding's mouth twisted in disgust. 'Fingerprints? Good God – I thought that place looked rundown, but if I'd known it was that dirty, I wouldn't have stopped there.'

'What were you doing there?'

'I can assure you, Detective Hunter, it wasn't by choice. You'll appreciate it's not the sort of place either myself or Patricia would frequent.' Redding sighed. 'I was driving back from London when I received a phone call asking if I'd be able to meet with a potential client the other side of Maidstone at short notice. Rather than come all the way home only to turn back again, I stopped at the

White Hart while I waited for confirmation of the meeting.'

He paused, and gave them both a sheepish smile. 'I only had a lemonade, of course. I learnt my lesson two years ago, believe me.'

Kay inclined her head towards the desk. 'What do you do, Mr Redding?'

'I develop online training courses for NASDAQ and FTSE 250 companies.' He smiled benignly. 'Not very exciting, I'm afraid.'

'How on earth do you manage that with no mobile signal?' Barnes said.

Redding chuckled. 'I only use my mobile to pick up voicemail messages and texts while I'm here. We tend to use the landline for everything else. There's a vicious rumour going around that they might put in fibre optic broadband soon here, but I'm not holding my breath and Trish won't let me have an antenna installed on the house. She says it'll make the place look ugly.'

'Back to the White Hart,' Kay prompted. 'What do you drive?'

'The sports car parked on the driveway. You probably saw it when you got here.' Redding tried and failed to hide a smug smile. 'I've wanted one of those since I was a teenager. Trish calls it my mid-life crisis toy.'

'Have you been back to the White Hart since that day?'

'God, no.' Redding shuddered. 'Like I said, I'd never been in before and it was only for convenience. The place was dead when I was there, and the bloke behind the bar was... slovenly. I certainly won't be going in there again.

Not if they haven't even cleaned the tables in three weeks. That's disgusting.'

'Do you own a firearm, Mr Redding?' Barnes asked.

'Not anymore.' The man crossed his legs, pausing to straighten the crease in his trousers. 'I lost my firearms certificate when I was charged with drink driving.'

'One last question, Mr Redding,' said Kay. 'Where were you on Wednesday night between eight thirty and midnight?'

'Here,' said Redding. He waved towards the large computer screen on his desk. 'Two successive video calls with clients – one in Chicago, and the other in Minneapolis. Patricia brought supper to me at about nine to keep me going.'

Kay rose to her feet and handed over a business card. 'Thanks for your time this evening. We'll let you get on with your dinner.'

'No problem, detective. Any time.'

After they were shown to the front door, Benji appearing in the hallway to make sure the visitors left, Kay walked back to the car beside Barnes and inhaled the fresh night air.

Somewhere beyond the trees, an owl hooted, and a shiver crossed her shoulders.

'What do you think, guv?' said Barnes. 'He seemed genuinely surprised at the fact his fingerprints were found at the pub.'

'He did.' Kay jerked her chin at the low silhouette of the sports car as they reached their own vehicle. 'And that would've stuck in people's minds if it'd been parked at the

White Hart last night. You don't see many of those around here.'

Lost in thought, they reached the end of the Reddings' driveway before Barnes spoke again.

'I don't like this, guv. Twenty-four hours later, and we've got nothing.'

'I know.' She blinked to counteract the tiredness seeping through her, and wound down the window a crack. 'Let's hope Lucas has some answers for us at the post mortem tomorrow.'

THIRTEEN

The next morning, Kay pulled into the last remaining parking space at the side of Darent Valley Hospital and peered at the menacing clouds gathered above the imposing building.

As if anticipating her dark mood, thunder rumbled in the distance when she switched off the engine, closely followed by a streak of forked lightning that illuminated the sky beyond the swooping wave-shaped arches that formed the entrance to the accident and emergency bays.

Rain started to spatter against the concrete pavers as she hurried towards a side door to the left of the ambulances and the general public, and when she pushed against the chrome handle, a second thunderclap shook the glass panels either side of it.

There was still no news from Sharp's team regarding the identification and apprehension of a suspect, and the atmosphere within the Maidstone incident room had been one of growing frustration during that morning's briefing.

She checked her text messages while the lift carried

her to the second floor, noted a meeting scheduled at headquarters for noon to update the chief superintendent, then tucked her phone away as the doors swished open and she stepped into a highly-polished corridor.

Muted voices carried from behind the doors she passed, a stark contrast to the cacophony of noise outside on the concourse and when she entered through the double doors to the mortuary department, a calmness filled the space.

After all, the patients that lay beyond the inner door to her right were in no hurry to go anywhere.

'Morning, Detective Hunter.' Simon Winter looked up from his computer screen and gestured to a visitor log on the desk beside him, his brown hair hidden under a protective blue bonnet. He glanced at the window as the rain gathered in intensity. 'Looks like you made it here just in time.'

'Beats getting a soaking.' Kay smiled, and scrawled her name in the next available space. She eyed the signature above hers and frowned. 'Who else is here?'

'Zachary Taylor,' said a familiar voice from behind her.

She turned to see Lucas Anderson pulling on protective gloves as he bustled in from the corridor, a large white envelope tucked under one arm.

'Who's he?'

'The ballistics expert I requested,' said the pathologist. 'Luckily he was able to come at short notice – I wouldn't have been able to proceed without him. Well, not unless I wanted to face Harriet's wrath afterwards. He's just getting changed. Do you want to do the same, and I'll see you in there?'

'Sure.'

Ten minutes later, clad head-to-toe in protective overalls over her suit trousers and blouse, Kay walked out of the changing cubicle and tucked her hair under a paper bonnet.

Simon gave her a grim smile, then pushed open the door into the examination room.

Cool air caressed her face as she followed him towards a stainless steel table at the far end, her pulse missing a beat as she approached the mangled body laid out ready for the autopsy.

The stench of bleach and antiseptic fluids invaded her senses, stinging the back of her throat, and she blinked to counteract the tears that prickled from the effect of the chemicals.

However bad those smells were, it was nothing compared to what would follow over the course of the next hour or more.

Two identically dressed figures stood at the far end of the room, their attention taken by six bright white screens fixed to the wall and a set of X-rays pinned under each.

The shorter of the two turned as she approached, and beckoned her over.

'Kay, come and join us,' said Lucas, his face obscured by a mask. 'This is Zachary Taylor, our ballistics expert.'

'Call me Zach.'

Kay shook the outstretched gloved hand and peered up at deep-set brown eyes. 'I'd say nice to meet you, but...'

'Don't worry – I get that all the time with this job.' The

skin around his eyes crinkled with humour. 'How's the investigation going?'

'It's going.' Kay tried to keep the frustration from her voice, and failed. 'I'm hoping you'll give me some answers that will help us this morning.'

Lucas gestured to the X-rays. 'We can certainly try. Before we start, we wanted to take a look at these. Harriet's team didn't find any bullet fragments at the scene so that told us they'd lodged in our victim's body rather than going through.'

'You can see them here.' Zach tapped the third and fifth screens. 'The one in the skull is stuck where the man's nose used to be, and you can see the other amongst what's left of his sternum.'

Kay moved closer, staring at the ominous white smudges within the tangle of bones and cartilage. 'You can hardly tell they're bullets.'

'Which makes me think that they're soft-nosed rounds or hollow points rather than full metal jackets,' Zach mused. 'It's the body that captures the kinetic power of the bullet, especially at such short range. What your killer used looks similar to what's used to hunt deer. We'll know for sure once we open him up.'

'We needed to know where they were before we started,' Lucas explained to Kay. 'There's no sense in my nicking one of these with a scalpel by accident – it could damage vital evidence.'

'Ever worked on a shooting investigation before, Detective Hunter?' asked Zach as they walked over to the examination table.

'Please, call me Kay while we're in here. I haven't in a

long while.' She grimaced. 'I'd forgotten how bad they can be.'

She ran her gaze over the man laid out ready for the post mortem.

Under the stark lighting of the morgue, his injuries were even more horrific to look at than when she'd first encountered him in the White Hart's car park on Wednesday night.

Simon had done his best to wash away the blood and worse that had clung to the man's skin but there was little he could do for the shattered face and chest cavity.

'We took swabs of his hands, arms, face and clothing before passing those on to Harriet's team,' he said to Kay. 'It'll help them work out whether there was more than one weapon involved, and how close the victim was to his killer when he was shot.'

'Okay, thanks. What about identifying him? He didn't turn up on any of our systems, and given the damage to his face…'

'While I was getting these X-rays, I had some taken of the remains of his jaw as well,' said Lucas. 'What was left of his teeth showed some expensive work had been done in the past, so I've passed everything on to a forensic orthodontist. We obviously can't promise anything, but if there are records available then we might be able to let you have a name in the next twenty-four hours or so.'

'Fingers crossed, then.'

'Indeed.'

'Lucas, before you start, would you mind if I take a look at the entry wounds?' said Zach. He held up a tablet computer. 'I'll take photos on this as well, if that's okay with you – that way, I can use them to work out trajectories, that sort of thing, for my report.'

'Of course – Simon, could you give me a hand?'

Kay took a step back as the pathologist and his assistant rolled the victim onto his right side, and watched as Zach bent over to photograph the back of the man's skull before moving to where a second hole punched through the spine.

'Thanks,' he said, straightening while Lucas rearranged the victim ready for the examination. He frowned, swiping through the photographs. 'Bigger than a .22, I'd say.'

'Well, we'll soon find out,' said Lucas, pulling a magnifying lens over his face and selecting a scalpel from a trolley beside the gurney. 'Shall we make a start?'

Moving along to the victim's feet and staying well out of the way while the two pathologists worked, Kay listened as they provided a running commentary.

A microphone hanging from a cord above the table recorded Lucas's every word, which would then be transcribed and checked before his report reached her email inbox later that week.

In the meantime, she soaked up the knowledge emanating from the experts around her, desperate for information that would help the investigation.

She turned away while Lucas used tweezers to pick apart the remains of the man's face, knowing she would remember every detail for years to come.

The memories never left her – they only faded a little until a random thought triggered a recollection.

And yet, she would never stop what she did.

It was the only way she could bring the victim and their families any justice for a life taken too soon.

'Here's the first one.'

Lucas's voice roused her from her thoughts and she looked over her shoulder to see him using the tweezers to hold up a tiny object to the light.

She crossed the slip-proof floor to where he stood, and waited while Zach took a number of photographs before the pathologist placed the bullet fragment into an evidence jar.

After sealing the lid, he handed it to her.

'One down, one to go,' he said.

'Can you tell me anything about it?' she asked Zach, eyeing the squashed metal fragment. 'I mean, it's hard to tell what its original shape was now, isn't it?'

'Despite the damage to it, I'd suggest I was correct in saying that it's a soft-point. Expanding ammunition, too – designed to do a lot of damage on impact.'

'So we'd be looking for someone with a sizeable rifle, then?'

'Yes, most certainly. Something like a .308 – like I said, typically used for hunting deer, or perhaps wild boar.' He gave a grim smile. 'Not what you'd use for a localised rabbit problem, or rats. There wouldn't be much left of them afterwards. It might also be a semi-automatic, something with a small magazine holding half a dozen rounds.'

'That would explain why our witnesses said they heard the two shots in quick succession then.'

'The killer wouldn't have had to pause to reload,' Zach agreed.

A cold chill flickered across Kay's shoulders as she handed back the evidence.

'And if he was using a semi-automatic rifle with a full magazine as you suggest, then he could still be walking around with a loaded weapon,' she said, rummaging under her gown and pulling her mobile phone from her trouser pocket. 'I need to tell Sharp.'

FOURTEEN

Gavin bit back a yawn and held a borrowed and chipped ceramic mug under the vending machine nozzle as a viscous black liquid spurted out.

It smelled like coffee, but he had already worked out that at least three sugar sachets were required to make it taste anything like the real thing.

He wasn't even sure it contained caffeine, and wondered if any placebo effect was starting to wear off.

Moving across to an empty table, he brushed crumbs from its laminated surface with a napkin and sank into one of the aluminium chairs with his back to the wall of the break area.

The plasterwork had been painted a plain cream colour and noticeboards were fixed to it in several places around the room.

He automatically ran his eyes over the posters and other documents, but there was nothing new. Instead, he turned his attention to the small television bolted to the wall in the corner, the sound turned down. Subtitles ran across the bottom of the screen, the captioning struggling to keep up with the two daytime television presenters perched on a sofa, bright white teeth gleaming.

'Late night?'

He blinked, jerking his attention away from the latest gossip about a pop singer he'd never heard of.

DC Paul Solomon stood next to one of the spare chairs, his face as weary as Gavin felt.

The detective had helped the Maidstone team with some information during a drugs investigation a year ago, and had impressed everyone with his knowledge of the local smuggling operations that were being slowly disbanded.

He pushed back his chair, held out his hand to the other man, and gestured to the vending machine.

'Paul, good to see you. Can I get you a coffee?'

'Not likely. It's only visitors who drink that stuff.' A friendly smile followed his words. 'Okay if I join you?'

'Sure.'

'I didn't realise you were here until I overheard Sharp talking to my DI. Are you working on the shooting case?'

Gavin nodded. 'The search and arrest part of it. Kay's managing the victim side of things from Maidstone.'

'Any news there?'

'Nothing yet. The post mortem was this morning though, so hopefully…'

'Yeah. I heard there wasn't much left of his face.' Paul wrinkled his nose. 'Poor bastard. Rumour around here is that he was trying to run away, too.'

'Looks like it. What're you working on these days?'

'We've got a sex crimes gang along the north coast

we're about to break. Bringing in girls from the continent, then selling them.'

Gavin pushed away his coffee. 'I don't know how you do that every day. We had a case like that a few years ago, and I'll never forget some of the stuff we saw.'

'Someone has to, right?' Paul paused as a pair of uniformed constables walked in, radios turned down enough to hear the next call-out without interrupting conversations. 'How're you finding your way around here? Settling in okay?'

'Yes, thanks.' Gavin exhaled. 'I didn't realise how big the place was. Compared to Maidstone, I mean.'

'It's filled up quickly, especially after they closed Sutton Road. Are you enjoying being in the middle of a major investigation?'

'Always. I mean I know we have a victim, and a family who've lost a loved one, but this is what it's all about isn't it? Getting into the thick of it, using all the resources we have.'

'True.' Glancing over his shoulder at the sound of someone calling his name, Paul gave a rueful grin. 'Looks like I'm wanted. Listen, any time you fancy moving over here permanently, let me know. We could always do with good people in major crimes, and I reckon you'd fit right in.'

'Thanks, mate. I'll bear that in mind.'

Gavin watched as the other detective wandered off to join a woman in a black suit who waited by the door for him, and then both rushed off to wherever they'd been summoned.

Paul's words echoed in his mind.

He'd already been hearing from others on the search and arrest team about the numerous roles available here in Northfleet, and he couldn't ignore the fact that by comparison Maidstone was rather like a satellite of headquarters these days.

Was that why Sharp had volunteered him for this role?

Was he testing his abilities?

'Piper?'

Sharp's voice carried over the heads of the assembled officers, and Gavin saw him beckoning.

He pushed back his chair, threw the leftover coffee into a nearby bin without a second glance, and hurried to join the DCI.

'Guv?'

'We've had some new CCTV footage come in from one of the local teams,' Sharp said as he led the way back to the incident room. 'It's from a private residence half a mile from the White Hart. Apparently the owners got home from Bruges late last night and only heard about the shooting this morning. They got in touch and provided a copy of all the recordings from the past week.'

He paused, shoved open the incident room door and then strode across to the spare desk Gavin was using. 'Given we've had no luck from businesses along any of the major routes, we need to refocus our search on the immediate vicinity.'

'No problem, guv.' Gavin pulled his chair closer to the desk and logged in. 'I'll do a preliminary review of the recording from Wednesday night, and if I don't spot anything there, I'll work backwards a day at a time in case either the victim or the shooter recce'd the White Hart first. It won't be easy but at least we know what the victim was wearing and a rough description of what his killer was wearing too.'

'Good man. I always said to Kay you'd go far.' Sharp reached out and slapped his shoulder. 'This case is going to test everything you've learned so far, Piper, but trust me – it'll be worth it.'

'Thanks, guv.'

FIFTEEN

Kay wolfed down the last of her tuna sandwich, dusted crumbs from her lap and swallowed before reading through the latest updates from Northfleet.

The Maidstone incident room was filled with phones ringing, people talking across each other, and – somewhere over by the ancient printer and photocopier – loud swearing.

She shook her head in frustration, and forced herself to read the rest of the report.

Despite new information being available, she knew first-hand how long it could take for CCTV footage to be processed, especially when the officers watching it were already working long hours in front of their computer screens.

'Guv?'

She peered over her screen to see Barnes replacing his desk phone in its cradle.

'What's up?'

'I've just heard back from Daniel's team – Mark

Redding's in the clear. They've got a copy on file of the form he sent in confirming that he destroyed his firearms certificate. Apparently, he sold his rifle to a friend within the seven day period after being convicted of drink driving, and they've got the matching registration from the buyer as well.'

'What about Clive Workman?'

'They've got nothing on file to suggest he's ever applied for another licence after losing his original after that fight, or that he's been in trouble since. His alibi checked out too.'

'Bloody hell.' She huffed her fringe from her eyes. 'We just can't catch a break, can we?'

'Only a matter of time, guv.'

Kay scrunched up her sandwich wrapper and scooted it into the wastepaper basket under her desk. 'We need to try another angle. We've only looked at one demographic so far, and I think it's time to widen the search.'

'Are they not having any luck over at Northfleet either, then?'

'It doesn't look like it. Not from Sharp's latest update, anyway.'

'Are they looking at the illegal weapons aspect as well?'

'Absolutely. In the meantime, we've got to eliminate all of the legal firearms. We can't simply rule out our suspect being a legitimate owner of a gun until we know otherwise.'

'What are you thinking?'

She rose to her feet, rolled her shoulders, and then beckoned to him to follow her.

After crossing the room to the whiteboard, she took a moment to read the latest notes Barnes had added, and then turned to her colleague.

'Daniel told me that there are several groups of people who are considered under the "good reason" process of elimination for firearms certificates. So far, we've ignored special interest groups so I want to look at those.'

Barnes frowned. 'Like who, guv?'

'Historical re-enactment groups, private collections...' She paused. 'We've already covered target shooting clubs in the first wave of enquiries in order to get lists of members and eliminated most of those.'

'Do we count museums within those private collections?'

'We might as well. Even if our victim and his killer weren't employees of these places, they might be known to them.' She lowered her voice, seeing the doubt in his eyes. 'We've got to try, Ian. We're running out of options.'

'I know,' he murmured. 'All right. How do you want to divide up the work?'

'Hang on.' Kay peered past him to where Laura was standing at the door talking to Daniel, and waved her over, then spotted PC Kyle Walker passing with two boxes of paper in his arms. 'Kyle, what are you up to at the moment?'

He grinned. 'Being bossed around by Debbie, guv. She's loving it.'

'I'll bet. Tell her I need to boss you around instead for a while.'

'Will do.'

She waited until he joined them, then set out her plan.

'Laura, have you and Daniel ascertained whether anyone with a licensed firearm has reported a theft in recent weeks?'

'Everyone our team spoke to was asked to check their gun cabinets, and we've got nothing reported as missing,' said the detective constable.

'Okay, I want to spend today filling in the gaps with regard to licensed weapons,' Kay explained. 'We won't rule out illegally owned firearms but we do need to make sure our suspect isn't someone with easy access to a firearm. That's why I'd like you both to lead a breakout team and look at local historical re-enactment group members and museums. Concentrate on the larger calibre weapons though, because Zachary Taylor has confirmed the rounds were .308s. Barnes, you're with me – we'll make a start on the larger private collections that haven't been covered through Laura and Daniel's initial review.'

'How does this help us identify the victim, guv?' said Kyle, frowning. 'If you don't mind my asking, that is.'

'Not at all. Although Sharp's been tasked with leading the search and arrest team, we still need to work out what the connection is between the killer and our victim,' said Kay. 'Sharp will be doing the same – something links them, so we have to look at this from every angle.'

She waited while they finished updating their notes, and then reached out to grab Phillip Parker's sleeve as he passed. 'Any news from missing persons about our victim?'

The constable shook his head. 'No one who matches the description of existing mispers on the database, or the national charity one, guv – and there have been no new reports since the incident on Wednesday either.'

'Our victim could be someone with no family, then,' Laura suggested as Parker walked back to his desk.

'Even so, you'd expect him to have friends who'd report him as missing,' said Barnes. 'It doesn't make any sense.'

'None of this makes any sense,' Kay muttered. She glanced at the clock on the wall above the printer. 'Let's get on with this. We'll reconvene back here for the briefing this afternoon. Hopefully by then, we'll have some information to share with Sharp's team over at HQ.'

SIXTEEN

Kay dropped her sunglasses over her eyes before running a hand through her hair to free the wayward strands that caught in one of the arms, and checked the dashboard GPS.

Tangled overgrown hedgerows crowded the pool car from both sides, the narrow and twisting lane leading away from the main Staplehurst road.

She braked at the top of a steep decline, slowing her speed to negotiate a sharp turning to the left and then the car rattled across a metal cattle grid.

Tufts of grass appeared between the cracks in the asphalt and she zigzagged to avoid the worst of the potholes on either side as a rabbit shot across the road in front of her.

'You'd think the council would do something about the bloody holes,' Barnes grumbled, looking up from his phone. 'Look at the state of it.'

Kay smiled. 'We left the council-owned road half a mile back. This is all private land.'

Barnes lowered his phone, his jaw dropping as he cast his gaze around the woodland on each side of the car, sunlight strobing through leaves that were starting to turn a golden hue.

'Bloody hell. I knew this bloke owned some land, but I didn't realise it was this much.'

'Wait until you see the house.'

A second cattle grid shook the suspension, and then the thick swathe of oak and hornbeam gave way to pasture. Kay changed gear, settling her speed to walking pace while she admired the small herd of deer grazing to their left.

The pitted asphalt was replaced with a newer surface and widened out as the driveway curved around to the left, and she grinned at her colleague's ill-disguised gasp.

In front of them was an imposing late-seventeenth century Grade II listed house nestling amongst rolling lawns that abutted the fields.

Tall stone chimneys rose into the air from each end of the gabled roof, the afternoon sunlight catching the upper windows.

'I thought you said this bloke had a few sheds?' said Barnes, finally recovering from his shock.

Kay laughed. 'He does. They're round the back, out of view.'

'And who did you say he was?'

'Porter MacFarlane. He's been supplying props and equipment to film and television production companies for the past forty years. The big stuff, too – horse-drawn carriages, things like that. If you or Pia have watched a historical drama lately, chances are that you saw some of

Porter's collection being used.' She switched off the engine. 'And he has an armoury business that supplies guns. A lot of guns.'

'Ah, right.'

'That's how I first met him. Every time a production company wants to film a scene involving weapons, they have to notify us in advance so we can avoid any problems. Things like members of the public panicking thinking it's a real situation and calling us to sort it out. I was asked to provide support on a TV drama a few years ago and got chatting to him.'

Climbing from the car, she led the way over to the enormous front porch where a stocky man in his early sixties with a shock of white hair waited beside open oak doors, a wide smile forming as she drew near.

'Kay, how delightful to see you.' He gripped her hand. 'I was so sorry to learn about the attack on Adam. How is he doing?'

'He's fine now, thanks Porter. That herd of yours has got bigger since I saw you last.'

'A few additions from a local rescue centre. Two of them were too young to be released into the wild.' He gave an indulgent smile. 'They're safer here, at least.'

Kay turned to Barnes, introducing him. 'Porter's a bit different to some of the other local landowners around here. He actively allows the deer to roam on his property rather than let anyone hunt them.'

'Hence why he knows your Adam.' Barnes shook the man's hand.

'Are you the police?'

Kay peered past MacFarlane as a slim man in his late

twenties appeared at the front door, rolling down his shirt sleeves and straightening his tie as he walked towards them.

'Ah, Detective Hunter – meet my son, Roman.'

She nodded to the newcomer. 'We're here to ask your father some general questions in relation to an ongoing investigation.'

'I understand you have quite a collection of weaponry as well,' added Barnes.

'Ah, yes. This wasn't a social visit, was it?' MacFarlane's smile faded. 'Do you want to take a look?'

'Thanks, Porter.' Kay jangled her keys in her hand. 'Shall we follow you down to the sheds?'

'No need.' The man gestured towards an oversized golf cart parked beside the front steps. 'Hop in that, and I'll take us. I can give your colleague a tour of the place at the same time.'

Kay bit back a sigh, knowing how much the man enjoyed his work. 'The *short* tour, Porter. I've seen how much stuff you've got, and we don't have all day unfortunately.'

'Understood.'

'Don't forget we've got that video conference with the producer from Manchester,' Roman said. 'We've already had to postpone it once.'

'I'll be there,' said MacFarlane, giving his son a wave over his shoulder as he started up the cart. 'Don't worry.'

Five minutes later, the golf cart halted outside two corrugated iron sheds, each the size of a small aircraft hangar and casting shadows over a well-worn concrete apron.

'Quickest way is through the vehicle shed,' said MacFarlane, giving Kay an apologetic glance. 'Sorry.'

'Why's he apologising?' Barnes hissed under his breath while they waited for the props owner to find the right key from a bunch he withdrew from a pocket.

'Probably because he knows what your reaction is going to be when you see what he's got in here,' she replied. 'Just remember we're due at the other place by four o'clock otherwise they'll be closed before we can speak to the curator.'

'Here we go.' MacFarlane pocketed the keys and swung open a wicket gate in one side of the large doors. 'Hang on a moment, there's a light switch just... Ah, there.'

Kay blinked as a series of lights flashed to life in the rafters high above her head.

Four rows of various carriages, vehicles and bicycles filled the space as far as she could see, a slight mustiness in the air. Dust motes sparkled around her despite the highly polished paintwork and chrome, evidence of the collection being maintained rather than used on a regular basis.

Her gaze fell upon a reconditioned eighteenth-century curricle to her right.

'You've had it repainted,' she said as they followed MacFarlane along the far left-hand side.

'Yes, for a job up in Northumberland in March,' said MacFarlane, a hint of disgust in his voice. 'The director was quite insistent, even though I told him the colours aren't consistent with the period. Apparently, he wanted it to look *pretty*.'

Kay watched as Barnes's jaw dropped at the sight of a vintage Lancia.

'How old is this?' he managed.

'Early nineteen fifties. One of only a very few left in the country,' MacFarlane replied, his chest visibly swelling. 'I've run it at the Goodwood Revival a couple of times in the past. A long time ago, mind. These days I only let her out of sight for very special occasions.'

'Not for wedding hire, then?'

'Perish the thought, dear boy.'

'The rifles, Porter?' Kay prompted with a smile.

'Oh, yes. This way.'

Barnes tore himself away from the classic car and fell into step beside her as the props owner hurried towards the back of the cavernous space.

The end of the shed appeared shorter on the inside than the outside, a design quirk that was soon revealed when MacFarlane used a second key to open an inner door.

A blast of warm air washed over Kay, evidence that the secure room was both airtight and heated by the confines of the reinforced ceiling that cocooned the collection.

When they stepped over the threshold, Kay swept her gaze over the rows of steel gun cabinets lining the walls. A large workbench took up the space in the middle of the room, with an array of tools lined up along one side of it and the distinct scent of gun oil in the air.

'Okay, let's make a start,' she said. 'You said on the phone that everything's where it should be, right?'

'Absolutely,' said MacFarlane, unlocking the first cabinet to reveal three rows of assault rifles similar to the ones she had seen Paul Disher and his colleagues using on

Wednesday night. 'We haven't had a request for weapons since May, and the next scheduled production doesn't require our services until January.'

'Is your work always during the winter?' said Barnes.

'Usually, yes. It's quieter, you see. Less people around, so it's easier for the film crews to get on and work without being interrupted.'

'Do you train the actors as well?' Barnes asked as MacFarlane closed the cabinet door and waited for the next one to be opened.

'Sometimes we'll have the actors meet here first, especially if they've never handled a weapon before,' he replied, wrinkling his nose. 'Nothing worse than watching someone holding a weapon the wrong way. Pure Hollywood, as far as I'm concerned.'

'Do you have anyone working with you?'

'Just my eldest son, Roman, who you met up by the house. He's taken over doing all the administrative work from me, which frees up my time to meet with prospective clients and take the guns wherever they're required for filming.' MacFarlane moved to the next cabinet. 'With all the streaming services available, there's a high demand for content so we're never at a loss for work.'

'But you've had nothing since May, you said.'

A genial smile crossed the man's face. 'That's right. It's a bit quiet at the moment but I'm sure it'll pick up again soon. Always the way in this business.'

'Are we the only visitors you've brought down here recently?' asked Kay.

'You're the only ones who've seen the collection in the last four months.'

'Don't you show this lot to prospective clients, then?'

'No – most of them know what they want and just tell me when and where. If they're not sure and want to see something, then I'll meet with them up at the house and take three or four weapons from here to show them.' MacFarlane paused, and slid out a battered laptop computer from a shelf between two cabinets. 'We keep a stocktaking system on here, and we record everything that's removed from this room. Even the samples I show my clients are recorded so we know where any weapon is at all times.'

'Sort of like our evidence logs.'

'Exactly.'

'We'll need a note of the last visitors,' said Kay. 'Just to rule them out.'

'No problem. I'll email you their contact details once I'm back in the office. It was a small production outfit from Leeds.'

'There's one last thing, Porter, and this is something we're asking everyone – where were you between the hours of eight and midnight on Wednesday?'

The man's eyes widened, his cheeks flushing, and then he spluttered. 'Are you...? Of course, you're serious. I'm sorry. Yes, I can vouch for my whereabouts. I was here, having a late video conference call with a counterpart in Los Angeles who's shipping one of my carriages over to New England for a film next week. I'll send you the details if you like.'

'Thanks, Porter. I appreciate it.'

After twenty minutes, the armourer closed the last

cabinet door and wiped a bead of sweat from his forehead with a cotton handkerchief.

'Let's get some fresh air,' he said with a smile.

Barnes gave the Lancia a last longing gaze when they passed it, then shook his head in wonder as Kay grinned at him.

'Now I understand why you didn't let any of the others come here,' he murmured. 'We wouldn't have seen them for hours.'

'Thanks again for your time this afternoon, Porter,' said Kay when they reached the door.

'No problem at all. I hope you catch the bastard.' Locking the shed, MacFarlane tucked the keys into his pocket and gestured towards the golf cart. 'Shall we?'

'Just one final question,' said Barnes. 'Those keys. Are they the only set?'

'They certainly are. And if I don't have them on me, they're kept in a fireproof safe at the back of my wardrobe.' MacFarlane gave a grim smile. 'We don't take any chances here, detective.'

SEVENTEEN

Laura cast a sideways glance at Kyle Walker as the tall constable climbed from the car and squinted at the array of industrial units and fenced-off yards on either side of the private road.

A row of enormous articulated trucks were parked side-by-side on the other side of a wire mesh boundary, signs fixed to the fencing at regular intervals warning of CCTV and alarms, and in the distance the hiss and spit of an air hose at work resonated off the brick wall beside her.

Farther along from that business, a mechanical digger chugged and groaned within the confines of a builder's yard, its driver spinning the machine around as deftly as a ballerina while he worked at moving a pile of ballast from one side to the other.

The roar of traffic on Sittingbourne Road underpinned all the other noises, and she wondered how the workers in the offices farther along the industrial estate managed to concentrate.

Especially with the noise from the heavy goods vehicle training track at the end of the road.

Suddenly the incident room overlooking Palace Avenue didn't seem so bad after all.

'I thought you said this bloke was an expert in World War Two history?' said Kyle, watching as a trainee driver sped past on the track. He winced as the man crunched through the gears of the tractor while the trailer behind it juddered alarmingly. 'Didn't he tell you he was recce'ing some buildings today? I can't see anything that old here.'

Laura grinned, then pointed at the entrance to a footpath a few metres away. 'He said if we follow that, we'll find him.'

'Lead the way, then.'

The path was little more than loose stones and dirt, but at least it was dry.

After a few metres, the brick wall gave way to wire fencing that provided a clear view across the wide expanse of the test track.

During summer months, the place was used for open-air exhibitions and fairs, the grass expanse filled with thousands of people from all over the county and farther afield.

She smiled, recalling assignments as a uniformed constable helping to manage the throngs that surged through the ticket gates day and night.

Within a few footsteps, the path gave way to a muddy overgrown track that wove its way around the back of the old airfield and towards a wooded area. A few metres away, she spotted large chunks of discarded concrete and broken walls covered in moss, tree roots crawling like possessive fingers over the decaying structures.

Pausing a moment, she held up her hand to Kyle and lowered her voice. 'I don't like this. He said he'd meet us here but this feels wrong.'

Kyle's suntanned features paled. 'Do you think this is a trap? He could be our suspect. I mean, we're only a few miles from the White Hart here.'

'He sounded all right on the phone.'

Her colleague snorted under his breath. 'They reckon the worst serial killers are the politest people you'd ever meet.'

Laura swallowed, then pulled out her mobile and checked the signal.

One bar wavered in the top left corner of the screen.

'There's someone over there, next to that pile of stones.'

She looked to where Kyle pointed as a balding middle-aged man dressed in jeans and a dark green sweatshirt emerged from what appeared to be a hole in the ground.

He raised a hand in greeting, dropped a battered canvas hat onto his head, and swished through the long grass towards them.

'Are you the detectives?' he bellowed.

'Yes.' Laura waited until he was closer, and then held up her warrant card and made the introductions.

'Elliott Windlesham,' he said. 'I understand you wanted to talk to me about guns? I take it this is about the shooting that was on the news?'

Laura exhaled, taking in the man's dishevelled appearance.

He didn't look like a killer, and his cheerful greeting allayed her fears a little.

'It is, yes. We just wanted to ask you a few questions about the members of your club.'

Windlesham thrust his shoulders back. 'I can assure you, detective, they're all upstanding members of their respective communities, and we take safety very seriously.'

'I'm sure you do,' Laura said soothingly. 'However, as you'll appreciate we do have to make sure we've spoken to everyone in the area who has access to firearms.'

'Of course.' The man relaxed a little, then gave a shy smile. 'Do you mind if I continue working while you ask your questions? As I said on the phone, I'm pushed for time today and if I don't get this done today I might not get another chance until the spring.'

'What is it you're doing?' said Kyle.

'Metal detecting around this old pill box.' Windlesham's smile broadened. 'It hasn't been done in a while, and the owners of the land around here don't often let us have an opportunity to explore.'

Laura peered across to where the man had emerged, and frowned.

The old wartime defensive structure was unrecognisable from the box-shaped buildings she'd seen dotted around the Kentish countryside – the front wall had tumbled forward and was now buried under an ancient tree trunk, and an ash sapling was sticking up through what was left of the roof.

'Do you expect to find anything?'

'The soil can shift over time, so I'm hopeful I might

dig up some new finds for the museum. They don't like us going inside anymore in case the rest of it falls down, but I couldn't resist a peek,' he said, and winked.

'Well, we'll try not to keep you too long from your explorations.' Laura nodded to Kyle as he removed his notebook from his utility vest. 'First of all, could you tell me where you were on Wednesday night between the hours of eight and midnight?'

Windlesham clasped his hands behind his back. 'I was chairing the monthly meeting for our historical group in the village hall at Detling. Quite a packed room, too – always reassuring to see. Some months, we only see half a dozen but we had a guest speaker from the MoD. Riveting stuff.'

'And what time did you leave the village hall?'

'By the time we packed everything away, it was getting on for half ten. After that, myself and two of the other club members went for a drink in Thurnham on the way home. I got back at about ten past eleven – my wife will vouch for me. She was watching the end of a rom-com on the telly.'

'If you could let us have the names of the people you went out for a drink with as well, please.'

She waited while he scrolled through his phone to find the numbers for Kyle. 'You're involved with one of the re-enactment groups here as well – do any of your members hold firearms certificates?'

'Yes, myself and four others all have certificates. We only ever use the rifles for demonstrations using blank ammunition. Everything's kept under lock and key at my place.'

'In Detling?'

'Yes. The gun cabinet's in my son's old bedroom. He left home about five years ago to study in the US and never came back – having too much fun, I suspect.'

He smiled, but Laura could hear the loneliness underlying the comment.

'Have there been any problems with members of the club recently, Mr Windlesham?'

'No, not that I've noticed.'

'What about any arguments perhaps, or disagreements?'

He shook his head. 'No, nothing like that. There are only fifteen of us, and only four with firearms certificates. There aren't enough of us, and we don't meet up often enough to warrant anyone falling out I suppose.'

'Does anyone else have access to that cabinet?' Kyle asked, then blushed as he caught her eye.

She gave a slight shake of her head – she didn't mind who asked the questions, as long as they got the answers they needed.

'Not even my wife,' said Windlesham. 'The other chaps have nowhere sufficiently secure to keep their rifles, which is why they're all kept at my place. Your firearms team are aware of the situation – I've kept them up to date about the collection.'

'And we appreciate that,' said Laura. She raised her chin as a cool breeze rustled the branches above her head. 'Along with your time this afternoon. We'll leave you to it before it gets dark.'

'Thanks. Hope you catch the bastard.' Windlesham shivered. 'Doesn't bear thinking about, a man wandering around shooting people like that. Just doesn't happen around here, does it?'

'We're doing our best. Thanks again.'

Trudging back through the undergrowth towards the footpath, Laura fought down her frustration as she replayed the conversation in her mind.

She didn't think the re-enactment enthusiast would be able to help with their investigation, but accepted the task as one that had to be done in order to eliminate anyone who might have knowledge of their suspect – or his victim.

'I hope the others have had more luck than us,' Kyle grumbled beside her.

Laura smiled as they made their way past the test track once more, the pool vehicle coming into sight at the end of the path.

'Me too. That's the way it goes sometimes – right?'

'All too often.'

She caught the keys he tossed to her. 'We're making good time, though. Fancy stopping for a coffee on the way back to the station?'

'I thought you'd never ask.'

EIGHTEEN

The narrow lane was quiet when Kay thanked Barnes for the ride home and closed the passenger door.

She watched until the rear lights from his car disappeared past the bend in the road beside the converted oast house, and then rummaged in her bag for her keys and trudged across her driveway towards the front door.

Her back ached, her backside was numb from sitting in a two-hour video conference call with headquarters, and her thoughts were starting to tumble one after the other with all the information she was trying to process.

The front door opened before she could insert her key, and she smiled.

Adam Turner, her partner for over a decade now, held a glass of wine in one hand and wore a cheeky grin.

'Figured you'd need this.'

She kicked off her shoes beside the stairs, closed the front door and sighed, some of the stress from the past three days seeping away.

'You're not wrong,' she said, stepping into his

embrace. Burying her nose into his T-shirt, she closed her eyes. 'I'm beat.'

'Barnes said you were on your way home. I've run a bath, and I made soup earlier.' He squeezed her shoulders, then kissed the top of her hair. 'Go on, get yourself upstairs. I'll pop up in a bit to make sure you haven't fallen asleep in the water.'

'I owe you.' She frowned as they drew apart. 'What's that smell?'

'A minor incident with a pregnant cow this morning. I'm just waiting for the first load to finish in the washing machine, and then I'll do my overalls.'

Kay wrinkled her nose. 'Poo.'

'And the rest.' He grinned. 'Go on – upstairs.'

Five minutes later, Kay was soaking in hot water, bubbles frothing up to her ears and her wine glass perched beside her.

Despite Adam's warning about not falling asleep, she closed her eyes.

She could hear him downstairs, the whirr of the tumble dryer starting up moments before the washing machine, and then he was whistling a tune from one of the TV shows they'd binge-watched over the summer.

All normal, and all a stark contrast to the reality that was waiting for her in a few hours' time.

'I knew you'd fall asleep.'

Her eyes opened in an instant, her hands thrashing in the water as she steadied herself before aiming a guilty look at Adam.

He was peering around the door, grinning. 'That water must be cold now. Come and have some soup – you'll be no good to anyone in the morning if you go to bed hungry.'

In reply, her stomach rumbled, and he rolled his eyes.

'Out,' he said, laughing as he disappeared, his footsteps on the stairs.

Kay smiled as she towelled herself dry and then pulled on old jeans and a sweatshirt while the water drained away.

When she entered the kitchen, Adam was spooning tomato and basil soup into two bowls on the centre worktop, a chunk of crusty bread on plates beside them.

She rinsed out her wine glass, poured some water and sank onto one of the bar stools, picking up a spoon.

'Did I tell you how much I love you?' she said.

'You did, and I love you.' He sat opposite her and took a sip of wine. 'What time are you due in tomorrow?'

'Six thirty. I'm on call, too.'

'Any news?'

She shook her head in between mouthfuls. 'Nothing yet. They think it's an isolated incident, and whoever shot our victim has gone to ground.'

'That's something, I suppose. Definitely not a random shooting, then?'

'They seemed to know each other – I mean, they were drinking in the pub together before it happened.' She tore apart some more of her bread and wiped it through the soup. 'How come you're up so late?'

'Apart from washing cow shit out of my clothes, you mean?' He smiled. 'I was watching an old eighties film on TV, then figured you'd be hungry when you got in. Eating tonight saves me worrying about breakfast anyway – I've got a client popping by the surgery early tomorrow with a spaniel that's boarding with us for a few days.'

Kay swallowed the last of the bread and looked around the kitchen. 'I'm surprised there's nothing here to greet me.'

'Honestly, after the cows this week, I haven't got the energy.' He ran a hand through his dark curls, his eyes weary. 'If anything crops up, I've agreed with Scott that he'll babysit. As it is, I've got to try to catch up with the farm visits I was meant to be doing today.'

Yawning, Kay gathered up her bowl along with his, put them in the dishwasher and then staggered back to where he sat.

'This isn't going to sound very rock 'n' roll,' she said, draping her arms around his shoulders. 'But do you fancy an early night?'

'Yes.' He laughed. 'God, we're getting old.'

NINETEEN

Ian Barnes rubbed his hand across his freshly-shaven jaw and glared at his computer screen.

Bright morning sunlight stabbed its way through the slatted blinds across the incident room windows, warming his back and softening the glare from the overhead LED bulbs.

Conversation around him was muted at the moment, the volume not yet at the level it would reach once everyone else turned up to start their shifts within the hour. The current undertone provided a calming white noise while he skim-read new emails, his gaze moving from the computer to his phone and back.

He blinked to counteract the grittiness under his eyelids, rued the fact he'd spent most of the night lying awake, and wondered how Gavin was getting on over at headquarters.

'No news?'

He glanced up as Kay dropped a paper bag under his

nose, the telltale aroma of a bacon sandwich making his mouth water.

'Not yet, and thanks.'

She moved around to her desk, switching on her computer. 'What time did you get here?'

'About half an hour ago. Figured I'd beat the traffic that way.' He paused, ripping open the bag and took a mouthful of sandwich before pointing at his screen. 'As well as trying to get a head start on these.'

'Anything useful?'

He shook his head, then looked at his watch. 'What time are you expecting Sharp?'

'Now.'

Barnes jumped at the voice.

The DCI smiled as he perched on Kay's desk. 'I don't suppose you've got any more of those lying around?'

'Sorry, guv, no.' She glanced at the door. 'I can go and get you something though, if you want?'

'Don't worry – I'll live.' Sharp shrugged. 'Besides, Rebecca's trying to get me to behave myself.'

Barnes swallowed, then tossed the wrapper into the bin under his desk. 'Any news on the search this morning, guv?'

'No, and if we don't get a breakthrough today, the media is going to crucify us at this afternoon's press conference. I take it you've had no success finding out who the victim is yet?'

'Not yet but we're about to start the briefing if you'd like to join us for that,' said Kay. 'At least then you'll have the latest update before heading back to Northfleet. There's a lot of information coming in from different teams – we were all out yesterday interviewing licensed firearms owners.'

'Sounds good.' Sharp rose to his feet. 'I'll have a wander round and speak to a few old faces while you're rounding up everyone.'

Twenty minutes later, Kay had taken her team through the morning's agenda, assigned tasks for the day and was bringing the briefing to a close when she saw Barnes raise his hand.

'I was thinking last night, guv…'

'I'm glad I'm not the only one who didn't get much sleep.'

A rumble of laughter filled the room, and she gave one of the constables a knowing smile. All of them had been working long hours since Wednesday night, and yet she knew none of them would rest until the victim's killer was in custody.

'And you'd be right,' Barnes continued. 'What worries me is that we've exhausted the list of legal firearms holders, and no one's raised any major concerns. We've had a couple given cautions about the age of their gun cabinets, but everyone we've spoken to has given us an alibi, and we've seen nothing to suggest there are guns missing. That leaves us with illegal firearms.'

He watched as Kay leaned against a nearby desk as if to steady herself, her gaze remaining on the whiteboard and its spiderweb of notes and photographs.

'It sounds like you and I have been having the same nightmares,' she said eventually. 'And if we're right, then it widens the scope for motive as well. Until we know who our victim is, we can't rule it out.'

'I can help you there, guv.'

Barnes swivelled in his seat at the sound of Kyle Walker's voice carrying across the incident room.

The constable cradled his laptop in the crook of his arm, excitement in his eyes.

'What've you got?' said Kay.

'We've just had an email come through from Lucas Anderson. He's heard back from his orthodontist expert, and they've got a match for our victim.'

The incident room exploded with voices as the team began talking over each other, until Kay raised her hand.

'Quiet.' She waited until the noise abated, then turned back to Kyle. 'Who is it?'

'A thirty-four-year-old by the name of Dale Thorngrove. They matched the samples to dental records from a practice in Sevenoaks. He had to have an implant three years ago after losing a front tooth in a fight outside a pub in Rochester.'

Barnes flipped open his notebook and wrote down the details. 'Have you got the dentist's name who did the work?'

'I'll email it to you now,' said Kyle.

'Thanks, I'll give them a call and find out if they've got a note of next of kin and an address for Thorngrove.'

'I'll go with you when you speak to them.' Kay was already updating the whiteboard, and glanced over her shoulder as Sharp passed behind her. 'Are you off?'

The DCI had his phone to his ear and nodded. 'I'll update my team there, and we'll start looking at that pub fight from three years ago. We might find out our suspect's name that way.'

'I'll call you later.' She turned her attention back to her officers. 'Okay, further actions for today. Laura – can you source a decent photo of Thorngrove we can use, and then take Kyle with you and go and speak with Len Simpson at the White Hart. Maybe the photo will help to jog his memory about whether he's seen him before Wednesday night. Ian, we'll speak to the dentist first to get next of kin details and then interview the family. Debbie – get that update from Lucas into HOLMES2 and then divide up the team. I need Daniel's lot to find out if Thorngrove's details show up in their database, and I want his photo shown to gun shops, dealers and shooting clubs in the area.'

She paused for breath, waiting while they caught up with their note-taking. 'And if that doesn't work, then we'll show his photograph to everyone we've spoken to these past three days. We're getting closer, everyone.'

Barnes pushed back his chair after Kay ended the briefing, a renewed energy surging though him.

Suddenly, he didn't feel tired anymore.

TWENTY

Kay tapped her fingers on the steering wheel, willing the traffic lights to turn green, and wondered who had managed to scrawl a lewd joke amongst the grime at the top of the trailer door on the articulated truck in front of her.

'What have you managed to find out about Dale Thorngrove?' She glanced over at Barnes, who was scrolling through emails on his phone.

He lowered the phone and pointed at the road as the lights changed, and she slipped the car into gear.

'Our victim was thirty-four when he died, single as far as Kyle could work out from his social media profiles, and worked as a tyre fitter at a garage in Aylesford for the past two years.'

'What about an address?'

'The one on the DVLA database is for a one-bedroom flat in Snodland from six years ago. Rented.' He tucked his phone into his jacket pocket and fished out his notebook, flicking through it. 'I've spoken to the management company but they reckon Thorngrove hasn't lived there for the past three and a half years. I'm hoping the dentist might have a more up to date address. Either that, or his parents ought to know. We managed to pull their details from his social media profiles as well.'

'Where are they?'

'Burham.'

'Interesting. I wonder why he didn't update his address with the DVLA?'

'Perhaps he forgot.'

'Or was avoiding someone.' Kay negotiated a roundabout and joined the A20 towards their first destination. 'I wonder why he went to a dentist in Sevenoaks? Maybe this is where he's been living.'

'We'll have to ask her.' Barnes frowned. 'I'm surprised there's nothing on our system about the punch-up if Thorngrove was injured that badly.'

'Maybe it fizzled out before anyone got a chance to call it in. You know what it can be like – they think getting into a fight solves everything until they realise it's not like they see in films and that it hurts like hell.'

Her colleague chuckled. 'True. Here, take the next left up there by the lights – it'll be quicker this time of day.'

She did as he suggested, eyed the GPS on the dashboard as it recalculated her route, and spotted the sign for the dental surgery two minutes later.

Parking in a spare space on a wide asphalt driveway, she followed Barnes to the front door of a dormer bungalow that had been converted into business use at least a decade before.

When she entered the reception area, the smell of

clinical-strength antiseptic assaulted her senses, and served as an unwelcome reminder that she was overdue for a check-up.

She pushed the thought away, walked past the two customers waiting for their appointments, and held up her warrant card to the twenty-something behind the counter.

'We've got a meeting with Dr Sharman,' she said.

The twenty-something shot her a high wattage smile, no doubt aided by the latest whitening products. 'She's just finished with a patient, so I'll let her know you're here.'

'Don't worry – I saw them arrive.'

Kay turned at the woman's voice, and took a step back. 'Jasmina?'

The dentist grinned in response, and reached out to take her arm after seeing her patient out. 'Come on through to my office.'

'I didn't make the connection with the name...' Kay managed as Barnes followed in their wake along a short hallway and then up a flight of stairs. 'How are you?'

'Bloody busy, but don't worry – I understand you need some help.' The dentist waved them into an office at the top of the stairs and closed the door. 'That's better. No need for the clients to hear us gossip about old times.'

Kay returned the smile, and introduced Barnes. 'Ian, meet Dr Jasmina Sharman – we used to be neighbours in my old uniform days.'

'Thanks for seeing us at short notice,' he said, shaking hands. 'That was over in Tonbridge, wasn't it?'

'A long time ago – or at least that's what it feels like.' Jasmina gestured to two visitor chairs. 'And Kay, I need to apologise for not returning your phone calls. Life has been… interesting these past couple of years. Hence the change of surname.'

'I'll give you another call once this investigation is over, and we'll have a proper catch up, don't worry.'

'Sounds good. Now, what did you need to know about Dale Thorngrove?' The dentist tapped her computer keyboard, peering at the screen. 'I've got his records here, and your colleague – Kyle, isn't it? – promised he'd email over the appropriate warrant as soon as possible. I wouldn't normally do this, but I'll make an exception – I'm guessing this is urgent, right?'

'Right. In confidence, we've had an orthodontist compare the records you sent against the victim of a shooting on Wednesday night—'

'I heard about it on the news—'

'And we're certain that victim is Thorngrove.' Kay leaned back in her chair. 'Now we have to piece together his last few days and try to work out who had motive to kill him. I realise it was three years ago, but do you recall him saying anything about the fight in Rochester?'

'Not at the time.' Jasmina gave a wry smile. 'To be honest, he was in too much pain and then relieved once it was all over. He wasn't very talkative at all that time.'

'That time? He's been back since?'

'Yes, four months ago. It's why my receptionist was able to retrieve his details so quickly for you – she recognised the name.'

'Is he a regular client then?' said Barnes.

'No, not at all – he chipped the implant I fitted, and wanted me to replace it.'

'Have you got a current address for him?' Kay said, already pulling her notebook from her bag.

'I have, yes. It's in Walderslade.'

After writing down the details, she drew two lines underneath it and frowned. 'Any idea why he'd use a dentist in Sevenoaks if he lived that way?'

'At the time, I was the only one able to do the work at short notice on a Saturday morning.' Jasmina smiled. 'My practice had only been open a few months and I was still building up my own client list after leaving that place in Tonbridge.'

'How did he seem when you last saw him four months ago?'

The dentist shrugged. 'He wasn't as chatty as some of my clients. Sometimes it's hard to get them to shut up long enough to do the work. I seem to remember him being polite, that's all.'

'Did you get the impression he might've had something on his mind?'

'Nothing that stood out to me. We got the work done and sent him on his way. I did suggest to him that he needed to see the hygienist soon because his teeth were in such a state, but we never saw him again.' Jasmina sighed. 'I'm sorry to hear that he's your victim though. What a horrible way to go.'

TWENTY-ONE

'I hate this part.'

Barnes shoved his hands in his pockets and waited on the pavement while Kay retrieved her bag from the back seat of the car, and scuffed a discarded tennis ball back and forth under his shoe before aiming it at the base of a nearby privet hedge.

'I know.' She joined him beside an open metal gate and checked her phone was switched to silent mode, then looked at the pretty garden beyond. 'Me too.'

'Ready?'

'As I'll ever be.'

Her colleague squared his shoulders and strode towards the front door, rapping his knuckles against a glass panel at the top of it.

A man in his late sixties opened it within seconds, his bushy eyebrows knitted together and green eyes perplexed.

'I'm not interested in buying anything, whoever you…' He broke off as they held up their warrant cards for inspection. 'Police?'

'Detective Inspector Kay Hunter, and my colleague DS Ian Barnes. Are you Derek Thorngrove?'

'Yes. What's this about?'

'May we come in, please?'

Perplexity turned to fear as the man stepped back and Kay entered a brightly painted hallway, noticing a vase of petunias on a small table underneath a mirror.

'Who is it, Derek?'

'Police.' He pointed to a door behind Kay. 'Best go through to the living room.'

When she entered the room, a woman raised herself from an armchair with the aid of an aluminium cane, her mousy hair streaked with grey and tousled.

'What's the matter?' she demanded. 'Is this about Dale?'

'Please, Mrs Thorngrove, would you like to sit back down?' said Kay. She positioned herself beside a radiator so she could face them both. 'I'm very sorry to be the bearer of such terrible news, but we believe your son was killed in an incident on Wednesday night.'

A shocked pause followed her words, and then Derek lowered himself to the arm of his wife's chair, his hands shaking as he reached out for hers. 'Wednesday, you say? What's taken you so long? Are you sure it's Dale?'

'I knew something was wrong,' his wife wailed. She gulped as tears streamed over her cheeks. 'I knew it. I tried to phone him yesterday but it went straight to voicemail. He never phoned me back. He always phones back.'

Derek wrapped an arm around her, burying his face in her hair as he wept. 'My boy…'

Kay gave them a few more moments, crossed to the

sofa and sat facing them. 'All I'm able to tell you at the moment is that Dale was killed following an argument in a pub just north of Maidstone. He was shot.'

'Oh my God.' Derek wiped at his eyes, shuffling around to face her. 'We heard about that on the news. Are you sure it's him?'

She glanced down at her hands. 'We were able to match his dental records earlier today. Yes, we're sure it's Dale.'

'I want to see him.'

'Sarah, love – they might not want us to.'

Kay took a deep breath. 'It's not a case of us not wanting you to, Mrs Thorngrove. It's simply that we think in this instance that it could be traumatic, and that you may prefer to remember Dale…'

'Y-you said he was shot.' Sarah dabbed at her eyes. 'Do you mean… in his face?'

'I do, yes.'

Her words were met with renewed sobs.

'We haven't released any of those details to the media in order to maintain privacy for both yourselves and our investigation,' she said. 'Again, I'm so sorry.'

'What can we do to help you find who murdered our son?' Derek gave his wife a hug, kissed the top of her head, and then rose to his feet. He crossed to the sofa and sat beside Kay, turning to face her. 'Tell me.'

She glanced at Barnes, standing by the door with his notebook ready, then back to Thorngrove's father.

'Are you aware of anyone who would want to cause your son harm? Has he mentioned anyone he's been worried about in the past few weeks?'

'No, he hasn't mentioned anything to me.'

'Nor me.' Sarah sniffed, then rummaged in the drawer of a small oak table beside her armchair and pulled out a packet of tissues. She blew her nose, then peered at Kay through red-rimmed eyes. 'And he never kept secrets from us. We were very close, especially after they decided to divorce.'

'When was that?'

'Six months ago,' said Derek. He sighed. 'He and Amy were only married for a couple of years.'

'They never should've gone through with it,' Sarah said, her mouth twisting into a moue. 'I told him she was no good for him – and look where it got him.'

'Do you still keep in touch with her?'

'No. We didn't take to her, and the feeling was mutual.'

'What's her full name?' Barnes looked up from his notebook. 'We'll need to speak to her, just as part of our ongoing enquiries.'

'Amy Evans. She still rents their old house in Snodland. Dale couldn't wait to leave the place.'

'We have an address in Walderslade for your son, is that correct?' said Kay.

'It is.' The man's father stood and crossed to a sideboard, reaching into a small blue and white ceramic dish before returning.

He held out a lone worn brass key on a leather fob with a shaking hand. 'We never used this – he just wanted us to have it, for emergencies, he said.'

'We ought to contact the letting agency,' Sarah added,

dabbing at her eyes with a tissue. 'They'll be wanting to rent out the apartment again soon I expect.'

'We'll need to sort out all of his stuff first, love.'

Kay handed the key to Barnes before turning her attention back to the couple. 'I assume you don't mind if we take a look at Dale's place?'

'If it helps you find out who killed him, then no problem.'

'Thank you. We'll do that, and arrange to return the key to you as soon as possible. Are there any other family members we can contact for you?'

'No,' said Derek. 'We have wonderful neighbours though, and there's only Sarah's aunt up in Glasgow to contact – although she hardly knows who we are these days, so…'

'I'll have one of our family liaison officers come over to provide you with whatever support you need,' said Kay. 'You won't be alone going through this, I promise.'

TWENTY-TWO

'Did we find Thorngrove's car?'

Kay hurried after Barnes, flipping up her coat collar to counter the breeze tearing across a pitiful attempt at a landscaped garden that separated the pavement from the housing complex.

Discarded tin cans, chewing gum wrappers and more flipped back and forth in the wind, and she wrinkled her nose at the distinctive stench of dog shit.

A pitted asphalt footpath led from the car to the blocks of flats, a pale-coloured metal railing off to Kay's right separating them from a ramp that led down to a row of garages that faced the residential buildings.

'Not at the pub,' he said, setting a brisk pace. 'I'm hoping we find a key to one of those garages in the flat – he might've parked it in there.'

'So we don't know how he travelled from here to the White Hart.'

'Not yet.'

A scruffy grass verge encroached upon the left-hand

side of the path, and she noticed that some of the residents had arranged flower pots beside the communal front doors in an effort to add some colour to the otherwise bland masonry.

Barnes jerked his head towards the first block. 'There are four apartments in each block. Looks like number nine is the third one along.'

He opened the main door for her, and they entered a cramped hallway with a scuffed tiled floor and bare cinder block walls.

'Lovely decor,' Kay murmured.

'Stairs, or take the lift?' said Barnes.

'Stairs – it's only one flight.'

She kept her hands in her pockets, wary of the greasy stains covering the laminated banisters, and led the way up. When she reached the top of the stairs, the landing angled around to the right with a fire exit door to her left.

The sound of something being dragged along the tiled floor echoed off the bare walls, and someone grunted under their breath.

As she rounded the corner, she saw a woman with her back to the two detectives, dragging a cardboard box towards the lift.

The door to Dale Thorngrove's apartment was wide open.

'Who are you?'

The woman jumped at Kay's voice and spun around to face them, eyes wide open.

'Who... who are you?' she managed, pulling a cashmere cardigan around her waist, her expression turning from fright to guilt.

'I asked first.'

'Amy Evans. My husband—'

'Ex-husband, or so we're told.' Kay flashed her warrant card, then walked over to where the woman stood and bent down, flipping open the top of the cardboard box.

It was full of books and bric-à-brac.

'Care to explain why you're removing this from Mr Thorngrove's flat?'

'It's my stuff.'

'Can you prove that?'

'Ask him. He'll tell you.' Amy glared at Kay, and flicked her long brown hair over one shoulder. 'When he left our house, he took some of my things with him. I want them back. Otherwise, the divorce will go through, and I'll never see them again.'

'Who gave you a key?'

'What?'

'Where'd you get a key from?'

'I, um…' The other woman blushed. 'I took his spare, the first time I was here.'

'You stole it?'

'No! I just… borrowed it.' Her eyes darted between Kay and Barnes. 'I was going to give it back, honest.'

'It's a bit late for that,' Barnes said.

'What do you mean?'

'Dale Thorngrove was found dead on Wednesday night.'

'Dead?' Amy staggered in her heels and reached out for the wall to steady herself. 'How?'

Kay gestured to the open door. 'Shall we discuss this inside the flat? Away from the neighbours overhearing?'

'I'm not lifting that again. It's too bloody heavy.'

'Let me.' Barnes picked up the box and led the way into the flat, placing the collection of books and ornaments by the door as Kay closed it.

Amy stalked past him.

'I left my bag in here,' she muttered.

The narrow kitchen was functional, and remarkable in its ugliness.

Beige cupboards were fixed to the walls, crowding over shallow worktops with an electric hob at the far end while a stainless steel sink was off to the right under a window. Through the net curtains, Kay could see a shopping centre beyond the dual carriageway that carved its way past the housing estate, the traffic noise penetrating the double-glazed panes.

A single plate, cutlery and an upturned pint glass were on the draining board, while the cheap tiled flooring crunched under Kay's shoes as her gaze scanned the room, crumbs scattered beside a well-used toaster and the lack of crockery suggesting that Dale Thorngrove might have had a tendency to walk around while eating breakfast.

'When did you last see Dale?' she said, turning to face Amy.

The woman slung a tan-coloured bag over her shoulder before running a hand along the worktop, tracing a path through the toast crumbs. 'Monday. We had a meeting with our solicitors.'

Kay pursed her lips as she walked out of the kitchen and along the hallway into the living room.

The landlord had opted for beige here, too.

Thorngrove had done little more than add a pair of

worn armchairs to the room facing a large television and a slim coffee table that was cluttered with remote controls.

Mismatched curtains hung at the window.

Sifting through a small pile of discarded envelopes and utility bills, Kay watched out of the corner of her eye as Amy appeared, her mouth downturned.

'When did you last speak with your ex-husband?' she asked.

'Monday.' The woman stood with her back to the window, arms crossed over her chest. 'Then we sent each other a couple of text messages on Tuesday.'

'What about?'

Amy shrugged. 'Just some stuff to do with the divorce. I think he thought he could talk me out of it.'

'Where were you on Wednesday night between eight and midnight?'

'What?'

'Answer the question, please.'

'Do you think I killed him?'

'Did you?'

'Of course I bloody didn't!'

'Where were you?'

'At home, having dinner with a couple of girlfriends who came round.'

'We'll need names and phone numbers.'

Amy rolled her eyes, then dug out her phone from her bag and recited the details for Barnes. She emitted a bitter snort when he thanked her. 'I need to go – I told my boss I'd only be gone an hour.'

'We'll be in touch if we have further questions,' said Kay, holding out her hand. 'And I'll have that key, thanks.'

'Whatever.'

Amy flung it at her, then spun on her heel and flounced towards the door, ignoring the box.

Barnes waited until it slammed shut, then exhaled. 'Well, wasn't she a little ray of sunshine?'

'Yeah, no love lost there.' Kay dropped the bills back onto the table. 'Can you ask Phillip to run her name through the system, just to make sure there aren't any problems we ought to be aware of?'

'Will do.'

'Thanks. I hope the others are having more luck than us.'

TWENTY-THREE

When Laura drove into the White Hart's car park, she emitted a low whistle.

'Talk about making hay...' Kyle said beside her.

'No kidding.'

Six new circular wooden tables with matching chairs now occupied the four parking bays under the pub's front windows, each with a bright red and white parasol fluttering in the breeze and shading the drinkers from the early afternoon sunshine.

The door to the pub was wide open and as Laura pulled the keys from the ignition and walked towards it, a steady stream of patrons moved back and forth to the bar, glasses refreshed and various bags of snack food tucked under their arms.

'He might even afford a cleaner at this rate,' she murmured.

'I reckon he's too tight for that.' Kyle peered at the walls on each side of the door frame. 'He's put hanging baskets up, though – look.'

Entering the pub, Laura blinked to counteract the sudden gloom that enveloped her, and spotted Len Simpson polishing a table off to her right, his back turned to her.

Lydia Terry was standing behind the bar, her face flushed while she pulled pints and lined them up in front of four customers, all holding cash in the air in an attempt to be served first.

Her eyes widened when she saw the two police officers hovering at the threshold, and called out to Simpson.

'Someone here to see you, Len.'

He scowled when he turned, said nothing, and jerked his chin towards a table near the back of the pub before traipsing after them.

'Busy day, Mr Simpson,' said Laura cheerfully. 'It looks completely different out there.'

'It took me all day Thursday to hose the blood off the car park,' he said, his lower lip sticking out. 'And you can't be here – you'll scare off the clientele.'

'Oh, I think you're quite capable of doing that yourself, Mr Simpson – especially once they see what comes out of that kitchen of yours.'

He glared at her in response.

Kyle pulled his phone from his utility vest and held it out. 'Recognise him?'

Simpson squinted at the screen, then reached into the top pocket of his shirt and put on a pair of grimy reading glasses and tried again.

'Sort of. Who is he?'

'The man who was shot in your car park on Wednesday night.'

The landlord held up his hands and glanced over his shoulder. 'Keep your voice down, all right?'

'Mr Simpson, I think you realise these people are only here *because* of what happened on Wednesday night, don't you?' said Laura. 'Does this man look familiar?'

'I don't know. I'm not sure.' He shrugged. 'Like I said to your lot that night, I only noticed them when they got up to leave, and I only saw the back of him.'

'Fine. We'll ask Lydia.' Laura pushed back her chair, then looked down as Simpson grabbed her arm.

'Wait here. I'll get her.'

He waddled over to the bar, elbowed Lydia away from the beer pumps and pointed towards Laura.

The woman wiped her hands on the back of her jeans and hurried over.

'I don't know what you want, but you'd better make it quick – he's in one hell of a mood.'

Kyle peered over Lydia's head as she pulled out a seat. 'What for? This is probably the busiest this place has been in years, right?'

'It is, but Len likes to know who's drinking in here. He doesn't like strangers turning up, even if they are thrusting money at him. Especially after what happened last week.'

'Interesting.' Laura watched while the landlord finished serving.

He glared at the backs of the drinkers as they walked outside, and then she spotted the "reserved" signs placed in the middle of the tables scattered around the bar.

'Are you expecting a party in here or something?' she said.

Lydia snorted under her breath. 'He doesn't want any of them in here. Says those tables are for regulars.'

'Right. Lots of those in at the moment, aren't there?'

'Look, what do you want? I told you – he's in a foul mood.'

'Do you recognise this man?' Kyle asked, tapping his phone screen to waken it, then turning it to face Lydia.

'Yeah, I do actually. That's one of the blokes who was here on Wednesday night, isn't it? Is he the one who was shot?'

'His name's Dale Thorngrove. Does that sound familiar?' said Laura.

'No. Is he local?'

'Walderslade.'

'Not too far away, then.' Lydia frowned. 'But that doesn't explain why he'd come here, does it? Plenty of other pubs between here and Snodland. Or north of there.'

'Have you ever seen him in here before Wednesday night?'

'No.' The woman's mouth quirked. 'It's not the sort of place you visit twice unless you're local.'

Laura sighed.

She couldn't fault Lydia's logic.

Glancing over her shoulder, she saw Len watching them, and stood. 'Okay, thanks – we'll leave you to it. Here's my card. If you think of anything that might help us, my direct number's on there.'

As they walked towards the car, she could feel the stares from the people gathered around the tables. No doubt there would be more gossip posted to social media within seconds of them leaving.

'Don't turn around,' she hissed to Kyle. 'Last thing we need is our faces plastered all over the internet.'

He scowled. 'I'm glad the only parking space left was at the far end. What do you want to do next?'

Laura waited until they were in the car, checked her phone for any missed calls and then pointed down the lane.

'Let's go and see Geoff Abbott. He doesn't live too far away, and I want to find out if he knows Dale Thorngrove.'

TWENTY-FOUR

Gavin looked up from his notes as Paul Solomon exited the M2 and aimed the car towards Rochester.

'Where does your first bloke live?' he said, tapping his fingers on the top of the steering wheel while he glared at a red light that was taking an inordinate amount of time to change.

'Just off Wouldham Road, past the chippy. It's one of the roads down to the left heading towards the river.'

Solomon slipped the car into gear as the lights turned green and edged into the left-hand lane. 'It's about five minutes away. Yell when you see the house number.'

'Will do.' He bit back a yawn, reached out for the can of energy drink in the pocket beside the passenger seat, then cursed under his breath as he realised it was empty.

'Need another of those first?'

'Best not. That was my third today.'

Solomon shot him a sideways glance. 'That's not healthy.'

'I know, but what with the hours we're keeping on this

case and the bloke in the room next door at the hotel having loud phone calls with his ex-wife at two o'clock this morning, I need the help.'

'I didn't realise you were staying local.'

'Sharp reckoned it made sense given the sensitivity of this one – if we get a sudden breakthrough then we're both on hand immediately, rather than having to travel from Maidstone.'

'Well if it goes on much longer and you want somewhere quieter to kip, me and the wife have a spare room you can use.'

'Thanks, I'll bear that in mind.' Gavin sat up straighter and pointed through the windscreen. 'Here we go. Number eleven should be down here on the right.'

'What's his name?'

'Peter Jones. He was arrested for assault three months after the fight with Dale Thorngrove, given a caution when the other party refused to press charges, and seems to have been behaving himself since.'

'Okay, well I'll follow your lead on this one.'

'Feel free to jump in if I miss something obvious.' Gavin loosened his seat belt. 'You're the local, after all.'

Moments later, they stood on the front step of a 1930s terraced house with a red-brick archway forming a porch sheltering the door, and bay windows jutting out from the ground and first floors.

Gavin wrinkled his nose at the ugly pebbledash covering the walls, but took in the well-maintained front garden and fresh paintwork and reckoned Jones – or someone in his household – was at least making an effort.

The door opened, and a man in his late thirties with a

receding hairline frowned as he took in their appearance.

'Police? What do you want?'

'DC Gavin Piper, and my colleague, DC Solomon. Are you Peter Jones?'

'Yes. What's this about?'

'Can we talk inside?'

'I'd rather not.' Jones lowered his voice. 'My wife's at work, and I've only just got the baby to sleep. Can you make this quick in case she wakes up?'

Gavin held up his phone. 'Do you recognise him?'

'Looks familiar, but I'm not sure from where.'

'You and a mate of yours got into a fight with him three years ago. He needed dental work afterwards.'

Jones rubbed his hand across his jaw and sighed. 'Not one of my finer moments. I broke two fingers that night.'

'Yet you got into another fight soon afterwards.'

'Yeah, and then I quit drinking. I've been clean since.' Jones handed back the phone and frowned. 'What's this about?'

'Dale Thorngrove – the bloke in the photo – was murdered on Wednesday night.' Gavin ignored the shocked expression that flitted across Jones's face. 'Where were you?'

'On the phone to that free NHS service. Charlotte had a fever, and we were worried it might be something serious.' Jones exhaled. 'It wasn't, but I don't want another scare like that.'

'And your wife will confirm that?'

'Of course. Phone her and ask her.' Jones recited her number. 'She'll be out and about at the moment but you can leave her a message and she'll call you back.'

'Have you had any contact with Dale Thorngrove since the fight?'

'No, why would I?'

'What was the fight about?'

'God knows. It was a long time ago. Knowing what I was like on the grog back then, it could've been anything.'

'The other bloke who was involved – Owen Chard – is he a good friend of yours?'

'Not anymore.' Jones shoved his hands in his jeans pockets. 'Once I quit the booze, I stayed away from the old crowd.'

'What does your wife do?'

'She runs a real estate company in Chatham. Doing really well, too.'

Gavin heard the note of pride in the man's voice. 'And you?'

'Full-time dad,' Jones beamed. 'Best job in the world.'

He glanced over his shoulder as a child began to wail in the background.

'We'll let you get back to it,' said Gavin. 'Thanks for your time.'

'Reformed character, that one,' Solomon remarked as they walked back to the car. 'Shame they don't all turn out like that.'

'I had a feeling this would be a waste of time. I mean, it's a big step from beating up someone three years ago to shooting them twice at point-blank range, isn't it?'

Solomon smiled. 'Still has to be done though. Where does the second bloke live?'

'About twenty minutes away.' Gavin yawned. 'And we'd better stop for coffee on the way there.'

TWENTY-FIVE

Darkness had swept over the town by the time Kay called her team to attention and ushered them towards the whiteboard.

The briefing was already an hour late due to the sheer amount of information coming in to the incident room, and she wanted them home and refreshed ready for another early start.

A weariness was evident as they took their seats, their movements sluggish and without enthusiasm and she knew she would need another breakthrough soon to keep them focused.

'First things first,' she began as soon as the last person's backside found a chair. 'Zach, if you want to join me up here and explain your findings on the ballistics from the crime scene then we can take any questions about that before moving on to other matters.'

She flipped over the whiteboard so the blank rear was showing, and then waited while the ballistics expert connected his laptop to the overhead projector.

Zach pressed a button and a sketch of the White Hart and its car park layout appeared on the makeshift screen. Taking a pen from Kay, he cleared his throat and faced the assembled officers.

'The following is based on the post mortem report, current information from the forensics team and an on-site visit I conducted earlier today to take measurements,' he began. He paused to draw two stick figures on the whiteboard. 'The first thing that I can confirm is that the trajectory of what we considered to be the first gunshot was correct. Thorngrove was turned away from the shooter when the rifle was first fired. By my estimations, and based on where he fell, he was standing here when the bullet hit him.'

Zach rubbed out one of the stick figures and then drew him farther away from the other. 'The gunman was standing here, on the fringes of the car park, when he took the first shot. There were no vehicles parked on this side of the car park, so we need to consider where the two men were heading when they exited the pub.'

Kay folded her arms over her chest and stared at the sketch.

'Thorngrove managed to stagger a few metres before the second shot hit him in the back of the head,' Zach said.

'How is that even possible?' Laura asked. 'He had a bloody great gaping hole in his chest by then.'

'It takes a while for the message to reach the brain and the body to shut down,' said Zach. 'It's the same if a deer is killed – it'll often continue to run a few metres before dropping to the ground. As it is, and based on the measurements I've taken, the killer took a few paces forward in order to take the second shot.'

'Maybe he thought he'd missed the first time,' Barnes said.

'I'm not so sure,' said Zach. He pointed to the two figures on the board. 'From the trajectories, I think he knew he'd killed Thorngrove with the first shot. This second shot was just to make sure.'

'Was Thorngrove armed at the time?' said Kay.

'There was no gunshot residue on his hands or clothing, so he didn't fire a weapon at his attacker. Nothing was found at the crime scene either, and Harriet and her team conducted a wide search of the area. If he was carrying a weapon, I have to assume his killer took it with him when he fled the scene.'

'We've received no reports of any weapons being found in the area,' said Laura. 'So whoever the killer is, he's still got it.'

'And that'll be vital for evidence.' Kay thanked Zach as he returned to his seat, and flipped over the whiteboard. After adding the ballistics expert's feedback to the growing list of notes, she faced her team. 'Debbie – can you make sure Gavin and DCI Sharp are sent a copy of Zach's report before you leave today, and let them know we're looking for the firearm as well? That way, if they do find our suspect they can make sure his clothing is preserved so it can be tested for gunshot residue.'

'Will do, guv.'

'Right, let's have a quick update on today's tasks and then you can get some rest. Laura, Kyle – how did you get on with Len Simpson?'

'He says he's never seen Thorngrove in the White Hart before, guv,' said the detective constable. 'Lydia Evans recognised him from Wednesday night, but confirmed he's not a regular and again she'd never seen him before.'

'We had a bit more luck with Geoff Abbott,' Kyle added. 'He said he thought Thorngrove looked familiar, but couldn't pinpoint from where.'

'I've got a note to follow up with him on Monday to see if anything's jogged his memory,' said Laura.

'Do that, thanks. Where are we with regard to Thorngrove's car, Ian?'

'Uniform found it in the garage next to the flats once we got in a locksmith to open the door,' said Barnes. 'I phoned around a few taxi firms in the Walderslade area, and one of the dispatchers confirmed a pickup from the housing estate to the White Hart last week. The debit card used was Thorngrove's so that explains how he got there.'

'Okay, good.' Kay checked her text messages. 'Gavin spoke to the two men involved in a fight with our victim three years ago but says we can discount them. Both have cleaned up their acts since then, and both have solid alibis for Wednesday night. How did we get on with local gun shops? Did anyone there recognise Thorngrove?'

'They didn't, guv, but there is something that came up while I was processing today's reports.' Phillip's voice carried across the heads of his colleagues, and she waved him over.

'What've you got?'

'I ran Thorngrove's ex-wife's details through the system out of interest, and got something you might find interesting. Four months ago, she went to her GP with bruising to her arm.' Phillip's cheeks flushed. 'It raised concerns for me, so I cross-checked that with Daniel, and he confirms that around the same time, Thorngrove had applied for a firearms certificate. He was turned down—'

'Because of the domestic violence accusation,' said Kay. 'His GP would've had to have signed off on the medical side of things and if they shared the same GP, he would never let Thorngrove be approved knowing he had a violent streak.'

'Amy Evans said nothing to us when we saw her today,' Barnes said, frowning. 'Surely she would've mentioned that, once she knew her ex had been shot.'

'There's something else, guv,' said Phillip. 'I checked the system to see if she made a complaint to us about Thorngrove, and there's nothing. I even spoke to some of our domestic violence team to see if they'd ever spoken to her but they hadn't.'

'What do you want to do, guv?' said Barnes.

Kay tapped the end of her pen against her chin for a moment, then made her decision.

'Bring Amy Evans in for a formal interview first thing tomorrow. Let's find out what else she omitted to tell us.'

TWENTY-SIX

Kay held her breath as a man in his early twenties with a blackening eye and vomit stains down his T-shirt was led past her, then turned her attention to the paperwork in her hand.

The police station was busy for a Sunday morning, with all the people arrested in the town overnight being processed and either released for future court appearances or being led away for a spell on remand until their cases were heard.

She hummed under her breath to counteract the noise from the violent argument carrying on farther down the passageway towards the cells while she flicked through the scant information her team had collated about Amy Evans.

Laura and Kyle were tasked with collecting the woman from her home in Snodland earlier that morning, and while she waited for them to appear she took a moment to write down some questions that were niggling at the forefront of her mind.

'Are you freakin' kidding me?'

She lifted her eyes from the page at the sound of Amy's voice and the thick door between the front desk and the interview rooms slamming against the wall to see the woman storming towards her, Kyle Walker in her wake.

'Sorry, guv, she burst in as soon as I'd opened the door.'

'It's all right, Kyle. I think Mrs Evans has calmed down now,' said Kay, eyeing the woman. 'Haven't you?'

'What's the meaning of this? Him and some woman banging on me door at seven o'clock, demanding I come here – why?'

'Guv, we asked politely,' Kyle said. 'Given the circumstances and that.'

'Everything okay, guv?' Laura hurried along the passageway towards her, a manila folder clutched in her hands. 'I heard her kick off…'

'We're okay. And we're going to make the rest of this conversation formal in the circumstances.' Kay shoved open the door to interview room two and waved Amy inside. 'Kyle, if you'd like to wait out here, please.'

Amy strode over to one of the chairs that surrounded a metal table screwed to the floor and pulled it out, the legs scraping across the tiles. 'Make it quick. I ain't even had a coffee yet this morning.'

'Would you like some water?' said Kay.

'No.'

The woman folded her arms across her chest and pouted while Laura set up the recording equipment and read out the formal caution.

'Do I need a solicitor?'

'Would you like one?' Kay asked. 'You're not under arrest at the moment.'

'Oh.' She frowned. 'What do you want, then?'

Kay held up the documents in her hand by way of response. 'I've got some more questions for you.'

'What about?'

'Your ex-husband's application for a firearms certificate.'

Amy frowned. 'Nothing to do with me. I didn't know he had one.'

'He hasn't. And that has *everything* to do with you.' Kay clasped her hands on top of the manila folder. 'When did the abuse start, Amy?'

'Eh?'

'Was it physical? Did he hurt you? We heard your GP was concerned about bruising to your arm, which was why Dale's licence application was turned down.'

Amy's gaze flickered from Kay to Laura, then back, her eyes widening. 'No, nothing like that.'

'It's okay, Amy. You can tell us. Why didn't you report him? We could've helped you.'

A tear rolled over the woman's cheek, and she sniffed. 'I didn't mean it.'

Kay sighed, and flipped open the folder, waiting.

'I-I just wanted to get my own back,' Amy said eventually. She choked back a sob. 'I just wanted to make him pay.'

'What did you say?' Kay reared back in her seat. 'Did you lie about the violence?'

Silence.

Kay slammed her palm against the table, the sound reverberating off the walls.

Amy jumped in her seat, a shocked cry escaping her lips.

'Did you lie about your ex-husband being violent towards you?'

'Y-yes.' Amy nodded, her face crumpling. 'I lied. I didn't want him to have a gun.'

'Why not?'

'I didn't want him to have *anything*. I just wanted to get him back for leaving me. He made me look stupid in front of all of our friends. I hated him.'

'What about the bruises on your arm?'

Amy sniffed. 'I did it myself. I wanted to make it look real.'

Taking a deep breath, forcing herself to remain calm, Kay waited until the woman raised her head, then glared at her.

'Do you know how many women we fail to save because of people like you making false allegations just to get back at someone?' she said, her voice shaking. 'Instead of running around following up a lead like this, I've got officers working all hours upstairs who could have been assisting colleagues to help women and children escape some of the worst situations you could ever imagine.'

'I'm—'

'Don't you dare,' Kay snarled. 'Don't you dare say you're sorry. You knew exactly what you were doing when you lied to your GP and told him your husband was abusing you. You're lucky I don't charge you with wasting police time.'

She slapped shut the folder and shoved back her chair. 'Interview terminated at eight fifty-three. Show Mrs Evans to the door, Detective Hanway. She can make her own bloody way home.'

TWENTY-SEVEN

'Did she really make Amy get a bus home?'

Barnes glanced across to where Laura was frowning at her phone screen, then back to the road.

A blue motorway sign flashed past, and he eased off the accelerator, swinging into the left lane and taking the exit for Aylesford.

'Well, she told her to make her own way home. I'm guessing she must've either waited for a bus, or taken a taxi.' Laura grinned. 'You should've seen her face when I showed her the door. It'd started raining by then, too.'

'It sounds as if it's almost worth my while asking Hughes to show me the security camera footage from the front desk.'

'I thought Kay was going to strangle Amy when she confessed that she'd made it up about the domestic violence. Even I was scared.'

'Just as well we're out of the way for a while. At least by the time we get back for this afternoon's briefing she might've calmed down.' Barnes shook his head. 'There isn't much that can piss her off, but that certainly would. Right, where does Thorngrove's boss live? Second left up here, isn't it?'

'Uh-huh. Then look out for a willow tree, he said. Apparently his house is along a track to the right of that. And he said don't worry about the dog that's usually roaming around – apparently it's old and doesn't have many teeth left.'

'Good to know,' Barnes murmured. He noticed the sign before he spotted the track, its faded black lettering almost lost to time against a white-washed wooden background, and gave a surprised grunt. 'I didn't realise he lived in a caravan park.'

'Apparently he owns one of the chalets, not a caravan. Number seventeen – go left after we pass through the gate down here.'

He slowed to match the hand-painted speed limit sign to their left and took in the well-maintained flower borders that edged against the track, nodding to an elderly couple who held up their hands in greeting when they passed.

'Friendly place.'

'Quiet, too.' Laura unclipped her seatbelt as Barnes parked outside a bright blue chalet. 'Not sure I could cope with that colour first thing in the morning though. Reminds me of a beach hut.'

The ground shook when Barnes climbed out, and then a train flashed past the row of conifers behind the chalet, their branches bowing in its wake.

He snorted. 'So much for being quiet.'

'You get used to it.'

He turned to see a man in his fifties leaning on a

wooden rail that ran the width of the small house, its raised position forming a shallow deck above the two parking bays.

The man smiled, straightening when they reached the three steps leading up to the front door.

'I presume you're Detective Barnes.' He held out a hand. 'Gerry Harlington.'

'Thanks for seeing us at short notice. And on a Sunday.'

Laura introduced herself, then Harlington grimaced.

'Least I could do in the circumstances. I wondered if something bad had happened to Dale when he didn't show up for work yesterday. I couldn't get an answer on his phone when I tried that.'

'Not Thursday or Friday?' asked Barnes while Harlington guided them through a sliding patio door and into a narrow living room.

'He asked for some time off when we finished on Tuesday. Said he had some personal stuff to sort out.' He sighed. 'I assumed he meant with his ex-wife. You know they were getting divorced?'

Barnes caught Laura's warning look, and reckoned the memory of Kay's reaction to Thorngrove's marital issues was still raw, despite her light-hearted comments. He cleared his throat.

'We had heard they were having some issues, yes.'

'Amy *was* the issue. Honestly, the woman was a nightmare.' He rolled his eyes, then moved across to a small kitchenette at the back of the chalet and held up a kettle. 'Want a brew?'

'No, we're good thanks.' Barnes put his hands in his

pockets and peered at a series of framed photographs on the wall above a well-used armchair. In each, a motorbike had been captured leaning into a corner, the speed evidenced by the blurred background and the rider dressed in bright racing colours. 'Is this you?'

Harlington looked over and paused mashing a tea bag against the side of a mug. 'A whole other lifetime ago. Well, about thirty years at least.'

'Was this at Brands Hatch?'

'It was.'

'How come you went from that to running a garage?' Barnes joined Laura beside a metal fold-out picnic table and took a seat as Harlington joined them.

'There's only so many times you go sliding across a racetrack on your arse before you realise you don't bounce as well as you used to,' he said with a rueful smile. 'I did all right out of the race wins over the years, and picked up some sponsors so when I quit, I started up the tyre place. The servicing side of things happened by accident, and before I knew it I had four blokes working for me.'

'Any problems with Dale while he'd been with you?' said Laura.

'None at all. He's been reliable.' Harlington paused to slurp his tea. 'He was trustworthy, and good with customers too. The sort of bloke you could leave in charge for a few days if you wanted a break. I'm going to bloody miss him.'

Barnes gave the man a moment, before turning his attention to the task at hand. 'Did he seem worried, or perhaps preoccupied, on Wednesday?'

'Not really. We were busy though. He'd asked for a

couple of days off and although I've got the other three working for me, one of them's still an apprentice. Dale wanted to make sure he got a couple of servicing jobs out of the way and an MOT so we had a few less things to worry about while he was off.' He tapped his fingers against the side of the mug. 'We were too busy for me to notice if anything was on his mind. I feel bad about that now.'

'Was he the sort of person who would tell you if he did have something on his mind?' said Laura.

'Depends what was bothering him I suppose. I mean, he didn't talk about the ex-wife much, or the divorce. I got the impression he was embarrassed about it to be honest.'

'Was he acting out of character, or on his phone more than usual perhaps?' Barnes asked.

Harlington sat back in his chair, his gaze moving to the photographs on the wall.

'There was one phone call now you mention it,' he said eventually. 'Monday morning – it would've been about half ten because Sam – that's the apprentice – was helping with a delivery that had just arrived. Dale's phone went off, and he took one look at the screen and went outside to answer it.'

'Do you think it was his ex-wife?'

'No, because I stuck my head out the door after ten minutes to tell him I needed him to finish an MOT inspection before the customer came back, and he was pacing the forecourt and yelling at whoever was on the other end.'

'Can you remember what he was saying?'

Harlington nodded. 'Only because it was out of

character for him, mind. I don't make a habit of eavesdropping on my staff. Like I said, it's all about trust.'

'Understood. What did he say?'

'He stopped yelling when he saw me, but there must've been a lull in the traffic going past, because I definitely heard him say "you're going to pay for this".'

Barnes looked up from his notebook. 'Were those his exact words?

'Yes.'

'In that case, Mr Harlington, I'd like to interview the rest of your staff. Today.'

TWENTY-EIGHT

Laura paced the grease-streaked concrete floor of Harlington's garage, alternatively scrolling through new text messages and peering out through the open doors to the forecourt beyond.

Rather than try to locate the three men who worked for Harlington, the owner had suggested he call them and arrange for them to be interviewed at the garage to save time, something which she and Barnes had seized upon with enthusiasm.

Her colleague was currently interviewing the older of the remaining staff members beside a steel bench strewn with power tools, their voices a murmur while they perched on a pair of well-used stools.

Despite the open doors, the air was musty with the pungent aromas of engine oil, lubricant and – in anticipation of the predicted early winter – antifreeze.

She shivered, the wind turning and creeping through the gap in the doors, and tucked her phone into her pocket before buttoning her wool coat before flipping up the collar to counteract the draught.

The sound of a car drawing closer piqued her interest, and she walked out to the forecourt as a sporty blue hatchback turned in from the road, sound system blaring.

A scrawny man climbed out, his brow knitted as he caught sight of her and pulled a sweatshirt over his head.

'Are you the detective?' he asked, aiming his key fob at the car and crossing to where she waited.

'DC Laura Hanway,' she said, holding out her warrant card. 'You must be Sam Hennant.'

'I am.'

'Thanks for coming in on your day off.'

He shrugged, adjusting the short ponytail at the nape of his neck. 'I reckon Dale would've done the same for me if he were in my shoes.'

'Come on, let's get inside. It's moderately warmer in there.'

'You'd never make a mechanic, detective.'

'Trust me, I know.'

She smiled and led the way through the doors and towards a pair of plastic garden chairs that Harlington had found at the back of the garage, now set out in the opposite corner to where Barnes and the other staff member were talking.

Sam nodded to his colleague, shoved his hands in the kangaroo pocket of his sweatshirt and sat opposite her. 'What do you want to know?'

'Do you work here full-time?'

'Part-time. I do four days here, and one at college. I've only got another eight months to go, and then I'm fully qualified.' He smiled shyly. 'Gerry's already offered me a full-time job when I'm done.'

'That's good. Takes some of the stress out of finishing the course, I expect.'

'It does, yeah.' Sam wiggled in his chair and leaned closer. 'So, do you know who shot Dale?'

'It's an ongoing investigation. What we're trying to do today is understand why Dale was killed, and what he was doing up at the White Hart. Did he seem out of sorts last week, perhaps nervous about anything?'

'Not that I noticed. We were busy Monday – Tuesday's me day off, so I can't tell you anything about that – and Wednesday was flat out. It's why I like working here. The time goes really quick.'

'Gerry mentioned Dale got a phone call last Monday and it got pretty heated. Do you remember that?'

Sam tucked his hands under his arms and frowned. 'Yeah, I do because I hadn't seen him like that before, not angry. I was supposed to be helping unload a delivery but I couldn't help notice it. He was pacing back and forth out there, telling whoever it was at the other end that they'd pay for something.'

'Any idea what?'

'No.' He shrugged. 'Didn't want to ask, to be honest. He came back in here in one hell of a mood.'

'Did you get on all right with Dale?'

'Yeah, we all did. He was teaching me a lot of stuff, especially when Gerry was too busy.'

'What sort of things did you talk about, other than work?'

'Football, mostly. And stuff we'd seen on TV.'

Laura paused as Barnes wandered over, the man he'd been speaking to leaving through the open garage doors with a nod to Gerry in farewell.

'Did Dale ever mention an interest in guns?' he asked.

Sam nodded. 'He wanted to take up shooting for some reason, and didn't know where to start but he said one of our customers offered to take him out to show him the ropes to see if he liked it last month.'

'And did he?' said Barnes.

'He wouldn't stop talking about it the next week. Bored the crap out of us.' Gerry beckoned them over to a set of metal lockers at the back of the garage, took a key from his pocket and opened one at the far end. 'This is a master key. And this is all Dale's stuff – I wasn't sure what to do with it.'

'Do you know which customer it was who offered the taster session?'

'Haven't got a clue, sorry.'

'Sam?'

The apprentice shook his head in reply as Gerry reached inside the locker and extracted a pile of magazines together with an empty drink bottle and a duffel bag.

Opening the duffel bag, Barnes held up a scrunched-up T-shirt. 'Gym clothes, by the look of it.'

Laura flipped the magazines over, running her gaze across the titles. 'He was reading up on rifles and hunting, then?'

'Yeah. All the time. He couldn't wait to get his licence.' Sam frowned. 'He was gutted when your lot told him he couldn't have one because his ex-wife had put in a complaint or something.'

'Can we take these?'

'You can take all of it if you like.' Gerry exhaled. 'I mean, I can't see his ex wanting any of it, and at some point I'm going to have to advertise for a replacement for Dale. We're not going to cope otherwise.'

'Thanks.' Barnes hefted the duffel bag over his shoulder. 'And thanks for organising everyone to come over. That saved us a lot of time.'

'Just find out who killed him, all right? He didn't deserve to die like that.'

Laura gathered the magazines together and carried them out to the car, glancing over her shoulder at the sound of footsteps to see Sam following, tossing his car keys from hand to hand.

'Thanks for your help today.'

'No worries.' He winked. 'And come back any time. You've got my number.'

Laura turned away before he could see her face flame, and elbowed Barnes in the ribs as he started to chuckle.

'I think you've got a new fan there, Hanway,' he said, unlocking the car.

'The cheeky bugger,' she hissed.

TWENTY-NINE

While her team gathered around the whiteboard for the Monday morning briefing, Kay looked at their downcast faces, heard the agitation that seeped through their murmured conversations, and wondered how on earth she would continue to keep them focused and energised.

Squaring her shoulders, she placed the agenda on a spare desk beside her and raised her voice.

'Let's make a start. Laura and Barnes – I take it from the reports you filed last night that you've managed to find out more about Dale Thorngrove?'

'We did, guv,' said Barnes. 'To keep it short for everyone here, when we interviewed his colleagues at the garage he worked at, they showed us some gun magazines he'd been keeping in his locker, and told us that one of their customers had spoken to Dale about rifles not so long ago.'

'We're currently waiting for his boss to give us a list of customers that have used the garage in the past six months so we can cross-check the names against Daniel's firearms certificate records.'

'I'll try to allocate a couple of officers to help,' said Kay, updating the board. 'I take it you all heard about Amy Evans?'

'Can we charge her for wasting our time?' Debbie asked once a rumble of discontented voices had died away.

'It'd take more paperwork than it's worth,' Kay said. 'I checked with a contact at the CPS late last night, and he reckons it'd never make it to court. We've put a record on the system against her name for future reference though. In the meantime, I've spoken to Sharp at headquarters, and unfortunately they're reducing manpower on this investigation. The ACC is of the view that this is an isolated incident and so our focus now becomes one of finding out which of Thorngrove's associates killed him. Ian – you said you were following up with Gerry Harlington about an angle on that?'

'When Laura spoke to Sam, the apprentice, he mentioned that someone had got Thorngrove interested in guns and went so far as to invite him to a shoot a few weeks ago.'

'That's definitely worth following up,' Kay said. 'Can you chase up Harlington if you don't get that list of names by early afternoon? I'd like to split them up between the team and start phone interviews as soon as possible.'

Barnes nodded in response.

Exhaling, Kay glanced across at the agenda, then back to her officers at a surprised exclamation from Laura.

'What've you got?'

'A text message from Hughes downstairs, guv –

someone's just handed in a mobile phone that was found on the roadside half a mile from the White Hart.'

'Go. Now.'

The detective constable didn't need telling twice. She dropped her phone and notebook onto her chair and raced from the room.

'Harriet never found a phone or wallet at the crime scene,' said Phillip. 'So maybe it's Thorngrove's?'

'Or his killer's, if it's a burner phone.' Kay paced the thin carpet tiles, unable to keep still. She looked up as Laura returned, slightly out of breath and holding a plastic evidence bag.

'Here you go, guv.'

'Okay, take a photo of this and send it to Gerry Harlington. Ask him if he or his employees recognise it as Thorngrove's. Did Hughes get the details of the person who handed it in?'

'Yes, a woman by the name of Nancy Allen – she was walking her dog when she found it.'

'Ian, I want you to call her and find out exactly where she picked this up,' Kay continued. 'Take uniform with you and search the area to see if Thorngrove's wallet was dumped there too.'

'Onto it.' Barnes jogged over to his desk, snatching the sticky note Laura held out to him as he passed her.

'Do you want me to phone Andy Grey over at digital forensics to say we'll courier this over to him?' Debbie asked.

Kay shook her head and eyed the evidence bag in her hand. 'No time, Debs. I'm going over to Northfleet with this now.'

THIRTY

Swiping her security card and sweeping through the lobby of Northfleet's Kent Police headquarters, Kay raised her hand in greeting to another DI from East Division, and turned for the stairs.

Taking them two at a time, ignoring the perplexed expressions she received from three administrative staff as she passed them at full pelt, she reached the next floor and hurried along a narrow corridor.

The security door at the end opened before she reached it, and Andy Grey stood to one side.

'When you said you were on your way, Detective Hunter, I didn't realise you were going to stretch the space-time continuum to get here so fast.'

'The A2 was clear for a change.'

'Have you been taking extra driving lessons from Barnes and Gavin?' He grinned, then held out his hand. 'All right, let's have it.'

She gave him the bag containing the mobile phone and watched while he pulled protective gloves over his hands, signed the chain of evidence form, and then broke the seal.

'You reckon this belonged to your victim, then?' said the forensics technician while he wandered over to a computer and plugged in the phone.

'We think so.' Kay huffed her fringe from her eyes, her heart rate slowly returning to normal. 'It was found about half a mile from the pub, so…'

'Chances are good.' He frowned. 'It's password protected.'

'Can you crack it?'

'I could, but that'd take time. You could phone the ex-wife and see if she knows it.'

'We're not exactly on good terms at the moment.' She told him what had happened. 'Anyway, surely he'd change the password if they'd split up?'

'He's a bloke.' Andy grinned. 'We don't like change. Ask her.'

Kay made the call, and after a curt reply, Amy Evans confirmed she did indeed know her ex-husband's phone password and recited it from memory.

Andy smiled when she ended the call. 'Has the ex-wife redeemed herself?'

'Not quite.' She pursed her lips. 'You're going to hate me for this, but how soon can you go through these phone records?'

The digital forensics manager sighed. 'It'll take a while.'

'You're a star.'

'So you keep telling me. It would help me if I knew if there was anything in particular you're after?'

'Thorngrove received a phone call around ten-thirty last Monday morning. His work colleagues reported a heated conversation, and his boss told us that he heard him say "you're going to pay for this". That's our starting point – if you spot anything else on there I should know about, I'll take that too.'

'Okay. Go and get a coffee and wait for my call. I'll see what I can find. And don't tell anyone you've seen me – it's supposed to be my rostered day off.'

———

'So, how's Gavin getting on?'

Kay followed Sharp to a table on the opposite side of the room to the vending machine and tore the packaging off a sweaty-looking cheese and tomato sandwich.

Curling her lip at the processed food but resigned to the fact there was nothing else available, she bit into it while the DCI sipped his coffee.

'He's impressing a few people,' he said eventually. 'Not that I'm surprised.'

'Me neither.' She swallowed. 'I figured dropping him in the deep end for a bit would do his confidence good.'

'I don't think there's a problem with his confidence, just lack of experience in some areas.' Sharp looked around at the gathered officers, and sighed. 'Plus, I'm worried that if he gets bored in Maidstone, we'll lose him altogether.'

Kay paused, her sandwich halfway to her mouth. 'Have you heard a rumour?'

'No, just a gut feeling.'

'That's worse.'

'Eat your food. I don't think he's going anywhere just yet.'

He gave what she suspected he thought was a reassuring smile, but her appetite had waned.

She dropped the rest of the sandwich back in the wrapper.

'How's the rest of your team getting on there?' Sharp said. 'I heard you've got some new faces helping out. Anyone worth keeping an eye on?'

'Phillip Parker's a solid officer – dependable, I mean. I'm not sure if he's detective material though. He's never shown any interest in taking the exams, put it that way. There's another uniformed constable... Kyle Walker.' Kay's gaze wandered to the window as she spoke. 'He was first on scene at an overdose we had to deal with a while ago. I was impressed with his attention to detail back then, and he's certainly settled in well on this case.'

'I'll pull up his file when I get a quiet moment.'

'What about you? How are you getting on with a reduced team?'

'However much that frustrates me, I can see it from the ACC's point of view. We're as understaffed as ever, and Paul Solomon's been working a trafficking case with a skeleton crew these past few months. They're about to break a smuggling gang so that took priority – as it should, of course.' His top lip curled. 'I do wish we'd had more success tracking down Thorngrove's killer first though. Despite all the resources we had, he still managed to get away.'

'Or her.'

'Pardon?'

Kay pushed her lukewarm coffee to one side. 'Just keeping my options open.'

Sharp's eyes narrowed. 'Do you think the ex-wife had something to do with it?'

'I don't know.' She yawned. 'Perhaps she affected me more than I thought yesterday.'

'Still angry with her for wasting our time?'

'Yes.'

'It's a big step from nicking things from your ex-husband's flat to shooting him twice with a .308 though.'

'I think—' She broke off as her phone began to ring.

Andy's name was displayed across the screen.

'That was quick,' she said.

'I got lucky,' he replied. 'And I might have a name for you.'

'I'm on my way up now.'

Sharp watched as she gathered up her things and rose from her chair. 'Progress?'

'God, I hope so, guv. Talk later, okay?'

By the time she'd raced along the corridor and reached the mezzanine landing, Andy was already at the top of the stairs, his backpack slung over his shoulder and a motorcycle helmet looped over his arm.

He held out a piece of paper when he reached her, stepping to one side to let a uniformed sergeant pass.

'Thanks,' Kay said, then bit back a gasp when she read his looping handwriting.

'I take it you know this bloke, then?' said Andy, leading the way down the stairs towards the exit.

'We spoke to him last week,' she said, crossing the lobby and shoving open the front door. 'Mark Redding has got some bloody explaining to do.'

THIRTY-ONE

'Guv?'

Kay replaced her desk phone in its cradle at the sound of Barnes's voice to see the detective sergeant hurrying towards her.

'Whatever it is, Ian, it's going to have to wait. We've got Mark Redding in for questioning downstairs and his solicitor's just arrived.'

He held up an evidence bag. 'Thorngrove's wallet was found by Harriet's team a couple of metres from where Nancy Allen picked up his phone this morning.'

'Anything in there to help us?'

'Unfortunately not. There were just some bank cards and a driving licence. A bit of cash – not much.'

'In that case, I need you with me.' She gathered up her notebook and a folder containing Mark Redding's previous statement, and thrust them at her colleague. 'Andy Grey confirmed the phone call Thorngrove received last Monday morning was with Redding. His number appears in the recent calls list on the phone at the same time his boss—'

'Gerry.'

'Yeah, him.' Kay waited while Barnes signed over custody of the wallet to Debbie for logging into the system, then headed towards the door. 'The timing matches up with when Thorngrove was seen arguing with someone on the phone.'

Her colleague pulled his tie from his jacket pocket and looped it over his head before adjusting his collar as they took the stairs. 'Who's representing him?'

'Andrew Gillow from Blake Arrow.'

'Christ, if he can afford him then that business of his must be doing better than I thought.'

'Which also means he's got a lot to lose.'

Barnes held his arm across the door to the interview suites before she could reach the security panel. 'Motive?'

She shrugged and said nothing.

'Okay.' He dropped his arm and stabbed the key code into the panel. 'Let's find out what he's got to say.'

When Kay led the way into interview room four, Mark Redding broke off his conversation with his solicitor and waited until Barnes started the recording equipment and recited the formal caution.

'My client is a busy man, detectives,' said Gillow brusquely. 'I hope this matter can be sorted out in a timely fashion.'

'That depends upon Mr Redding's willingness to cooperate,' Kay replied.

Dressed in a light grey suit and a blue shirt, Redding

ran a hand along the side of his head, smoothing down his hair before raising his gaze to meet Kay's.

'Tell us about Dale Thorngrove,' she said.

'The chap from Harlington's garage?'

'That's the one.'

'He looks after my car.'

'Do you socialise with him?'

Redding glanced at his solicitor, who gave a slight nod, then cleared his throat. 'Only on one occasion. I'd been out shooting that weekend and bagged a bird for a friend. I was on my way to his place when I dropped into the garage to book the car in for an MOT. Dale saw the bird on the passenger seat and we got talking. He was interested in having a go, so we made arrangements for him to come with us one Sunday when he wasn't working.'

'When was that?' Barnes asked.

'About, oh… four weeks ago.'

'What were you using?'

Redding smiled indulgently. 'Only a small .22 rifle. Anything else, and there wouldn't be much of a bird left to cook.'

Kay opened the folder, pulled out a single page, and spun it around to face Redding and Gillow. 'Care to explain how you were using that rifle given that your firearms licence was revoked when you were caught drink driving?'

Redding spread his hands. 'Look, I only go shooting these days if I'm invited to do so on private land, and I know for a fact that the two people who invite me have firearms certificates. That's not wrong, is it?'

'It is, if you're claiming responsibility for another person you invited along with you,' said Barnes.

'They vouched for Thorngrove as well. Ask them – they'll tell you themselves.'

'I will. What are their names?'

Kay waited while her colleague took the details, then eyed the man in front of her once more, ignoring the glare from his solicitor. 'Remind me where you were last Wednesday night between eight and midnight.'

'I told you. I was in business meetings. Video calls. Both in different time zones in the US. My wife brought me a light meal at nine o'clock because I'd missed dinner.'

'What time did your second call end?'

'Around ten to midnight.' He gave a weary smile. 'Needless to say, I was shattered the next day, especially as I had to meet with a new client based in Singapore at seven that morning.'

'Why did you phone Thorngrove last Monday?'

'Pardon?'

'Dale Thorngrove's mobile phone and wallet were found earlier today in the lane between the White Hart pub and your house,' Kay said. 'Your number was in his recent calls list, and ties in with an argument his colleagues overheard last Monday morning. What were you arguing about?'

'God, I don't remember.'

'You can do better than that, Mr Redding. You're currently our only suspect.'

He paled. 'I was querying the invoice for the car service, that's all.'

'Wasn't that the sort of conversation you should've been having with Gerry Harlington?'

'Dale did the work. I wanted to query it with him.'

'What was the problem?'

'He replaced the exhaust manifold without asking permission.' Redding snorted. 'I could've done without the nasty surprise on the bill, that's all. He got quite irate – to be honest, I wish I had spoken to Gerry. He'd have been much more understanding.'

'We're currently processing Thorngrove's wallet for fingerprints. Now would be a good time to tell us if yours are going to be present when we do.'

'Why on earth would my fingerprints be anywhere near his wallet? I've told you – I had nothing to do with that man's murder.' He turned to his solicitor. 'This is getting preposterous.'

Gillow sighed, capped his fountain pen and closed his notebook. 'I believe we're finished here, Detective Hunter. My colleague has reiterated his previous statement, provided you with a clear explanation regarding his telephone call with Mr Thorngrove, and moreover has provided you with the names of two colleagues who can vouch for Mr Thorngrove's invitation to use firearms under their supervision. I believe we're done here.'

Barnes ended the recording and led the way from the interview room, his eyes downcast while Redding and his solicitor marched towards the exit.

Kay switched on her mobile phone, her heart sinking as she read the new message that appeared on the screen.

'Shit.'

'What's up?' said Barnes.

She held up the phone to him in response. 'Laura phoned Redding's wife while we were speaking to him. She's confirmed what he said about taking in his supper that night while he was in meetings, and the time he came to bed. She couldn't sleep so she was watching a film.'

Barnes growled under his breath. 'Fuck it, we're back to square one.'

THIRTY-TWO

'Somebody give me *something* to move this case forward.'

Kay stormed across the incident room ahead of Barnes, slapped the manila folder on top of a pile accumulating on the corner of her desk and put her hands on her hips.

She ignored the shocked stares from some of the junior administrative staff, instead stalking towards the whiteboard.

'Come on. It's been a week, and all we have is Mark Redding telling us his argument with Thorngrove was nothing more than a complaint about an invoice, and two alibis for him being in possession of a firearm without a valid certificate. Help me out here.'

Phillip scurried across to her, a pen tucked behind one ear and a report in his hand. 'Guv, we've dusted the wallet – we've matched Thorngrove's prints to the ones on file, but so far there's nothing to suggest Redding handled it or the phone.'

'Christ, Phillip – that's not what I meant by helping.'

Kay ran her hand through her hair as the constable's face fell. 'What about those two names, Barnes?'

The detective sergeant held up his hand, his phone to his ear, then pointed across the room to where Laura was also speaking to someone on her phone, her voice little more than a murmur.

Kay eyed the darkened sky beyond the windows, checked her watch and bit back a surprised snort.

No wonder her team were looking exhausted.

It was already seven o'clock.

'Phillip, do me a favour – go and see if Daniel's still here, and ask him to run Redding's alibis for the pheasant shoot through his database, will you?'

'On it, guv.'

The constable dashed off, the relief in his expression evident at having a reason to escape the incident room.

'What are we missing?' Kay murmured, turning her attention back to the whiteboard and gazing up at the photographs of Thorngrove's prone body splayed across the White Hart's car park. 'What the hell were you up to?'

'Redding's alibis check out, guv.' Barnes joined her, peering over his reading glasses. 'I spoke to Royce Maxton – he owns some land out west of Staplehurst, and he confirmed he invites Redding and the other bloke, Ambrose Weatherley, to go shooting every now and again. Laura's spoken to Ambrose to cross-reference the facts, and he's confirmed what Royce said, and that Mark brought along Thorngrove to give him a taster the other week.'

'Bugger.' She peered past him as Phillip reappeared.

The constable shook his head.

'So Redding's out of the picture, then,' she said.

'Do you want me to give Andy a call and find out if he's managed to get anything else off of Thorngrove's phone?'

'No, that'll do for today, Ian. Let's get everyone home for the night. We've got a long day ahead of us tomorrow.'

Her phone pinged while she was walking back to her desk, and when she saw the text message from Adam, she smiled despite the late finish.

Meet you in the pub X.

'Sounds like a bloody good idea to me, Turner,' she muttered.

She texted a quick reply to him, and minutes later was zipping through the light traffic towards Bearsted, her thoughts alternating between the investigation and the thought of a relaxing drink with him.

She knew her team were doing all they could with the information available, but it was the lack of any leads via the media appeals and house-to-house enquiries that frustrated her.

Parking outside her house, she wandered back along the lane a few hundred metres to their local pub and found Adam at the bar, chatting to the landlord.

The place was a welcoming contrast to the White Hart, with a separate public bar at the front of the building that used to house the smokers before the nationwide ban sent them out into the gazebo by the front door, and a larger main bar area that swept around to a dining room.

Low music played in the background, and she nodded to the regulars gathered beside the beer pumps, their friendly banter interspersed with loud laughter.

'Here she is,' the publican beamed, already pouring a pint of lager for her.

'Thanks.' She sighed as some of the stress left her shoulders, and kissed Adam, tasting beer on his lips. 'Been here long?'

He held up his glass. 'This is my first. Honest.'

Waiting until she'd taken a gulp of lager, he pointed to a corner table. 'Come on, we'll sit over there, out of the way.'

Sinking into one of the old church pews adorned with plush cushions, Kay took another sip of her beer and tried to push away her frustration with the investigation.

As if sensing the strain she was under, Adam sidled closer and reached out for her hand.

'That bad?'

'We're not getting anywhere.' She eyed him for a moment, then lowered her glass. 'Wasn't today the day you were interviewing a new vet?'

His lips quirked. 'Remember when you were interviewing prospective candidates for the DS job a few years ago?'

'Yes…'

'It's been like that, but worse.'

'Go on.'

She listened while he told her about the three candidates he and Scott had met that day, each progressively worse than the last, and covered her mouth to stifle her giggles as a couple of the regulars peered over their shoulders at them.

'If that wasn't bad enough,' Adam continued, 'the final candidate kicked off the interview by telling me he'd read my last journal article, and then proceeded to tell me everything that was wrong with it. Scott and I couldn't get a word in edgeways, let alone ask a question.'

He waited until she was taking another sip of lager. 'Halfway through the interview, Theresa knocked on the door saying she'd had an urgent call from a farmer over at Lenham with another pregnant cow that was in difficulties. I left Scott to it. I couldn't get out of there fast enough. I figured being up to my armpits in cow again was better than listening to the bloke any longer.'

Despite her irritation about the investigation, and despite the weariness that seeped through her body, Kay snorted with laughter.

Beer shot up her nose and she began coughing, then slapped Adam on the arm.

'You bastard,' she wheezed. 'You waited until I took a sip on purpose.'

THIRTY-THREE

Kay snuffled, a loud insistent ringing dragging her from her dreams before Adam elbowed her in the ribs.

'Your phone's going off.'

'Shit.' She threw back the duvet, rubbed sleep from her eyes and peered at the screen.

'Ian? It's five thirty – what's going on?'

'Guv, we've got a problem.'

'What's the matter?'

'I'm on my way to Porter MacFarlane's place – control just took a call about a suspected break-in, and in the circumstances I said we'd attend. How soon can you get yourself over there?'

Twenty minutes later, ruing the fact she hadn't even had time to fill a travel cup with coffee on her way out the door, Kay powered her car along the narrow lane and gritted her teeth.

Overgrown branches smacked against the paintwork and the wheels slammed into potholes that she would normally have taken care to drive around.

Not today.

She stomped on the brake when she spotted the entrance for the MacFarlane property, anger and frustration at the turn of events mixing with an underlying fear that the situation was quickly deteriorating.

Almost a week later, they still had no idea who had murdered Dale Thorngrove in cold blood.

And now this.

Sunlight sparkled on fresh dew in the paddocks either side of the driveway, and a pair of grazing deer raised their heads in curiosity as her car shot past them, kicking up dust and stones that clicked and spat out from under the wheel arches.

She could see a patrol car parked outside the MacFarlanes' house, and a uniformed constable climbed out as she approached, pointing to the track that led around the property.

She slowed and wound down her window. 'Have they found anything?'

'No, guv. DS Barnes is down at the shed with the owners.'

Shoving the car into gear, she eased down the winding track behind the house.

A small truck with a black box-like trailer was parked outside the shed where the MacFarlanes kept their props. There was a TV production company's logo emblazoned down the side and two men hovering beside the open back doors, their expressions worried while they watched her park next to them.

The older of the two stepped forward as she got out her

car. 'Do you know when we'll be able to get on the road? We're due to be in Northumberland by three o'clock.'

'Best you let your boss know you're going to be late,' she said, and walked over to where Barnes was standing beside Porter MacFarlane before following them into the shed.

Goosebumps flecked her arms in the coolness of the interior, and she buttoned up her jacket. After her eyes adjusted to the gloom, she saw Roman finish speaking with Kyle Walker at the far end and beckoned them over.

'Right, what's going on? Barnes said something about a break-in.'

The uniformed constable eyed the MacFarlanes, then turned his attention to her. 'There was no sign of forced entry, guv. Apparently the doors were locked when they came down here with the production crew just after five.'

'So what's the problem?'

Porter flushed a deeper shade of red and walked over. 'There seems to be an error with our inventory system, Detective Hunter. Most unusual.'

'What error?'

'We're missing two .308 rifles,' said Roman.

'*Two*?'

'Older models, and two that I had in mind to sell,' Porter added. 'They're hardly ever rented out these days, so I figured I could still make a few hundred quid on them—'

'Who else has access to this shed?'

'Apart from us, no one unless they're collecting stock, like these two gentlemen are. They're waiting to take some replica sixteenth-century swords for a TV show being filmed up north.'

Kay shielded her eyes from the rising sun's glare and peered out the shed doors to where the production crew were leaning against the truck, both smoking while the older of the two kept looking at his watch. 'Do you accompany your clients at all times when stock's being removed?'

'Yes, most times,' said Roman.

'Most times?' She turned back to him. 'Why not at all times?'

Porter cleared his throat. 'If one of our regular clients turns up and there's a lot to load then we all lend a hand to get them on their way as soon as possible…'

'It could be that one of them took the rifles,' Roman added.

'How would they have got into the inner room? It's locked all the time, isn't it?'

'Somebody might've slipped in while we were distracted,' mumbled Porter.

'I thought you used a cloud-based system to keep a note of all of your inventory?'

'We do, yes.'

Kay moved out of the way of one of the uniformed constables who carried a fingerprint dusting kit. 'Then why isn't it updated every time a firearm is checked out?'

'It is, but against the purchase order so we know what we have to invoice for at the end of the month.'

'The system also helps us to see what we've loaned out and what's in stock when we're negotiating new deals,' Porter explained. 'I mean, most of the time I know what's down here off the top of my head. It's Roman here who organised everything into a database of sorts for ease of reference.'

'When did you last audit the stock?'

'At the end of June.' Porter sheepishly glanced sideways at his son. 'That's my fault. Roman suggested a few weeks ago that we ought to go through everything to make sure our licences were up to date and see whether we should sell some of the firearms that weren't in demand. The problem is, it takes so much time out of the day when I could be finding us new work instead... I only got around to doing it today because your last visit reminded me how important it was.'

'So, what you're saying is that despite having an inventory system, you have no idea when the two rifles were stolen.'

Both men shuffled their feet.

'No, we don't,' said Porter eventually. 'Sorry.'

Kay bit back the curse that nearly flew from her lips. 'While I remember – Roman, where were you last Wednesday night between eight and midnight?'

'In here, cleaning the carriage we've just shipped over to New England for filming.'

Kay looked over to where he pointed, and saw a large space where the horse-drawn carriage had been parked on Friday afternoon.

She led the way back outside. 'We'll need the contact details for everyone who's entered this shed since the date of the last audit. Not just company names, mind – I want names, addresses and phone numbers for each person. And that includes any private tours you've given, Porter.'

'I understand.'

'Who else might have had access to the property?' She pointed to the gangly horse chestnut and oak trees that crowded the boundary line. 'Is all of that fenced off from the road?'

'It's hard to say – there's a public footpath that runs diagonally across our boundary about half a mile beyond those. There's a wire fence that runs alongside it but I suppose anyone could've ducked underneath it if they knew what was here.'

'They could've staked out the shed for days,' said Roman, squinting against the sun that broke through the trees. 'And then taken the rifles when we were busy with clients, I suppose.'

'Bloody great,' said Kay, and turned to Kyle. 'Seal off that woodland, and work with Phillip to get the search underway.'

'What can we do to help?' Porter asked, wringing his hands while he watched the uniformed officer hurry away.

'You can come back to the house with us and give us that list of names,' said Kay. 'And you can make me a bloody coffee.'

THIRTY-FOUR

Laura bounced her heels off the carpet tiles in time with the pulsing music playing through her earbuds and stared at the satellite image on her computer screen.

After receiving a text message from Barnes at six, she'd raced into work and phoned Kyle to help coordinate the search of the woodland around the MacFarlanes' property, and was now trying to work out how someone could have accessed the storage sheds from the nearest road.

A notification popped up at the bottom of the screen to let her know she'd received a new email, and she hit pause on the music.

The sender was Roman MacFarlane and the message was short and to the point, merely stating that the list of names and addresses that Kay wanted was attached.

'Perfect.'

Laura whipped out her earbuds and raced across to the printer as it whirred to life, ripping the pages from it as they appeared and running her eyes down the text.

There were fourteen companies in total, and she sighed before wandering over to Debbie's desk.

'How many bums on seats can I have to help me go through these?'

The constable peered past her to take in the staff strewn throughout the incident room, the place crowded despite the early hour. 'I can't, Laura. Sorry. headquarters made the decision over the weekend to lower the threat level, and we've lost six already to other cases this morning. Where are Kyle and Phillip? Don't they usually help you with this sort of thing?'

'They're still at the MacFarlanes', traipsing through woodland.'

'Lucky them.' Debbie gave her a sympathetic smile. 'Look, tell you what – give me some of those and I'll give you a hand until Kay gets back.'

'You're a superstar, thanks.' Laura handed her a copy of the list, relayed Kay's instructions and made her way back to her desk. She blew out her cheeks, picked up her phone, and dialled the first number.

Five minutes later, berated by a stressed-out third assistant director, she replaced the phone and crossed out the name, her ears still ringing.

Across the room, she could hear Debbie's raised voice and wondered if all production crew were as cranky first thing in the morning.

She dialled the second number, and held her breath.

'Sophie Grannard.'

'Ms Grannard? I'm sorry to call so early. My name's Detective Constable Laura Hanway. I'm with Kent Police.'

'Hang on.'

She waited while the woman spoke in a low tone, then a child's cry reached her before the voice returned.

'Sorry – just trying to get the kids out the door for school.'

'I can phone back later if now isn't convenient?'

'No, that's okay. My husband's taking them this morning.' There was a rueful laugh. 'We were just going through the usual routine with my youngest about why she has to go to school. Where did you say you're from?'

'Kent Police. We got your details from Porter MacFarlane.'

'Porter…?'

'He and his son run a props and armoury company down this way.'

'Oh, Porter. I know who you mean now. Is he all right?'

'He's fine, Ms Grannard. We're just making some routine enquiries with his clients from the past three months. I understand your production team rented some rifles from him in August?'

'Yes, we were filming a couple of scenes for a drama in West Sussex – Porter's company came highly recommended.'

'Who arranged to view the guns you wanted to hire?'

'Two of my production assistants. You'll have to check with them about what was ordered though.' Grannard gave a small laugh. 'That's what I pay them for. Do you want their details?'

'It's okay, I've got them here. Did you have any issues

with the weapons or with Roman or Porter during filming?'

'No.' There was a pause at the other end. 'Look, is everything all right? What's going on?'

Laura plastered a smile on her face, hoping it would reach her voice. 'Nothing to worry about, Ms Grannard. Thanks for your time.'

She ended the call as the incident room door opened and Kay and Barnes walked in, their faces grim.

'Anything to report?' said the detective inspector. 'How're you getting on with those names?'

'Early days, guv and nothing untoward yet.' Laura pointed to Debbie. 'There are only two of us working on the list at the moment though, so it's going to take a while.'

'Give some of them to Ian, and I'll take a couple once I've caught up with Sharp.' Kay glanced at the clock above the printer. 'I'm supposed to be giving headquarters an update in ten minutes. Kyle and Phillip are on their way too – we just saw them pull in to the car park.'

'Thanks, guv. How's the search at the house going?'

'The team there haven't found anything yet.' Kay thanked a passing administrative assistant for the cup of coffee that was thrust into her hand and took a sip. 'There are six officers completing the search but I don't think they'll find anything. God knows how much wildlife has traipsed through there. Trying to find footprints is going to be a nightmare—'

'Especially when the MacFarlanes have no idea when the rifles were stolen,' Barnes growled.

Laura shot Kay a look. 'Is that right?'

'Yes. Despite them telling us they've got a system to record every firearm's whereabouts.' Kay took another swig of coffee, then straightened her shoulders. 'I guess I'd better get this phone call out the way.'

THIRTY-FIVE

'Detective Hunter, I understand there's been a development.'

Assistant Chief Constable Tess Bainbridge leaned closer to her laptop camera, her green eyes keen. 'Care to update us?'

Kay eyed the notes beside her own computer, then made sure the door to Sharp's old office was closed and looked back to the three faces staring at her from her screen.

Both Sharp and Chief Superintendent Susan Greensmith appeared relaxed despite the hastily scheduled video conference, and she wished she possessed a modicum of their calmness in the face of one of the force's highest commanders.

Then she realised their resilience was honed by years of experience.

Experience that had been gained first hand, in situations like this.

She took a deep breath. 'Earlier this morning, control

took a triple nine call from the MacFarlane residence. The MacFarlanes were interviewed earlier in this investigation because they hold one of the largest firearms collections in our division. At that time, we conducted a spot check of weapons against their computerised inventory, interviewed both Porter MacFarlane and his son Roman, and concluded that they weren't involved in Dale Thorngrove's murder last week.'

'I sense there's a "but" here,' said Bainbridge.

'When we attended the property this morning, the MacFarlanes informed us that they'd discovered two .308 rifles were missing. They only found out because a TV production company turned up to take delivery of some stock. Porter decided to audit the firearms while he was up early. Apparently his son's been nagging him to do that for weeks.'

Sharp hissed through his teeth while the two women stared at their screens in shocked horror.

'Do they know when the rifles were taken?' Greensmith asked.

'No, they don't.' Kay bit her lip before continuing. 'It transpires they've been relying on purchase orders to note stock going in and out on the inventory database and Porter hadn't conducted a full audit since June. I've currently got Daniel's team reviewing their firearms certificates, and we'll obviously be making further enquiries before deciding whether to revoke those, bearing in mind that a substantial portion of their business is reliant on firearms.'

'Do they know who took them?' said Bainbridge.

'Neither man has been able to suggest who might've

taken the rifles. They allow production crews to go in and out of the building while stock is being loaded under their supervision. My team here is working through a list of production companies that have been to the MacFarlanes' property since the last audit. I've also got a team on site concluding a search of the property for any indication as to how anyone else might've accessed the shed. It's locked at all times and there was no sign of a break-in, but the building is surrounded by woodland and it isn't visible from the house.'

'Given the amount of time that's elapsed since their last audit, that theft could've been any time in the past three months,' said Sharp.

'Exactly, guv. We also have an additional problem that has only come to light since I've returned to Maidstone. Roman MacFarlane has advised that an amount of ammunition was taken as well. Over two thousand rounds, to be exact.'

A stunned silence met her words.

Kay paused a moment to check she'd covered everything in her notes, then raised her gaze to the screen once more. 'We're understaffed here, and I could use an experienced pair of hands to help work through all the information we've got, and to help me coordinate with Paul Disher once we locate the weapons.'

Bainbridge managed a wry smile. 'I take it you want Piper back there?'

'Yes, please. As soon as possible.' Kay tried to keep the desperation from her voice. 'He's one of the most experienced detective constables on my team, and I need him to work with some of the uniformed ranks to focus on tracking down those rifles. I also need someone I can trust to dig into Porter MacFarlane's background and activities – without drawing attention to themselves.'

Bainbridge turned her attention to Greensmith and Sharp. 'I'm inclined to agree. Do either of you have any pressing matters you need Piper for?'

'Now that the focus has centred on the Maidstone area, I'm happy to release him,' said Greensmith. 'We can retain a watching brief from here utilising the team available to us with respect to any suspicious activity that might lead us to the gunman.'

'Agreed,' said Sharp. 'Unless and until the killer breaks cover, our hands are tied.'

'Very well. I'll release Gavin Piper from the team here with immediate effect,' said Bainbridge. She winked. 'Look after him, Detective Hunter. I want him back at Northfleet one day.'

THIRTY-SIX

Kay stretched her arms over her head and leaned back in her chair, groaning.

A muscle cricked at the base of her skull, and she reached out for her coffee mug before realising it was empty and sighed.

Pushing it away, she turned her attention back to her computer screen and the hundreds of emails that had arrived over the past twenty-four hours, scanning the subject lines for anything that could be discarded, and any others that could be delegated straight away.

That done, her eyes flicked to the clock in the corner of the screen.

Seven o'clock, and half an hour since she'd sent her team home.

The atmosphere had been subdued while they'd slunk away, half-hearted goodbyes and attempts at humour falling flat in their wake.

A few had resisted her orders, citing an opportunity to

catch up with their work and try to get a head start on the next day, the quiet murmur of conversations carrying across to where she sat.

A stale air clung to the room, stuffy now that the building's central heating system had been switched on for autumn and lulling Kay into a sleep-deprived fug while she scrolled back and forth between the messages.

Although she wouldn't admit it to anyone else, Mark Redding's solicitor's words had rattled her.

Despite herself, she knew Andrew Gillow was right.

They didn't have sufficient evidence to charge anyone, or any idea behind the motive for Thorngrove's brutal murder.

They had nothing.

And the more time that passed, the easier it would be for the killer to distance himself from the crime scene and his victim.

An email from someone called Elliott Windlesham sent fifteen minutes ago snagged her attention, the subject line pertaining to a new list of names, and she clicked on it to see that it had been addressed to Laura and copied to her automatically by the system.

'Please find attached the list of past and present members' names, with apologies for the delay,' she read.

Then she spotted the signature line.

'Ah, the re-enactment lot,' she murmured, and sent the attachment to the printer.

Walking over to it, she nodded in farewell to a pair of uniformed constables, and ran her eyes down the list while debating whether to pick up a takeaway on the way home.

Her stomach rumbled as she returned to her desk, still scanning the list.

Then she paused, stock-still between Gavin's empty chair and her own.

'I know that name.'

Wracking her memory, she tried to dredge up where she'd heard it before, and then dashed across to her computer and opened up the HOLMES2 database entry for the investigation.

Scrolling through all the documents Debbie and her team of administrative assistants had filed in chronological order, she worked her way back through all the witness statements and house-to-house enquiry logs until her eyes fell upon the familiar name.

'What the hell…?' she muttered.

She found Windlesham's mobile number at the end of his email.

The man picked up after two rings.

'Hello?'

'Mr Windlesham, it's Detective Inspector Kay Hunter of Kent Police. I hope this isn't too late to be calling?'

'Is this about my email?'

'It is. I wondered if I could ask you a couple of questions.' She didn't give him a chance to respond. 'You've got a man by the name of Clive Workman on the list of past members. When did he leave?'

'Um, off the top of my head I'd have to guess about four years ago. A while back, at any rate.'

'Why was that?'

'He lost his firearms certificate. He didn't say why. I

suppose without being able to take part in the re-enactments anymore, he lost interest. He never renewed his membership with us anyway.'

'When was the last time you saw Mr Workman?'

'Around about the same time, I reckon.' There was a pause, then, 'He's not really the sort of bloke I liked to hang around with.'

'In what way?'

'Always had a bit of a temper on him, from what I remember. Easily offended. Not really the sort of person we want around when we're interacting with the public. We never had him manning the static displays or the membership tent – he'd always get into an argument about the slightest thing.'

'Right. Okay, thanks for your time.'

Kay ended the call before opening another tab on her computer screen and finding Laura's report about her interview with Workman.

Scanning the text, she reviewed the questions the young detective constable had asked, and frowned.

The man had never answered her colleague's inquiry whether he knew anyone who owned a firearm. Instead, he'd changed the subject, asking about the shooting at the White Hart before providing an alibi for his whereabouts.

The alibi, Matty Oakland, had confirmed what Workman had said, but it still left the question open regarding who else the man might know – and what information he might be withholding.

Otherwise, why not answer the question?

Was he trying to protect someone?

Kay swiped her phone screen and pressed speed dial for a familiar number.

'Ian? Can you meet me at Clive Workman's house? I'll text you the address.'

'No problem, guv. When?'

'Now.'

THIRTY-SEVEN

Kay drummed her fingers on the steering wheel and checked her mirrors as another car swung in behind hers, its lights going out before the sound of a door slamming reached her.

Seconds later, the passenger door opened and Barnes dropped into the seat, his gaze fixed on the house farther along the street.

'I take it he's in, then?'

'Seems to be. I walked past earlier and I could see lights beyond the curtains at the front.'

'How do you want to do this?'

'Carefully. Until we figure out what Clive Workman's trying to hide by avoiding Laura's question, we assume he's a suspect.'

'Want me to call for back-up, just in case?'

She shook her head and gestured to the houses on either side of the road. 'I don't think he'll try anything. Not with this many witnesses.'

'It didn't bother the bloke who shot Thorngrove last week.'

Kay shivered. 'True.'

'Ready?'

'Yeah.'

Setting a brisk pace, Kay strode up to Workman's door and rang the bell before rapping her knuckles against the uPVC surface, then took a step back.

Half past eight on a Tuesday night, and given there were no lights on anywhere else in the house she could see, she didn't think the man would be expecting visitors.

Light pooled through the frosted window pane in the door from a room to the right, and a chain rattled before Workman peered out.

Light stubble covered his jaw, and he wore a pale blue shirt over a grey T-shirt, grease spots down the front of it.

'Who—'

Kay held up her warrant card and made the introductions. 'A quick word, if you wouldn't mind, Mr Workman.'

She stepped forward, but he held the door firm and glared at her.

'I've just sat down to eat my dinner…'

'Like I said…'

'So, be quick.' The door opened a little more but he stood his ground, folding his arms over his chest.

'We have some follow-up questions. Specifically, who do you know who owns an illegal firearm?'

Kay saw his Adam's apple bob once.

'No one,' he spluttered, his eyes darting between her and Barnes. 'Who told you I did?'

'You avoided the question last time my colleague asked. That makes me suspicious. So, do you want to have a quick think about it – given that your dinner's getting cold – and try again?'

Kay cocked an eyebrow and waited.

His jaw worked a moment.

'Look, it was a long time ago,' he said eventually. 'I still had my own licence back then. A bloke I knew in passing had an old Ruger he got from his grandad. Apparently he'd picked it up during the war, and gave it to him. He was asking me whether he ought to hand it in or sell it.'

'Where's that revolver now?'

'I dunno.' He frowned. 'I never saw it. He just told me about it, that's all.'

'I'll need a name.'

Workman told her, and then chuckled bitterly. 'Not that it'll do you any good – he died in a boating accident off Sheerness a year or so ago. It was in all the papers.'

'Why didn't you tell my officers this when they first spoke to you?'

'It slipped my mind.'

'You avoided the question at the time.'

'Look,' he said, spreading his hands. 'They were firing questions at me left, right and centre. I did my best. I've got nothing to hide.'

'Where were you between the hours of eight and midnight on Wednesday?'

His gaze turned cold. 'Exactly where I told the last two I spoke to. Down the pub – my local one – playing pool with a mate. That bird who was here last time wrote down his name – Matty Oakland. He's already spoken to one of your lot and confirmed that. Now, if you don't mind, I'm going to go and finish my dinner.'

The door slammed shut and Kay turned away, fuming silently.

'I'll run the name through the system anyway, and the accident,' said Barnes as they walked back to their cars. 'I'll also try to find out what happened to the old gun to close the loop on that.'

'Thanks, Ian.' Kay unlocked her car and tried to batten down her disappointment. 'Unfortunately I don't think it's going to help us find Dale Thorngrove's killer.'

'Tomorrow's another day, guv,' he said, turning to go. 'Catch you in the morning.'

'Sorry to drag you out for nothing.'

'It's never nothing.' He stopped and peered over his shoulder. 'It's like you tell the rest of the team – if we don't ask, we don't find out.'

She managed a smile. 'I reckon I should listen to my own advice more often.'

THIRTY-EIGHT

Gavin shouldered his backpack and locked his car before setting a brisk pace across the car park outside the Archbishop's Palace.

He eyed the CCTV cameras pointing at the fading paintwork of the parking bays, their position next to the streetlights that bathed the uneven surface providing a clear view of everyone passing by.

An involuntary shiver crossed his shoulders at the memory of watching himself being attacked under those same cameras a few years ago, and he shook his head to clear the thought.

His footsteps echoed off the centuries-old pavers under a stone arch, and then a stiff breeze buffeted him as he crossed the disused cobbled cart track between the Palace and All Saints' Church. Flipping up his coat collar, he dodged around a pile of dog shit then hurried past the tilting gravestones that crowded the path when he saw the lights turn green at the pedestrian crossing.

He joined half a dozen commuters who shuffled onto a concrete island on the other side, and waited for the passing traffic to grind to a standstill while he eyed the red-brick exterior of Maidstone's police station at the curve in the road a few metres away.

Until this morning, he hadn't appreciated how compact the box-like structure was compared to Northfleet's modern headquarters.

The darkened privacy glass peppering the upper floors stared blankly out across the cluttered skyline, smeared with grime from the passing nose-to-tail traffic that clogged Palace Avenue. Unlike the smooth rendered exterior of headquarters, the rough outer masonry seemed dull against neighbouring buildings.

Jogging over the crossing as soon as the lights changed, Gavin slowed his pace as he drew nearer, staring at his feet while he wondered what Sharp was saying to his team during his early morning briefing, and whether his absence would be noticed.

He hadn't had time to explain his sudden departure to Paul Solomon, or the two uniformed constables he'd shared a corner of the incident room with, their desks cluttered by files and paperwork.

'Morning, Gav.'

A familiar voice jolted him from his thoughts, and he raised his head to see Laura standing on the front steps of the station, grinning.

'Hey.' He smiled, held open the door for her and swiped his security card across the panel beside the front desk.

'So, how was it over there?' she asked once they were climbing the stairs up to the first floor. 'Glad you're back?'

'Yeah, I am.'

She stopped on the landing, turning to him with a frown. 'You don't seem too sure about that.'

'It's different over there.'

'In what way?'

'It's hard to explain.' He paused a moment. 'It's good to be back among familiar faces, though.'

Laura reached out and lightly punched his arm. 'We missed you too. Come on, otherwise we'll be late.'

Kay was already standing beside the whiteboard when they walked into the incident room, and after storing his backpack under his desk Gavin wandered over to join her.

'Morning, guv.'

'Good to see you.' She smiled, and he saw then how weary his mentor looked.

'Sharp said you had something for me.'

'Yes.' She reached up and tapped one of the photographs pinned to the board. 'This is Porter MacFarlane.'

'The armourer who's missing two rifles? Has anything turned up?'

'No, and the search team came up empty-handed as well.'

'Okay. What do you need?'

She folded her arms, lowering her voice. 'I want you to look into Porter's background. A deep dive. We've got all the obvious records to hand, things that had to be covered for his firearms certificates...'

'But you think there's something else.'

'I don't know.' She sighed. 'I could be completely wrong, but the fact that they have that many firearms and aren't controlling their stock scares the living shit out of me, Gav. I mean, what else might be missing?'

'Not being funny, guv, but Laura's more than capable of doing this.'

'She is, you're right – but I need someone I can trust.' She stopped, waiting until a gaggle of uniformed constables passed, then looked at the photograph again. 'Adam knows Porter.'

'Ah.'

'They're not friends or anything like that, but he does look after the deer herd, and Porter used to take his old springer spaniel over to the surgery. I'd like to keep that connection under wraps until we know more because otherwise—'

'You'll have to claim an interest in the investigation and hand it over to someone else.'

'Exactly. And I'm not prepared to do that. Not yet.'

Gavin exhaled, his gaze moving to where Laura and Barnes sat at their desks, heads bowed while they worked through the first emails of the morning. 'All right. Leave it with me. Do you want to give me something else to do during today's briefing that I can use as a cover? Otherwise Laura's going to want to know what I'm up to.'

Kay grinned. 'Oh, don't worry. I'm sure I can come up with something.'

'I'll bet.' He turned to go.

'Gav?'

'Yes, guv?'

When he glanced over his shoulder, Kay was watching him, a wary look in her eye.

'Did Bainbridge offer you a job over there?'

'No.'

'Let me know if she does. I'd like the chance to convince you otherwise.'

THIRTY-NINE

Kay elbowed open the door of the café and emerged into a crowded Jubilee Square, errant pigeons doing their best to weave in and out of the foot traffic while scavenging for scraps of food.

She held a large takeout cup of coffee in each hand, ruing the fact that the café had run out of cardboard trays while the hot drinks burned her fingers, and vowed to take in the teetering stack the team had accumulated next to the recycling bin in the incident room before the week was over.

Shivering as her body adjusted to the cooler outdoor temperature, she made her way past the town hall and along a narrow pedestrianised lane overlooked on all sides by small businesses that had taken up residence in the old town buildings.

Low doorways displayed painted signs and brass plaques advertising solicitors, real estate agents and more but none of the bright wording caught her attention.

Instead, her thoughts returned to her conversation with

Gavin and the surreptitious glances that had been aimed his way by his colleagues during the morning briefing.

She sensed a wariness towards him in the incident room now, but realised some of that was borne from the fact he had only just joined the investigation team and was desperately trying to catch up with all the new information that had been generated.

Crossing the street, she made her way along the concrete footpath beside the River Medway, the wind buffeting her coat and creating a chop across the water.

A flock of ducks bobbed on the wavelets, creating a lazy zigzag as they swam back and forth in search of morsels while halyards slapped and clanked against the mast of a small dinghy on the opposite bank, the owner lowering it before navigating the low bridge under the ring road.

Rounding the back of the church, she spotted a familiar figure slouched on a bench seat, his eyes downcast.

'Cheer up, sunshine – I brought coffee.'

'Thanks.' Barnes huddled into the wool collar of his coat and glared at the water. 'Why do we always come down here when it's blowing a gale?'

'Because no one else is stupid enough to sit here, that's why.' Kay smiled. 'And we know we won't be overheard.'

He shuffled along the seat to make room for her. 'All right, what's on your mind?'

'Gavin.'

'Thought so.'

'Christ, I was hoping it wasn't that obvious.'

'Probably not to the others. I've known you longer.'

'True.' She took a tentative sip of the coffee, the hot

liquid scalding her lips. 'Do you think he's going to settle back here all right after being at headquarters?'

'I hope so. I think the trick is to make sure he knows we need him, and that we don't take him for granted.'

'That'll only keep him happy for so long, Ian. It's only a matter of time before he wants more.'

'Yeah, but more what?' Barnes turned to face her. 'I can't see him wanting the paperwork that comes with a DS role like mine – he likes being in the thick of it too much. Gav's the sort of person who thrives in an active investigation like this.'

'There are plenty of bigger investigations underway at Northfleet,' Kay countered, then sighed. 'It'll only take something like a major long-term one to pique his interest.'

Barnes took another gulp of coffee and scowled at a seagull that swooped over their heads. 'Do you think he'll do something like working undercover?'

'No.'

'You sound pretty sure.'

'I think he and Leanne are getting pretty serious.' She smiled. 'I can't see her being happy with him taking those sorts of risks. No, I think Gavin will always be a team player but he definitely shines when he's under pressure. I'm worried that if he only gets to investigate minor crimes down here most of the time, we'll lose him.'

Barnes grinned. 'Maybe we could become criminal masterminds, just to make sure we don't.'

'Yes, I can imagine that conversation at your next evaluation meeting with Sharp.' Kay drained the dregs of her coffee and rose to her feet with a groan. 'We should get back.'

Holding out her empty cup to her colleague and waiting while he dispatched both into the nearest waste bin, she fought down the worry and turned her focus back to the investigation.

'Hopefully Laura's had some success talking to the production companies this morning,' she said as they walked up the path towards the main road. 'Even if we could—'

She glanced down as Barnes's mobile started ringing and he dug around in his coat pocket, swearing under his breath as the material snagged on the phone.

'Debbie? What's up?'

Kay watched as his jaw dropped, and then he started to weave his way between the cars queued at the lights, pulling her with him.

'Ian? What's going on?' she said as he ended the call and took off at a jog towards the police station.

'We've got to get over to the waste and recycling plant,' he called over his shoulder. 'They've found something in one of the industrial bins that were delivered this morning.'

FORTY

Kay paused at the door, her eyes widening at the expansive layout within the hangar-like space.

At the far end of the facility, wide open aluminium doors led out to a red and white barrier beside what looked like a guard hut. A waste truck rumbled up to the barrier, and she saw the driver lean out of the window while he spoke to a man in a high visibility vest who emerged from the small building.

Below the concrete jetty where she stood overlooking the delivery bays, a truck emptied its load onto a towering pile of waste. A pervading stench of rotten food, grease and general rubbish wafted across the building to where she watched, and she wrinkled her nose, shuffling her feet within the borrowed steel-capped boots she now wore.

'You're lucky we keep a few spare pairs for visitors,' Cliff Exley said. The site manager glanced down at her feet. 'Sorry we didn't have your size though.'

'These will do.' Kay grimaced while she curled her

toes to stop them sliding around in the size twelves, and ignored the smug look that Barnes gave her.

'Okay, so concluding the health and safety checks, if you could both sign your names here,' Exley said, holding out a clipboard and pen, 'then I'll show you what we found this morning.'

Kay scrawled her name at the bottom of the page and handed over the paperwork to Barnes.

'I never appreciated what went on behind the scenes here,' she said.

'We process over fifteen hundred tons of industrial waste and eight hundred tons of household waste every month,' said Exley, smiling indulgently. 'And then we've got all the recyclable waste that gets sorted and redirected to other facilities as well.'

'Impressive.' She paused and took the high visibility vest he held out to her, shrugging it over her shoulders. 'Where did you find the rifle parts?'

'Over here – mind your step, and make sure you hold onto the railing. It can get slippery.' He guided them down a steel staircase and onto the concrete floor of the facility. 'We've paused processing the waste – that truck was the last one we'll offload until you tell us otherwise.'

Kay struggled to hear the site manager over the noise of machinery and loud voices, and raised her voice.

'Who found the parts?'

'Natasha Perrott, one of our permanent staff. She's been with us for over six months now, and seen all sorts of things so she didn't hesitate when she spotted what looked like a rifle scope. Her shift was due to finish twenty minutes ago but she offered to stay until you could speak to her.'

'How many workers are on the floor at any time?'

'Very few.' Exley pointed to a box-like structure that jutted out from the mezzanine level. 'That's the control room, so we can observe what's going on from a safe position. There are cameras throughout the facility, including the storage bunkers and the conveyor belt. The supervision team up there can see everything from those windows, and only come down here if there's a problem. Like this morning.'

They walked past a precariously sloping pile of rubbish, and Kay ran her eye over the tin cans, takeaway cartons and assorted household waste before realising there were four further identical mountains beyond that.

An enormous steel claw dangled from a cable in the ceiling above the storage bunkers, its teeth open in anticipation.

'Do you know where each of these piles originates from in the area?'

'Roughly.' Exley paused while a forklift truck negotiated a stack of flattened cardboard boxes, then waved them forward. 'My brother's a copper in Hampshire though, and as soon as Natasha radioed through what she'd found, I put two and two together. I figured the parts had to be something to do with your murder. Otherwise, why would someone throw them away?'

'Were they found within household waste like this, or—'

'No, the non-hazardous industrial waste – the bins are emptied from commercial premises, restaurants, that sort of thing. We sort out what can be recycled and incinerate the rest to provide power for the local population.' He smiled. 'Much better than contributing to more landfill.'

'How quickly are these bunkers emptied?' Barnes asked, pointing at the nearest one that appeared to be near to overflowing.

'Every few hours. That furnace is a hungry beast.'

'Does that mean that anything delivered yesterday has already been burned?'

'That's right.'

'In that case, Mr Exley, we'll need the details of every staff member who's had access to these bays this morning.'

'Of course. No problem. Now, if you'd like to follow me up these stairs, Natasha's waiting in the control room.'

When Kay followed Exley through a door into the narrow room, she was first struck by how clean the room was, and then stepped away from the window as a fleeting sense of vertigo caught her by surprise.

'You get a good view from up here.'

She turned to see a woman dressed head to toe in bright orange overalls, silver visibility stripes on the arms glinting under the lights in the ceiling and her hair scraped back into an efficient bun.

Kay flipped open her warrant card. 'Detective Inspector Hunter.'

'Natasha Perrott.' The woman nodded in greeting, then gestured to the large comfortable-looking chair overlooking the facility below that was taken by a man in his thirties who barely registered their presence.

His hands cradled a clipboard while on either side of

the seat a set of panels blinked and shone, a joystick at the edge of each.

'Josh here usually has the next shift, although I think he's going to have a quiet one this afternoon, right?'

'Thanks for staying. Do you want to show us what you found?'

'Sure. Over here.' Natasha took a few steps back and pointed to a collection of objects on top of a low cabinet at the far end of the control room. 'We kept them up here out of the way. We figured you wouldn't want everyone gossiping about this.'

Kay and Barnes shuffled past the enormous chair while the woman and Exley hovered at the open door, the small room already cramped.

Pulling a pair of disposable gloves from her trouser pocket, Kay reached out and picked up a metal object slick with grease.

'What is this?'

'Part of a rifle's trigger assembly. Reasonably clean, too. Not often used. I couldn't see the guard rod though.'

Kay frowned, turning the long metal spring in her gloved hands, then looked across to where Natasha stood in the doorway, hands clasped behind her back. 'You'd have to know something about weapons to spot this amongst all that rubbish. What did you do before you started here?'

'Three tours with the British Army. None of which I'm authorised to tell you about.' The woman's lips quirked, and then she walked over to the cabinet and gestured at the other items. 'Someone knew what they were doing. The bolt assembly's been taken apart, too – I only found the bolt carrier but I reckon the bolt and gas piston will be in there somewhere.'

'I don't suppose you were wearing gloves when you handled this lot?'

In reply, Natasha held up a pair of thick work gloves. 'Standard workplace health and safety. Besides, I didn't think you'd thank me if I added fingerprints to whoever's are on there already.'

'Thanks. Mr Exley, you're right – we're going to have to ask you to stop processing that waste until we've had our forensic examiners go through it,' said Kay.

The site manager's face fell, but he gave a stoical shrug. 'I expected you might.'

Barnes raised his chin and peered through the window to see another truck was pulling up to the barrier beyond the open doors of the waste facility, engine rumbling while it idled, then at the enormous metal claw that dangled above the stinking pile of detritus waiting to be processed, before turning back to Kay.

He grinned. 'I can't wait to see Harriet's face when she gets here.'

FORTY-ONE

Kay walked into the incident room, a discordant mixture of raised voices and phones ringing assaulting her ears as she made her way across to her computer.

After leaving Harriet and her team at the waste management facility, she had updated Sharp about Natasha's find and now needed to rally her colleagues and ensure they remained focused at such a late hour.

Darkness had blanketed the town over two hours ago, but there was still much to be done.

Although the administrative staff who were employed on normal hours had left on time, a rag-tag group comprising her detectives and various uniformed personnel remained, and she intended to make the most of their presence.

'Briefing, now,' she said, beckoning them towards the whiteboard. 'Come on, we need to get on with this while our killer thinks they've got away with it.'

'Unless he was at the facility,' said Barnes, his face

clouding as he dragged a seat across and dropped into it with a groan. 'In which case...'

'We don't know that for sure yet,' Kay replied.

The final stragglers scurried to lean against desks or pull up abandoned chairs, hastily forming a rough semi-circle beside the board, and the conversation died down.

After explaining the events at the waste facility, Kay glanced down at the notes she'd scribbled while Barnes had driven them back to Maidstone.

'Given the circumstances, this can't wait,' she began, 'so apologies if you had plans for this evening. First of all, Laura – can you work with Phillip to speak to the eight staff members who had access to the waste storage bunkers earlier today. Their shifts ended between seven o'clock and ten o'clock this morning, so hopefully by now they've had some rest and won't get too antsy with you if you call them after this. We need to work out whether the rifle parts were dumped in one of the industrial bins collected from the Maidstone area, or by one of the contractors employed by the facility.'

'Would it be better if we spoke to them face-to-face?' Laura asked.

'We don't have time. I'll leave it to the pair of you to use your best judgement in the circumstances. If you're speaking to someone on the phone and they sound cagey, then by all means organise a formal interview – but quickly. Once people hear that we're investigating the discarded rifle parts in connection with Thorngrove's murder, our killer will have time to react, and we're already dealing with the aftermath of what that might be.'

'Understood, guv.'

'Thanks. Daniel – where are you?'

A hand thrust upwards from the back of the small crowd.

'Can you and your team take a copy of the list of names we've got from the facility and cross-check those against the firearms licensing database? Let Laura know immediately if anyone is flagged so she can adjust the interview strategy if she needs to.'

'Will do, guv.'

'Gavin – I'm going to need your help leading a team to go through the CCTV footage we've acquired from the facility. We've obviously got two lines of enquiry here – the rifle parts were dumped elsewhere and captured within a standard collection, or someone there tried to hide them. I'd like you to monitor activities from when the first shift started at six o'clock this morning and let me know the moment you spot anything suspicious.' She bit back a sigh. 'If you don't, then we're going to have to try and find out where the contents of that storage bunker originated from and—'

Kay broke off as the incident room door opened and Harriet Baker strode towards her, a determined expression on the forensic manager's face.

She wore no make-up, and her cheeks still bore the imprint of the protective mask she'd been wearing while assisting her team of CSIs with their search.

'Excuse the interruption but I figured you'd rather have an update from me as soon as possible,' she said, slightly out of breath. 'And give me a moment – the bloody lift is out of use and I'm not used to running up stairs.'

A good-natured murmur of sympathetic laughter

rippled through Kay's team, and she held up her hand for silence.

'I take it you found more?'

'We did.' Now recovered, Harriet smoothed back her long fringe and took a deep breath. 'So, as well as the trigger assembly part that Natasha Perrott found, we located the metal guard rod. We also discovered the gas piston and two discarded magazines – one with two rounds missing. I've just dropped them over to the lab for testing, and we've taken swabs to run against our databases too.'

Kay tried to ignore her racing heartbeat, her throat dry with anticipation. 'Fingerprints?'

'Patrick's checking for those now. I'm going to head back to help but like I said, I figured you'd want the latest news ASAP.'

'Did you find anything else?'

'No, that's it – we searched the two bunkers either side of the one where the parts were found too, but found nothing.'

'That's great, Harriet. Thank you – you'll call me when you have more to report?'

'I will, and you'll get my full report from this afternoon's search sometime tomorrow.'

As Harriet left the room, Kay waited a moment to let the team digest the information, then dismissed them and turned her attention to Gavin. 'So, they've only found enough parts for one rifle, and until those have been tested we can't assume it's one of the ones stolen from the MacFarlanes. Even if it is, we've still got one missing so I need you to keep on top of the lab and pull in some favours to get more information tonight if you can.'

'One of Harriet's team owes me so I'll give him a call now.'

'Thanks.' Kay glanced at her watch as he walked back to his desk, then sent Adam a short text message to let him know she would be home late.

It was going to be a long night.

FORTY-TWO

Ian Barnes uttered a muffled curse, swallowed the last of his bacon sandwich, and glared at the grease spot now pooling in the middle of his burgundy polyester tie.

Up early, unwilling to wait until he'd had breakfast at home with his partner Pia, he'd rushed into work and was sitting at his desk by six thirty.

Kyle looked up from the desk arrangement he was currently sharing with Debbie West, and grinned.

'Mouth not big enough, sarge?'

'Up yours,' Barnes replied. He opened his desk drawer, breathing a sigh of relief when he spotted the spare tie rolled up beside a stapler and switched it for the stained one, placing that in the front pocket of his backpack.

No doubt he'd remember it sometime next month.

He turned his attention back to the briefing minutes from the night before that had been left on his desk, Kay's sprawling handwriting crowding the margins where she'd added her thoughts about the direction the investigation should take next.

'What time did she leave last night?' said Debbie, walking over and handing him the latest report out of HOLMES2.

He squinted at his screen. 'The last email I have from her is time-stamped twelve oh four. I think she sent everyone else home by eleven.'

The uniformed constable snorted. 'I'd better make sure there's fresh coffee on when she gets in.'

'Speaking of which.' Barnes held up his empty mug, and smiled.

'You know where to find it.'

'It was worth a try.'

After fetching a refill and taking an appreciative slurp, Barnes dropped back into his seat and searched through the case management system until he found Laura's last entry for the previous day.

According to her notes, she and Phillip had spent most of the evening talking to contractors employed by the facility to ascertain whether any of those might have been responsible for dumping the parts in the storage bunkers.

Their conversations had been frustratingly brief and no suspects had emerged, especially once Daniel confirmed that none of those names appeared on the National Firearms Licensing Management System either.

Gavin's report was equally disappointing, with the detective constable summarising that after spending several hours reviewing the facility's CCTV footage, none of the workers could be seen throwing anything into the storage bunkers.

In fact, none of the workers went anywhere near the bunkers while the facility was fully operational – all of the waste was sorted and managed by Natasha Perrott and her colleagues from the control room overseeing the waste hopper while it moved back and forth.

Recalling his conversation with Kay yesterday morning, Barnes hoped the young detective wasn't regretting the move back to Maidstone and the onerous tasks that the case now entailed, especially as the outcome of last night's endeavours meant that they would all be phoning local commercial waste collection companies this morning.

'Sarge?'

He looked up from his screen to see Kyle walking towards him, the constable's brow creased with worry.

'What've you got?'

'I just had Hughes on the phone. He says there's a Mrs Yvonne Maxton downstairs who wants a word. Apparently she's nervous as hell, and will only speak to someone on the Thorngrove enquiry.'

Barnes removed his reading glasses and pinched the bridge of his nose. 'Where do I know that name from?'

'She's married to Royce Maxton – the chap Mark Redding said he goes shooting with sometimes.'

'That's it.' Wagging his finger at Kyle, Barnes slipped on his jacket then straightened his tie. 'Let's go and see what she wants to talk about then.'

———

Yvonne Maxton was perched on the edge of one of the chairs in interview room two when Barnes and Kyle walked in, her musky perfume lending a pervasive scent to the otherwise stuffy interior and allaying some of the body odour that always lingered from previous occupants.

She wore a smart navy skirt suit, large gold hoops peering out from under a choppy black bob, and peered at the two men with watery green eyes while they took their seats opposite.

'Do you mind if we record this conversation, Mrs Maxton?' Barnes began, his voice gentle. 'It's standard practice.'

'I… no, of course. My husband won't hear this, will he?'

'This is a formal interview, and won't be shared with anyone outside of our investigation unless and until the matter goes to court.'

She chewed her lip for a moment, then nodded. 'All right. I suppose so.'

'Thank you. We have to start with a formal caution, but it's nothing to worry about.' Barnes recited the words by rote after Kyle started the recording equipment, and then leaned back in his chair, affecting a relaxed pose. 'My colleague on the front desk said you needed to talk to us about the Thorngrove case, Mrs Maxton. What did you want to tell us?'

'P-please. Call me Yvonne.' She tugged at a silver bracelet and twisted the chunky links between her fingers, keeping her eyes lowered to the table. 'I… um…'

'Take your time. Maybe a deep breath, too.'

The woman forced a nervous smile. 'I had this all planned out in my head while I was on my way into work this morning.'

'Where do you work?'

'Um, a firm of accountants. Up near the square.'

'Do you normally start this early in the morning?'

'Oh, gosh no. I don't usually start until half eight. I just wanted to see if I could talk to someone beforehand.'

'And here we are.'

'Yes.' A few more seconds ticked by on the clock above the door, and then Yvonne exhaled. 'Look, I don't want to sound like I'm telling tales or anything like that. It's just that I've been worried since Royce got a phone call from one of you earlier this week. He's been in a bad temper ever since.'

'Your husband?'

She met his gaze and nodded.

Barnes took a moment to run his eyes down the report Kyle had printed off before running downstairs after him, tracing the lines of text with his forefinger. 'Right, I see. DC Laura Hanway called him on Monday to ask about the pheasant shoots he organises from time to time.'

'They're rare – maybe one or two each season.' Yvonne blushed. 'Knowing Royce, he probably made it sound like we have hundreds of acres. It's really just a smallholding with a few chickens but we do have six acres of woodland next to the paddock. And it's not even as if he invites lots of people. Maybe three or four at most.'

'And he follows all health and safety procedures for guests?'

'Yes, of course.'

Barnes clasped his hands on top of the report. 'But there's still some sort of problem, I take it?'

'One of the men who turned up at the last one brought

his own rifle.' Yvonne shuffled in her seat, lowering her eyes.

A silence followed her words, and he let it go on, willing the woman to reveal what seemed to be troubling her so much that she had sneaked into the police station before work.

Finally, she sighed. 'Look, it's just that – and I might've got this wrong, perhaps mixed him up with someone else Royce mentioned – I thought he'd lost his licence a while back. I couldn't understand how he'd got this gun.'

'Have you mentioned this to your husband?'

'No. I… he likes having these shooting parties – his words, mind. He says it enables him to suss out potential investments before the rest of the market. I usually tune out when they turn up, I'm afraid – all they talk about is this deal and that deal, and it can be boring.' She flashed a rare smile. 'As long as I make sure the kettle's on and the brandy's ready when they get back to the house, I don't think they even know I'm there.'

'When was this?'

'Four weeks ago.'

'Do you know the man's name?'

'I'm sorry, I don't. I don't think this man was involved in that shooting, but it… it does worry me that someone might be walking around with an illegal weapon. I just thought you ought to know. I mean, after what happened. It's on my conscience, that's all.'

'Is your husband at home today?' Kyle asked, looking up from his notebook.

'Yes – he's a day trader. Stocks and shares, that sort of

thing. We turned the formal dining room into an office for him six years ago.' Yvonne sat up a little straighter. 'He's doing really well with it.'

'All right, Mrs Maxton – Yvonne. Thank you.' Barnes rose to his feet.

'Oh.' She gathered her handbag from the floor beside her and joined him by the door, glancing at Kyle over her shoulder. 'Is that it?'

'It is, and thank you for coming in. We'll be in touch if we have any further questions.'

He waited until Hughes had shown her out through reception to the front door, then turned to see Kyle looking at him, an excited gleam in his eyes.

'Reckon her husband's friend is our killer, sarge?'

'I don't know, but I'm sure the guv will want to ask him.'

FORTY-THREE

Kay swept her gaze over the stony turning circle outside the Maxtons' red-brick farmhouse, and wondered how much money Royce was making from day trading on a regular basis.

A brand new four-by-four sparkled off to one side of the driveway, its paintwork freckled by a recent rain shower that had Barnes reaching for the wipers on their way out of Maidstone.

'So when was the last time she saw this bloke?' she said to him as they walked towards the front door.

'Last month, which ties in roughly with when the blokes at the garage said Dale Thorngrove had a go at shooting for the first time. Too much of a coincidence for my liking.'

'But she couldn't give you the man's name?'

'No. Apparently her husband never introduced her.' He rang the doorbell, then shrugged. 'I figured it was worth a punt anyway.'

'Nothing ventured…'

She jumped as a security panel behind her squawked to life, and a voice bellowed from the speaker.

'Who is it?'

Barnes pointed to a small camera above the door, and she held up her warrant card.

'Detective Inspector Kay Hunter, Kent Police. I'd like a word please, Mr Maxton.'

'What about?'

'Easier to talk face-to-face, Mr Max...'

'I'm in the middle of something.'

'Or we can do this down the station. It's up to you.'

She heard him curse under his breath, and then there was a rattling sound at the other end before he returned. 'Come around the side of the house. The office has its own entrance.'

A clatter ended the call, and she hurried past the front windows to a gravelled path that ran down the side of the house.

'These stones are a good burglar deterrent,' Barnes murmured appreciatively.

'So are those.' She pointed to the security cameras at each end of the house, then knocked on a thick wooden door below a protruding stone arch. 'Fancy place.'

'Doing all right with the share trading then.'

The door was wrenched open a moment later, and Royce Maxton appeared.

A shock of grey hair framed bushy eyebrows, under which piercing blue eyes glared at them.

'This is most inconvenient,' he snapped. 'The US market is about to open, and there's an IPO up for grabs. If I don't...'

'The sooner you answer our questions, the sooner we can have you back to your computer,' said Kay.

'Fine. Come through here. At least I can keep an eye on things while we talk.'

They stepped over the threshold into the utility room for the house, a washing machine and dryer side-by-side next to a sink unit and a selection of dog bowls and scattered cat litter spread across the tiles in one corner beside a tray that reeked of urine.

'Sorry – the woman who cleans for us is running late.'

A door to the left led through to what turned out to be Maxton's study, where two large computer screens took up a desk, one displaying a complicated spreadsheet that hurt Kay's eyes just to look at, and the other showing a share trading website.

Maxton gave the screens a forlorn glance, then crossed his arms and turned to them. 'Okay, let's make this as quick as possible.'

'We understand that you have a regular private shoot in the woods adjacent to your land,' Kay said, after reciting the formal caution.

'The woodland belongs to us, detective. We can do what we like there.' His brow furrowed. 'Has that idiot Tapper been making complaints again? You do realise they're unfounded? His property boundary is nowhere near our fence line.'

'Nothing like that. When was the last shoot you held here?'

'About four weeks ago, I think.'

'Can you check that?'

He pulled a mobile phone from his trouser pocket and dabbed at the screen. 'Yes. Four weeks ago. A Sunday.'

'How many of you were there?'

'The usual three. Myself, Ambrose Weatherley, and Mark Redding. Plus a guest of Mark's – Dale someone or other.' He lowered the phone. 'Hang on a minute. You already know all of this. I spoke to someone only a few days ago.'

'You did, yes. Thanks for that.' Kay waited until he put the phone away. 'Which one of you owns an illegal firearm?'

'I beg your pardon?'

The bushy eyebrows disappeared under his shaggy fringe while his jaw dropped open.

'One of the men you invited here that day doesn't have a firearms certificate, and yet we have reason to believe he brought his own rifle with him. Who was it?'

'I…'

'Careful, Mr Maxton.' Kay moved closer, taking some satisfaction in the man's discomfort. 'I'll remind you, you're under caution and my colleague here has a tendency to take extremely accurate notes. Any failure on your part to tell the truth right now could result in you losing your own firearms licence as a minimum.'

Maxton swallowed, then flushed. 'I wondered at the time… I didn't want to embarrass Ambrose, that's all, and I did want to ask about it but I never got the opportunity. My wife came outside as we were getting ready to set off, and I was worried she'd overheard us.'

'And you never thought to ask him after that day?'

'No.' His gaze slid to the computer screens, then back. 'Look, I'm terribly sorry.'

'This Ambrose Weatherley – how long have you known him?'

'Years. We went to university together, and stayed in touch. He retired from his architecture practice last year, and took up shooting soon after. Mind you, I was happy to vouch for him when he applied for his licence. No problems there.'

'Hang on. Which one of your guests that day has no licence?' said Kay, confused. 'Are you saying Weatherley lost his licence less than a year after it was approved, or—'

'Good God, no. I was talking about Mark Redding, of course. I don't know – I suppose I thought he was a safe pair of hands, and it *was* only the first time I'd seen him with his own gun. Other times, he was always happy to use mine. Said he lost his licence but was hoping to get it back. That's sort of why I didn't worry too much. He didn't seem bothered by it at all, so I assumed by the end of the day that he'd had his licence reinstated and all was well…'

Kay exhaled at the sound of Barnes snapping shut his notebook, and turned for the door. 'We'll be in touch, Mr Maxton. We can see ourselves out.'

They left the day trader standing in the middle of his study, stunned.

'What do you think, guv?' Barnes said as they sprinted back to the car. 'Is Redding our killer?'

'I don't know,' said Kay, staring through the windscreen as the front curtain twitched back into place. 'I still can't work out what his motive might be.'

She thrust the car into gear, peering over her shoulder

as she reversed it to face the exit, and then stomped on the accelerator.

'Where are we going, guv?' Barnes asked, adjusting his seatbelt after the rapid manoeuvre.

'To bring in Mark Redding for formal questioning again. If there's one thing I *do* know, it's that he's been lying all along.'

FORTY-FOUR

When Kay got back to the Maidstone police station, she found Gavin hovering at the top of the stairs, consternation etching his face.

'Ian, can you make sure uniform bring in Mark Redding?' she said, sending the detective sergeant on ahead of her. Waiting until he'd disappeared into the incident room, she turned to her younger colleague.

'What's the latest?'

'We were finishing the phone calls to the commercial waste collection companies in the area while you were gone,' he began, wandering over to a plaster wall in desperate need of a repaint and leaning against it. 'We'd concluded all the interviews when I got a call back from one of the smaller ones – not only did they have collections yesterday morning that were then dropped off at the waste facility, but they collect from the White Hart pub.'

'They what?' Kay blinked. 'Really?'

Gavin smiled. 'Really.'

'Interesting. Did you get anything else?'

'I did. I spoke to the delivery driver who was working yesterday. He said he doesn't usually see Len Simpson – probably because his pick-up time is around eight o'clock in the morning and I'd imagine Simpson would still be in bed – but yesterday he was hovering at the back door next to the bins, watching. The driver said he thought he might want a word so he was going to wander over and see what he wanted after the bin was emptied but by then, Simpson had disappeared back inside. He mentioned it to his shift supervisor when he got back to the depot, who in turn confirmed she'd phoned Simpson to enquire if he had any questions or concerns about his collection service. Simpson – her words, mind – was rude, sexist and put the phone down on her before she'd had a chance to finish speaking.'

'Sounds like Simpson to me.' Kay folded her arms, mulling over the new information for a moment before speaking. 'I think we ought to formally interview him before we speak to Mark Redding. Do you mind bringing him in, Gav?'

She saw some of the worry leave his eyes in response to the request.

'I don't mind at all, guv.'

He pushed away from the wall and followed her towards the incident room. 'About that other matter…'

'Porter MacFarlane?' She paused, her hand on a metal door panel that was smeared with fingerprints. 'How did you get on?'

'I've got one more lead I want to speak to in person – a bloke by the name of Douglas Chilton. He hung up the phone when I called him earlier, and won't respond to any of my messages.'

'That's odd.'

'I've got his address off the DVLA. I was going to pop round to his house and see if I could speak to him in person.'

'Okay – can you do that after you've fetched Len Simpson for me?'

'No problem.'

'What about Porter?'

'Nothing to report, guv. Nothing on any of our systems, at least. I only found out about an unpaid parking ticket from a mate at the council, but MacFarlane's only just been sent the reminder so…'

The door gave way under her touch, and she dropped her hand as Barnes emerged, a pair of manila folders under one arm that he handed to her.

'Guv? I'm ready to go through these and prepare for Redding's interview if you are.'

'Be with you in a minute.' She stepped aside to let him pass, then turned back to Gavin.

'I'll catch you later. Take Laura with you when you go over to the White Hart to fetch Len Simpson, all right? No heroics, either.'

'Understood. Good luck, guv.'

'You too.'

FORTY-FIVE

Laura held on to the strap above the passenger window while Gavin wrenched the steering wheel to the left and braked to navigate around a black wheelie bin at the edge of the White Hart car park.

He stopped before reversing until the vehicle blocked the entrance and shot a grin at her.

'Just in case he decides to try and make a run for it.'

'I knew Simpson was hiding something,' she said, getting out and leaning on the roof of the car as she looked at the pub. 'But he can't be the shooter, can he? I mean, he was inside the pub when Thorngrove was killed.'

'Yes, but he's obviously involved somehow – otherwise why were the rifle parts found in a load collected from those commercial bins over there?'

She shrugged, then glanced down as her phone pinged. 'Got a message from the boss.'

'What's it say?'

'"Find out where he was for the thirty minutes before

calling triple nine too.'" Laura tucked the phone into her bag and slung it over her shoulder. 'Good question.'

'Didn't you believe his story about keeping his head down then?' Gavin peered across the car and grinned.

'I don't know.' She frowned, then held up her hand. 'Do you hear that?'

They both turned towards the pub, the sound of raised voices carrying out through the open door.

Laura threw her bag back into the car, reaching for a telescopic baton. 'Reckon this might come in handy?'

'Kay said no heroics – remember?'

'Right.'

They hurried forward, sliding to a standstill on the gravel surface as first Len Simpson then Lydia Terry emerged from the building.

She looked apoplectic, her face red while she stormed after the overweight publican.

'Don't you fucking dare,' she shouted. 'Not after all the bloody hours I've worked for you and helped you out. You can't run this place without me.'

'I told you, you're fired.' Len spun on his heel, towering over the diminutive woman. 'I won't stand for gossip.'

'It doesn't usually bother you,' Lydia spat. 'You're always asking me about people. What they're up to, who's sleeping with who, who…'

'Erm, excuse me?' Laura called. 'Everything all right here?'

The landlord turned around, his eyes widening.

Behind him, Lydia started to laugh. 'Well, this should be interesting.'

'What's going on?' said Gavin, edging closer, keeping his baton lowered. 'Are you all right, Mrs Terry?'

'Oh, I am now,' she said, still grinning. 'Was it me or Len you were after?'

'Mr Simpson, a word please,' said Laura. She waved him over, and lowered her voice. 'What's going on?'

'I fired her, and she doesn't like it,' he replied. 'What do you want?'

'Parts from a rifle were discovered in your commercial waste collection. We'd like to know why.'

Len paled. 'You what?'

'You heard me. Rifle parts. We're currently testing them to find out if they match the weapon used to kill Dale Thorngrove here last week. Anything you'd like to tell us?'

'Such as where you really were for the thirty minutes it took you to call triple nine,' said Gavin, moving closer. 'Care to explain?'

'I got nothing to say to you.'

'Now, Mr Simpson, I think you know as well as us that's not true,' said Laura, giving him her sweetest smile. 'Shall we try that again? What were the rifle parts doing in your bin?'

'I've got no idea. I don't own a gun. Never have, not since I left the army and even then, those were kept under lock and key when we weren't firing them for practice. I only ever carried a weapon when I was based overseas, out on patrol and the like.'

'So, what were you doing for those thirty minutes?'

'I know what he was up to,' Lydia said, raising her

voice to be heard from where she still stood outside the door.

Len turned, lunging towards her before Gavin caught him and pulled his arms behind his back.

'Steady, Mr Simpson,' he said. 'No need for that.'

'Lying bitch,' Len hissed.

Laura ignored him and walked over to Lydia. 'Do you know, or are you just trying to cause trouble?'

'Oh, I know. That's what we were arguing about.' Lydia shot her a wicked smile. 'I suppose it doesn't matter now. He can't fire me twice, can he?'

'What's he been up to?'

'Distilling his own gin.'

Laura blinked. 'He what?'

Len squirmed within Gavin's grip, then swore under his breath as the detective slipped handcuffs over his wrists.

'Yeah, I know.' Lydia tried, then failed to contain her amusement at her ex-boss's discomfort, her smile widening. 'Apparently he got pissed off when the cash 'n' carry put up their prices six months ago and decided to start making his own. Had it all set up in the back bedroom above the kitchen.' She jabbed her finger to where Simpson stood beside Gavin, glaring at her. 'He decided to go and dismantle the still before phoning the police last week in case you lot found out he hadn't been paying the duty on it. Shoved it up in the attic while we were lying terrified on the floor instead of phoning for help. Bastard.'

'Is that true, Mr Simpson?' said Gavin. 'Care to give us the guided tour?'

Len sneered. 'It's just her word against mine, and she's

pissed off because I fired her. You can all bugger off. You ain't got nothing on me.'

'Actually, Mr Simpson, based on what was collected from your bins this morning, we have.' Gavin reached into his pocket, unable to hide his smile. 'And we've got a search warrant.'

'You won't need it,' said Lydia. 'It's all in the pickup truck over there.'

Laura took one look at Gavin, then hurried over to a light grey truck beside the empty wooden picnic tables.

A tarpaulin covered the contents of the tray, the shape cylindrical and bulky.

She flipped back the tarpaulin, and blinked.

A grubby copper still lay on its side, the pipework and fittings cluttering the floor beneath.

Turning back to Gavin, she grinned. 'I reckon Weights and Measures are going to want a word with Mr Simpson after us. Probably the Inland Revenue as well.'

Len glared at her. 'I ain't saying nothing until I've got a solicitor.'

'We can arrange one for you at the station,' said Gavin, leading the publican towards their car. 'In the meantime, you do not have to say anything…'

FORTY-SIX

'So Redding's being brought in because he was withholding information about his relationship to Dale Thorngrove and an illegally-owned rifle, and I plan to speak to his wife as well.'

Kay leaned against the wall of the corridor outside the interview suites while she watched the landlord from the White Hart being led to the cells by Hughes, then switched her mobile phone to her other ear. 'And we're about to speak to Len Simpson.'

'What's your thinking on that one?' Sharp spoke to someone in the background before returning his attention to her. 'Sorry – what did you say?'

'I said I reckon Len's got to be involved somehow,' she repeated. 'First of all, he didn't call triple nine straight away that night because he was too busy trying to cover up an illegal distillery operation and second, we've got evidence to suggest the discarded rifle parts found at the waste facility originated from the bin outside the White Hart.'

'He hasn't got previous convictions though, has he?'

'Nothing on the record. Mind you, that doesn't mean he's innocent, guv. Especially after what Laura and Gavin found him trying to hide.'

Sharp gave a mirthless chuckle. 'What are your next steps?'

'Barnes and I are about to interview him to see what he's got to say for himself.' She glanced up as her colleague walked towards her with a fresh batch of folders in his grip and a determined look on his face. 'Maybe being interviewed here rather than the pub will shake some answers out of him. He's been a bit too confident for my liking up to now.'

'Do you think he's been supplying black market weapons?'

'He'd know what he was doing – ex-army, and all that. It'd be better pay than whatever he's making from that crappy establishment he calls a pub, that's for sure, even if he is illegally selling alcohol and dodging duty tax.'

'True. All right, thanks for the update. I'll let you get on.'

Ending the call, Kay took the documentation from Barnes with a grateful smile and started to read.

'What are the highlights in here?'

'I had Laura dig into Simpson's past a bit more while we were waiting for a duty solicitor. She got in touch with the last brewery who employed Simpson as a tenant. According to her, the bloke she spoke to said they couldn't wait to get rid of him – he caused more trouble than he was worth, and apparently when he left the last place they had him in, it needed a complete redecoration.

Took over a year to claw back the reputation of the place, too.'

Kay frowned, scanning the reports. 'How the hell did he get his hands on the White Hart then?'

'Bought it cheap a few years ago when the bottom fell out of the trade.' He lifted out another document from the folder, turning it over for her. 'This is a copy of the original licence application he submitted. There was nothing untoward on it, and he had the money, so it all went through just fine. From what I can gather, the pub company that used to own it was keen to get shot of the place so it wasn't exactly as if they went into any detail regarding references.'

She closed the file and handed it back to him. 'Thanks, Ian. Tell you what – you lead this one. Given Simpson's previous conversation with us, I'd like to see how he handles being questioned by a bloke instead.'

Minutes later, the lights from the recording equipment blinking out of the corner of her eye, Kay looked up from her notebook to see Simpson staring at her, a familiar leer on his lips while Barnes read out the formal caution.

His chins shook while he confirmed his name and the address of the White Hart, and an overbearing stench of sweat and beer fumes wafted across the table to where she sat.

Barnes launched straight into the questions after establishing the duty solicitor's details, evidently suffering from the same sensory overload and wanting to get the interview underway as soon as possible.

'Care to tell us why parts from an illegal firearm were found in a collection of waste from your premises?'

'No idea.' Len shook his head. 'I've never had a firearms licence, let alone had an illegal weapon. I might not look like much to you, but trust me – being in the army gives you a whole new appreciation of guns and the damage they can do.'

'And yet a man was shot outside your pub, with a rifle matching the parts found in your kitchen waste.'

'Detective, I find it hard to believe that you have evidence to support such a spurious claim,' said the solicitor. 'Unless the waste facility can categorically prove that load came from Mr Simpson's bin, you're wasting our time.'

Barnes kept his gaze locked on Simpson. 'You're ex-army. Dishonourably discharged. That means no pension, right? Must be tempting to skim a bit off the profits now and again, not to mention distilling your own illegal booze.'

Kay watched as Simpson's face turned a darker shade of red.

'We found the still, Len. And we know it came from the spare bedroom in the pub because we have a witness statement to that effect, and our officers found leftover bottles and piping during a search there after your arrest. Did Dale Thorngrove find out? Did you arrange his murder?'

'I don't know who shot him.'

'But you knew his killer wouldn't come inside the pub, didn't you? Otherwise, why risk taking the time to hide the still before phoning triple nine?'

'I didn't want no one finding it,' Len said. 'That

bloody Lydia is a gossip. It's all her fault you found it anyway.'

'Seems to me you have your priorities mixed up, Mr Simpson,' said Kay. 'Did Thorngrove get on the wrong side of you? Did you argue with him like you were seen arguing with Lydia this afternoon?'

'How long ago did you start dealing in black market weapons?' Barnes asked. 'Where do you get them from? Or do you steal—'

'Detective, I must insist—'

'I don't deal in fucking guns, and I ain't a bloody thief,' Simpson spat, ignoring the warning hand his solicitor placed on his arm. Instead, his belly pressed against the table as he leaned towards Barnes, a dangerous flash in his eyes. 'I didn't kill that bloke outside my pub, either.'

'Do you know who did?'

'No. I told you that.'

Barnes slipped on his reading glasses and flicked open one of the folders, pulling out a photograph. 'Do you recognise this man?'

He spun it to face Simpson, the image showing a cropped picture of Mark Redding that had been copied from his social media profile.

Simpson leaned forward, but didn't touch the photograph.

He frowned.

'Is he one of the blokes who were in last Wednesday?'

'You tell me, Len. You were there.'

'No. I don't know him.'

'Funny that, because he says he was in the White Hart

the week before. Monday lunchtime to be exact.' Barnes removed his glasses and glared at the pub landlord. 'Given the state of your place, I can't imagine it was heaving with clientele that day. Recognise him now?'

A sly smile crept across Simpson's face, and then he turned and grinned at his solicitor. 'I don't work Monday lunchtimes. That's when I go to the cash 'n' carry to get whatever we need for the kitchen and stuff.'

'Who was minding the place while you were there?'

'The cook, Tom. Big bloke. You would've seen him when you were there on Saturday.' He shrugged. 'Like you said, it's not busy on Mondays so it's the one time I can get out and about.'

'What's his full name?' said Kay, then wrote down Len's answer and hurried to the door, handing the slip of paper to Hughes, who hovered outside.

He took it with a slight nod, and she returned to her seat satisfied that Tom would be receiving a phone call from him within the next few seconds.

After another five minutes of questioning, Barnes had exhausted their strategy, and sent Simpson away with a reminder that he was still a person of interest in the investigation.

As the landlord left the room with his solicitor in tow, the detective sergeant turned to Kay with an exasperated sigh.

'It's not him, is it?' he said as Hughes stuck his head around the door.

'And it's not the cook, guv,' said the uniformed officer. 'That Tom bloke says he can't remember Redding either after I texted him the photo. I know Simpson said the place is usually quiet on a Monday but Tom reckoned a party of walkers came in and he was rushed off his feet serving food as well as running the bar.' He jabbed his thumb over his shoulder. 'Redding's solicitor just turned up too, guv.'

Kay closed her notebook, made sure the recording equipment was switched off, and pushed back her chair.

'So who dumped the rifle parts in Simpson's bin?' she said. 'I mean, okay – that bin would've been collected along with a couple of others that day, but those were nowhere near the shooting.'

'I'm wondering *why*.' Barnes collated the photographs and shoved them back in the folder as he stood. 'I mean, Simpson isn't a pleasant character but if he didn't shoot Thorngrove, who did, and why did they try to set him up for getting rid of the murder weapon?'

'God knows, Ian. Come on – let's see what Mark Redding has to say.'

FORTY-SEVEN

Kyle Walker was standing outside the interview room when Kay and Barnes arrived downstairs, the young constable glaring at the door before turning his attention to them.

'Everything all right?' Kay asked, keeping her voice low.

He scowled, jerking his chin towards the "Engaged" sign showing on the silver panel three quarters of the way up the door.

'Redding was driving away from his house when we found him,' he replied. 'We stopped him in the lane just beyond his driveway and found a suitcase in the back. He reckons he was going on a last-minute business trip to the Netherlands.'

'Did he now?'

'Mind you, he couldn't tell us what flight he was on, or which ferry.' A mischievous glint flashed in Kyle's eyes, his mouth quirking. 'And he was a bit pissed off when I took his passport off him.'

'Where is it now?'

'In there.' Barnes pointed at one of the folders in her hand, and waited while she flipped through the meagre contents.

'Was his wife aware of the trip?' Kay said.

'She wasn't there when we arrived. We tried knocking on the door in case he was lying but there was no answer. She was out – shopping, he said.' Kyle checked his watch. 'We probably only missed her by half an hour, mind, but I thought we'd better bring him straight back given your instructions.'

'Did he tell you who he was meeting with in the Netherlands?'

'Only that it was a private matter. I figured you'd prefer to wait until you had him in here to push him.'

'Thanks.' Kay closed the folder. 'Any luck tracking down Redding's wife?'

'No answer, guv – it keeps going to voicemail.'

'Okay. Keep trying. Give it another fifteen minutes. If that doesn't work, take Phillip over there with you and find out where the hell she is.'

'Will do, guv.'

Kyle took off at a jog, and then Barnes opened the door to interview room three for her.

She frowned when she spotted Redding's solicitor, the man drawing away from his client with a confident nod.

Andrew Gillow cleared his throat, unbuttoning his jacket. 'I hope you've got a good reason for dragging my client back here.'

Ignoring him, she settled into her chair, and waited

until Barnes had started the recording equipment and read out the formal caution.

'Tell me why you possess an illegal firearm, Mr Redding,' she began.

'I—' he tried, then pursed his lips. 'I'm not sure I understand what you mean.'

'Fine, if that's how it's going to be.' She pulled the hastily photocopied statement given by Royce Maxton from the folder prepared by Barnes, and slid it across the table. 'According to Mr Maxton, the last time he held a shoot at his property, you turned up with your own rifle instead of borrowing a spare from him like you usually did.'

Redding paled. 'It was a private event. He assured me he wouldn't...'

'People can change their minds about keeping secrets once they realise someone's been murdered,' Barnes said. 'So we'd suggest you start telling us a few of yours.'

'I only used it that day,' Redding said, desperately looking at him then Kay.

'Why?' she said.

'Because I took a guest with me. I didn't know if Royce had another spare.'

'Awfully decent of you.' Kay eyed the man in front of her as he lowered his gaze, the indignant manner he'd displayed during his previous interview quickly disappearing. 'Why did you kill Dale Thorngrove?'

Redding's head snapped up. 'I didn't kill him!'

'Why did you take Thorngrove to the private shoot?'

'Because we got talking while he was changing the tyres on my car the other month. He wanted to give it a go, but couldn't because he didn't know anyone who could let him try it out.' Redding snorted. 'That stupid bitch of an ex-wife of his made sure he'd never get a licence, either. Lying through her teeth about him beating her up.'

'So you took pity on him?'

'Yes.' He shrugged. 'Seemed a decent enough chap.'

'Where did you get the illegal rifle from?' said Barnes.

'I can't say.' Redding shook his head.

'Mr Redding... Mark. Why did you obtain an illegal rifle to take him to the shoot?' Kay pressed.

'I... I suppose I wanted to show off. Let him see that I was connected.' Redding's shoulders slumped. 'Ego, I suppose. I realised my mistake as soon as I'd opened my bloody mouth to invite him. I usually used Royce's spare when I went over to his place, and I knew he didn't have another. I'd have looked bloody stupid if I'd taken a guest to a shoot where there wasn't a rifle for him, wouldn't I?'

Kay waited a moment while Redding chewed his lip, his face one of misery.

'Mark – did Thorngrove know the rifle you were using was obtained illegally?'

'Eventually, yes. Not the day of the shoot though.' He looked up. 'Neither did Royce, so don't blame him. I told him I borrowed it for the day.'

Kay wrote the same on a clean page of her notebook, not answering.

As a firearms licence holder, Royce was still under an obligation to ensure all his guests were compliant with the law, no matter their circumstances. He should have reported Redding weeks ago.

'Tell me about last Wednesday night,' she said eventually. 'Why the White Hart?'

Redding held his head in his hands and stared at the table. 'I panicked.'

'Go on.'

'Dale enjoyed the day out – he kept phoning me, asking me when we could go again, who else I knew had land he could shoot at without a licence.' He swatted his hand in front of his face, his eyes reddening. 'He wouldn't shut up about it, and I was worried someone would find out about the rifle.'

'The illegal one.'

'Yes.'

'What happened?'

'I was stupid, that's what. After the shoot that day, I might've had a bigger nip of brandy than I thought…'

Kay jotted down another note. 'Drink driving as well as being in possession of an illegal firearm, Mr Redding. That's quite the day out you were having.'

Redding sighed. 'I must've let slip that I knew someone who traded in black market firearms.'

'Loose lips…' Barnes murmured.

'He threatened me, detective. He phoned me three weeks ago and said if I didn't tell him where I got it from, he'd tell your lot. Of course, I refused. I couldn't have him telling anyone else if he found out. I mean, there's no knowing the sort of person who could end up with a firearm like that, is there?'

'What happened?' said Kay.

'He kept pestering me, and in the end I ignored the phone calls. That's when things went south,' he mumbled.

'He started to blackmail me. Money, not just the threat of telling the police.'

'How much?'

'Five thousand. The bastard addressed the letter to my wife and I. I was bloody lucky she was out that morning when the post arrived.'

'Did you pay?'

'The first time, yes. And then he demanded more.'

'How long did this go on for?'

'I got another demand last Monday. So I phoned him and told him I needed to see him. I said to meet me at the White Hart. Nobody knew us there.'

'Tell us about that,' said Barnes, gently pulling the manila folder out from under Kay's arm and flipping it open. 'When we first interviewed you, you said the only time you'd ever been to the White Hart was at a lunchtime and that you weren't there last Wednesday. You lied, Mr Redding. You *were* there.'

Andrew Gillow eyed his client, and then turned his attention to the older detective. 'Unless you've got some evidence to—'

In reply, Barnes pulled out an enlarged photograph of a battered four-by-four vehicle, the background of which was clearly the Reddings' driveway.

'You knew that sports car of yours would be too easily recognised, so you drove your wife's vehicle to the pub, isn't that right? We're going to be speaking to her too, Mr Redding. Lying under caution won't look good for either of you.'

Kay held her breath, berating herself for not taking the time to read the briefing notes properly in her haste to start the interview, then gave her colleague an appreciative nod.

'Trish didn't lie to you,' Redding said. 'She brought me supper at nine o'clock like I told you. She knew I had a late-night meeting scheduled. She didn't know that I'd cancelled it at the last minute. I-I managed to reschedule it to this week. She said she was going to go and watch a film upstairs and maybe read her book until I came to bed. Benji went up with her, so I figured with the noise from the TV he wouldn't bark when I went out.'

He gulped a breath before continuing. 'I had to speak to Dale. I was desperate. I left the house through the French windows in my study and… God, I almost took the sports car. Then I saw Patricia's four-wheel drive, and thought why not? It was dark-coloured, there are plenty of them around here… it wouldn't be recognised.'

'What happened when you got to the White Hart?' said Barnes.

Redding wiped at his eyes with his jacket sleeve. 'I wanted to meet him somewhere public in case he became unreasonable. I know people will say Dale was the most laidback person they knew but trust me – he had a temper. He was just good at hiding it. That much was evident once we got back outside that night.'

'What happened?' said Kay.

'I'd told him I'd put him in touch with the seller. I told him we'd be at the Hart. Dale got more and more agitated the longer we waited for contact to be made, and I knew then that I'd made a mistake. He wasn't the sort of person who should be given a weapon – of any kind. I told him as we were leaving that the deal was off, and that I was going to phone the seller and tell him. I knew it was a risk, but I thought I could call Dale's bluff. I stopped believing then that he'd ever report me to the police in case it backfired on him. I could have him for blackmail after all, couldn't I?'

Kay held her breath, waiting.

'We went outside – last orders had been called by then, and I just wanted to get Dale far enough away from the door that we wouldn't be overheard. He started going on about how he'd find out the seller's name and that he'd tell him I'd told the police all about his black market scheme, and that I was a dead man. We got to my car… I saw the rifle on the back seat.'

'You put it in your wife's car before driving to the pub?' said Kay. She turned to Barnes, who wore a similarly shocked expression. 'What the hell were you thinking?'

'I wasn't. I-I don't know. I panicked, I suppose.'

'You planned to kill Thorngrove.'

'No, I swear it.' Redding splayed his hands. 'I tried to reason with him, Detective Hunter, really I did. But he wouldn't listen.'

'So you shot him.'

'No!' Spittle flew from Redding's lips, spraying the table and Kay leaned back in disgust. 'I didn't even pick it up. I closed the door and was going to tell him I'd take my chances with you lot when… when… Oh, God. One minute we were on our own, and the next he just appeared from nowhere with a rifle. He must've been hiding in the shadows, waiting for us.'

'Who?'

Redding shook his head miserably in reply.

'Mark, if you didn't shoot Dale Thorngrove, then who did?'

He exhaled, his face turning grey. 'He's a psychopath. He'll kill me if I tell you.'

Kay's gaze flickered from Redding to his solicitor. 'Mr Gillow, at present your client is our only suspect and his alibi is – at best – flimsy. I won't be asking the CPS for a manslaughter charge. This was an execution. We'll be asking the CPS to seek the maximum sentence when this reaches court.'

'Mr Redding, if I may?' The solicitor leaned over and murmured in his client's ear.

Kay watched while Redding's face went from grey to puce as he listened, and when Gillow was finished she could see the man's hands shaking.

She felt no pity for him.

'Well? What's it going to be?'

'I... I'll tell you. But not until you can vouch for my safety. Like I said, if he finds out I've been talking to you, he'll kill me too...'

FORTY-EIGHT

Gavin stared through the windscreen at the converted stable block and tried to read the small signs outside each of the doors.

The U-shaped buildings were accessed via a narrow driveway that wound around the back of a farmhouse, the entrance to which bore the name of the craft centre and a list of the businesses that now thrived where horses were once kept.

He edged the car forward, sure that the one he sought was the larger premises at the far end, and found a parking space between a battered pickup truck and a hatchback that looked like it had seen better days.

A few people milled about the place, a small café nearer the farmhouse doing a thriving business in hot drinks and pastries, and he groaned under his breath as his stomach rumbled.

Checking the details once more on his phone, he walked towards the building, casting his gaze over the reclaimed stone troughs filled with lavender and bright flowers placed outside the open door.

Various pieces adorned a wooden rack, some with price tags on that reflected the craftsman's reputation as a carpenter, and the reassuring aroma of fresh sawdust reminded Gavin of woodworking classes at school.

The sound of sandpaper scraping against timber carried through the open door, and he blinked to counteract the gloom before knocking on the glass panel above the handle.

'Hello? Mr Chilton?'

Stepping inside, he heard the sanding stop, and then a figure appeared from the back of the workshop in a cloud of sawdust motes.

'That's me.'

The man walked over and placed a sandpaper block on a cabinet behind the counter before turning to him, blue eyes inquisitive.

'Can I help you?'

In reply, Gavin held up his warrant card. 'DC Piper, Kent Police. I've been trying to call you.'

Curiosity turned to fear, and Chilton hurried around the counter before pulling the door shut. He glared at Gavin.

'What the hell do you think you're doing?'

'I'm trying to progress a murder investigation. You haven't returned any of my voicemail messages.'

'I can't talk to you.'

Chilton moved back to the cabinet, then picked up the sandpaper, turning it in his hands as he retreated to the back of the workshop.

'I only have a few questions.' Gavin nodded towards a

lathe and other machinery that stood silent, waiting for the craftsman to resume his work. 'How long have you been a carpenter?'

'Since I left school.'

'I understand you were involved in the film industry for a while.'

Chilton shuffled his feet, scuffing a path through the sawdust that sprinkled the concrete floor. 'It was a long time ago.'

'What did you do?'

'I was a set designer. Then I started an independent production company with a friend of mine.'

Gavin looked around at the various items hanging from the walls – cheeseboards, house signs, knife blocks. 'Why did you quit?'

'I'd rather not talk about it.' Chilton turned away and busied himself with what Gavin realised was a cradle, gentling sanding the surface.

The workmanship was incredible, with intricate carvings detailing the outside of the rails and animal silhouettes in the boards.

'When did you start this business?'

'About two months ago.'

'Looks like you're doing well.'

A shrug. 'It's okay. Keeps me out of trouble.'

'What sort of trouble?'

In response, Chilton turned and tossed the sandpaper block onto a workbench, then folded his arms over his chest.

'I meant what I said. I'm not prepared to talk about it.'

'Let me put this into perspective for you,' Gavin said,

running his fingers over the smooth surface of the wooden frame. 'We've already interviewed Porter MacFarlane and his son in relation to a murder north of Bearsted last week...'

'I saw it on the news.'

'What you won't have seen is that two rifles were stolen from the MacFarlanes sometime after the end of June. We believe one of those rifles was used in the shooting. Out of all the production companies we've interviewed who had access to their stock, you're the only one left. And you've been avoiding our calls. Why?'

He saw it then – the slight shake in Chilton's hands, the trembling lips while he raised his gaze to the ceiling as if seeking divine guidance.

'Mr Chilton?'

'You can't tell him you've spoken to me,' the craftsman said eventually. 'He'll kill me if he finds out.'

Gavin stepped forward, his heart racing. 'Who? Porter MacFarlane?'

'No.' Chilton snapped. 'That son of his. Roman.'

FORTY-NINE

'How come the carpenter bloke fell out with Roman MacFarlane then?'

Barnes clung on to the strap above the passenger window, his backside clenching as Kay took a narrow bend without lifting her foot off the accelerator.

'Gavin says Chilton was commissioned by one of the streaming companies to make a documentary series about true crime, and they needed to hire some replica weapons for a few scenes in one of the episodes. They were on a tight budget and didn't want to hire real ones.' Kay slowed to a crawl as she approached a crossroads, then took off once more, swerving to avoid a pheasant. 'While he was in the shed with Roman, he spotted that one of the handguns he picked up from the workbench had no valid proof marks…'

'So it was imported into the UK, then sold illegally.'

'Exactly. And Roman realised that he'd worked that out. Chilton didn't push the matter – he said Roman had a funny look in his eye as if he was daring him to say something. He got worried, especially as he was on his own that day, so he just took the weapons he'd hired for the production and left as quickly as he could. He asked one of his assistants to drop off the guns the next day and told them not to hang around – he says he was too frightened to go back there himself.'

Barnes frowned. 'What scared him?'

Kay's lips thinned. 'The fact that Roman phoned him at one in the morning threatening what he'd do if he told anyone. Chilton closed down the production company as soon as they finished the documentary.'

'Shit.' He waited until the car rumbled over the cattle grid at the end of the MacFarlanes' driveway, his thoughts tumbling. 'Do you think Porter is part of this as well?'

'I don't know, Ian. They live in the middle of nowhere and neither of them have ever been flagged for a misdemeanour or anything else to give Daniel's team cause for concern. But who knows what the pair of them have been up to?'

He loosened his grip on the strap as she slowed to a standstill outside the house, then held up his hand. 'Wait here. I'll see if anyone's in first.'

Shutting the car door, silencing her protests, he strode across the gravel, his gaze roaming the windows facing the driveway.

No one stood looking out, and not a single curtain twitched.

Throat dry, he forced himself to relax his shoulders and bounded up the steps to the door in case either of the MacFarlanes were watching from a distance, not wanting to alert them to why he was there.

Just a routine call, he thought with a grim smile.

He rang the bell and took a step back.

No answer.

He pressed the bell once again, the chimes resonating through to where he stood.

Turning, he shook his head and hurried back to the car as Kay wound down her window.

'Nobody there.'

She climbed out, pointing to a path that ran around the side of the property. 'Let's see if the back door's open. If Porter's out in the garden or something…'

'Hang on.' Barnes went around to the back of the car, opened the boot and pulled out two telescopic batons before handing one to her.

'Thanks,' she said, her face grim.

Neither of them voiced the fear that the batons would be useless against a gun, but as Barnes flicked his open, he felt slightly better being armed with something.

He paused, hearing sirens on the wind.

'There are two patrols on the way here,' Kay said. 'I asked for back-up to meet us here before we left Maidstone.'

'But you don't want to wait.'

She exhaled, and he saw the strain she was under.

'We could just have a look,' he ventured. 'They'll be here any minute.'

'Come on, then.'

He crept around the side of the house, trying to place his feet as slowly as possible to prevent the noise of crunching gravel alerting Porter or Roman, then held up his hand and peered around the corner.

'Back door's open,' he hissed over his shoulder.

'Anyone in the garden?'

He looked down the expanse of undulating lawn that led away from a pretty patio area, squinting as he tried to spot any dark-clothed figures lurking amongst the trees at the bottom of the garden that formed a border between the house and the outbuildings, then shook his head.

'Coast is clear.'

'Slowly, then.'

He checked over his shoulder as the first of the patrol cars braked beside theirs, then crouched and shuffled along the back of the house.

Passing beneath a window that overlooked the garden, he stopped and raised his head enough to be able to see over the sill.

An empty dining room was beyond the glass panes, a large elongated table in the middle set for twelve, but there was nobody present.

Nobody aiming a gun at him.

He ducked and hurried towards the open door, then paused and peered around the frame.

'Empty,' he murmured. 'It's the kitchen.'

'Maybe they're out,' said Kay.

'Huhmmph.'

'What was that?' Kay grabbed his jacket sleeve. 'Did you hear that?'

'Stay here.'

After taking a couple of deep breaths to try and still his thrashing heartbeat, Barnes stepped into the kitchen, baton raised.

'Help me...' said a weak voice.

It came from an open door off the side of the main kitchen, and as he approached he saw shelves laden with bags of flour, potatoes, and sugar while bunches of fresh herbs stood in jars on a counter underneath.

He heard voices outside, and realised the uniformed patrol had joined Kay.

Then he saw two feet poking out from behind a washing machine and tumble dryer next to another exterior door.

Dropping the baton onto the counter, he rushed forward.

Porter MacFarlane lay sprawled on the tiles, his forehead bloodied and his eyes closed.

'Kay? In here!' Barnes called over his shoulder as he dropped to the floor.

Running steps followed his words, and then: 'Where are you?'

'In here – butler's pantry.' He reached out and gently patted the man's cheek. 'Porter? It's Ian Barnes, Kent Police. Can you hear me?'

MacFarlane's eyes flickered open. 'He hit me. My own son…'

'Where's Roman, Porter? Where's your son?'

The man mumbled under his breath, his eyes closing.

'He's concussed, guv.' Barnes straightened and signalled to the young constable who peered past her, his radio already to his lips. 'Get an ambulance here.'

Kay knelt on the floor beside him and leaned closer to MacFarlane. 'Porter, stay with me. We think Roman could hurt someone. Where did he go?'

'He said… He said he had to get the other rifle. He

said he was going to make Redding pay...' MacFarlane frowned, then ran his tongue over his lips. 'I don't know who Redding is. I didn't know he owed us any money.'

'It's not that sort of payment I'm worried about,' Kay muttered, then beckoned to one of the uniformed officers hovering at the door. 'Stay with him.'

Barnes followed her out of the kitchen and along the hallway, opening the front door in readiness for the ambulance crew's arrival. 'Roman will be armed, guv. We need Disher's lot to meet us there, or someone could get hurt.'

'Christ.' Kay stumbled across the front step, her face turning pale. 'I told Kyle to go to Redding's house and pick up Patricia if he couldn't get through on the phone.'

He pulled out his phone and hit the speed dial for the constable's mobile number.

'Fuck, there's no answer,' he said through gritted teeth. 'Who's with him?'

'Phillip.'

He shook his head. 'No answer from his phone either.'

Spotting another constable on the path beside the house who was pacing back and forth while he listened to his radio, he raised his voice. 'Tell control we'll need tactical to meet us at Mark Redding's house. I want you and another car to follow us there, got it? Tell them it's urgent – there are two constables on scene and they need to make radio contact with them. They might be in danger.'

The young constable froze, too stunned to move for a split second, and then took off at a sprint towards his vehicle, relaying Barnes's instructions as he ran.

'Let's go.' Kay turned towards their car.

'Hang on – we need to check the shed to see if there's anything else missing,' Barnes said. 'At least then we can give Disher a head start on information about what he and his team might be walking into.'

'Get in. I'll drive.'

FIFTY

'Blimey. He must be making a fortune.'

Kyle climbed from the patrol car, easing the cramp from his long legs as he peered up at Mark Redding's house and then stared at the sports car parked off to one side of the sweeping driveway, elegantly poised to ensure its gleaming paintwork could be appreciated by all.

A battered four-wheel drive had been driven alongside, in stark contrast to Redding's car. Its sides were slicked with dried mud that clung to the paintwork, various scuff marks showing on the bumper and front wing.

'That must be the one he drove to the pub, then,' said Phillip. 'Anything from Hunter about how the visit to the MacFarlanes is going?'

'There's no phone signal here.' Kyle chucked the mobile phone into the footwell, disgusted. 'How the hell can he run a business with no phone signal?'

Phillip pointed up at a plastic box jutting out from the side of the property beside a set of French windows. 'Hunter said he's dependent on the landline.'

'I guess the twenty-first century hasn't reached here yet,' Kyle muttered, tucking his radio into his vest and slamming the car door shut. 'All right – let's find out where Mrs Redding is.'

'That's her four-by-four, isn't it?'

'So why didn't she answer the phone? Or at least call me back when she got back from shopping?' He jerked his chin towards the curtains pulled across the downstairs windows, chinks of light escaping around the edges. 'She's in.'

'Or she's out walking the dog.'

Kyle blew out his cheeks, cursing the low light that now cloaked the house and surrounding trees, casting the exit from the driveway into shadows.

His guts churned, but he couldn't reason with the uneasiness that was crawling across his shoulders.

Hand moving to the radio clipped to his vest, he tapped the top of it with his forefinger, wondering whether to call control, or—

A furious barking exploded from inside the house.

Hurrying across the driveway to the front door, he slowed as his brain struggled to catch up with what he was seeing.

Phillip stomped away from the car and followed, then emitted the words that were slowly working their way from Kyle's brain to his lips while he stared at the splintered wooden frame and the security chain hanging from it.

'Shit.'

A mud-streaked scuff mark was scraped across the bottom of the door.

The two constables looked at each other for a moment, then automatically reached into their vests for their telescopic batons.

'Pepper spray?' hissed Phillip.

'Okay, but for Christ's sake don't get the dog with it. We'll never hear the end of it from Hunter.'

His colleague nodded in response, and Kyle gently pushed the door.

He exhaled as it opened without squeaking and slowly edged into the hallway, the sound of the barking emanating from a closed door to his left.

Frantic scratching clawed at it, then the barking stopped and the dog whimpered while it snuffled along the crack underneath.

Kyle reached out for the handle.

'Leave it,' Phillip said under his breath. 'We need to search the rest of the house first.'

He nodded, letting the more experienced constable take the lead.

They stalked their way towards what Kyle's father would call a well-appointed kitchen, an array of spotlights in the ceiling illuminating the central worktop.

A chopping board was covered in slices of carrot and broccoli florets, and Kyle could smell burnt onions emanating from the large stove set against the back wall.

He walked over to it, found the food already spoiled and burned, and turned off the gas before glancing at his colleague.

'Where next?'

The sound of a heavy object tumbling to the floor

resonated through the wall, and as he strained his ears he thought he heard a muffled voice.

Phillip jerked his head towards the door. 'Come on.'

The dog continued scraping at what Kyle assumed was the living room door, and as they passed the bottom of the staircase, he noticed that it hadn't been fully closed.

Every time the animal pawed at the frame, the door inched open a crack before swinging closed once more.

'Hey.'

He turned his attention back to Phillip, who was waiting beside another closed door, and hurried over to join him.

'Redding's office is this way I think,' he whispered.

'It's right next to the kitchen. That's where the noise came from.'

The other constable set off once more, his baton raised.

With a quick check over his shoulder to make sure they weren't about to be ambushed from behind, Kyle trailed after him, heart racing.

Beyond an anteroom, the door to Redding's study was open, a soft hue escaping through the gap illuminating Phillip's stocky form as he inched forward.

'Mrs Redding? It's the police. Are you all right?' he called.

Kyle heard a muffled groan, and then his colleague glanced over his shoulder and nodded once before he burst into the room.

He was racing after him before he had a chance to think.

Something hard, metal, hit Phillip's arm, the man's

yelp of pain carrying over the crack of bone and he dropped to the floor, his baton bouncing off the thick plush carpet.

Kyle swung around, ready to fight.

'I don't think so,' said a calm voice. 'Drop it.'

Roman MacFarlane was standing beside the door, a handgun held against Patricia Redding's forehead.

He dropped the poker next to the fireplace with a *clang* then dragged Patricia towards her husband's desk.

She was bleeding, a nasty cut above her right eye bright red against her pale face.

'Are you okay, Mrs Redding?' Kyle managed, his gaze flickering to where Phillip knelt on the carpet cradling his broken wrist.

'The door hit me when he kicked his way in.' Patricia trembled as Roman shoved her into the leather seat and pressed the gun harder against her temple. 'I only opened it because he said he was with the police. Please, do as he says.'

Kyle raised his hand, then crouched and lowered the baton to the floor, keeping his eyes on Roman. 'We can talk about this, Roman. There's no need to harm her.'

'Give me your radio.' The gun swung around to face him, then Phillip. 'And his. The pepper spray and your batons too. Slowly.'

Crossing to his colleague, Kyle took the radio he held out, seeing the anger in his eyes at the situation they were now in.

He gave a slight shake of his head, snatched away the radio and walked towards the desk.

'Put them down. Next to the keyboard,' said Roman.

There wasn't a trace of fear in the man's voice.

Instead, a cold calmness emanated from him as he eyed the equipment.

A babble of codes and instructions were being bandied around by the dispatchers at force control, and as he listened to the early evening's banter between his unsuspecting colleagues, Kyle bit back the rising panic in his chest.

'Both of you – sit in the chairs over there where I can see you.'

Moving across the carpet and helping Phillip to his feet, Kyle spotted the brass poker that he'd been struck with now lying on an ornate rug where Roman had dropped it, and paused to examine his colleague's wrist.

A tiny bone protruded through the skin, and the other man swore under his breath as his shirt sleeve brushed against it.

'I said sit!'

Kyle looked over his shoulder. 'I think he needs a doctor. So does Mrs Redding.'

'I don't care what you think. Sit down. Now.'

Roman took a step away from Patricia, his jaw set as the gun swung precariously between the two men.

Taking the armchair closest to the desk, Kyle kept his eyes fixed on the man while Phillip sat in one of the other chairs, his breathing ragged.

Then the radio crackled to life, and his heart jumped as Kay's voice rang out.

'Kyle, Phillip? Control have been trying to reach you. Listen to me – do not enter the Reddings' house. Do you hear me? We believe Roman MacFarlane to be armed and—'

Roman reached out and switched off the radios one after the other.

He wore an ugly smile when he turned back to them.

'It's a bit late to tell you that, isn't it, officers?'

FIFTY-ONE

Kay stood at the side of the narrow lane beyond the Reddings' driveway, her mouth dry while she watched two ambulances crawl to a standstill beside a tactical response vehicle.

Shouted commands carried from the outer cordon as officers from the Traffic division cut off access along the lane and redirected locals, their faces stony while they worked.

A light drizzle misted the air, slowly soaking her hair and clothes and leaving a tangy ozone scent to the verges and hedgerows. She slicked her fringe from her eyes as a shiver wracked her spine.

This can't be happening, she thought.

Paul Disher's team were silhouetted by the headlights from the assembled cars, their response vehicles hulking shadows beyond the dark-clothed men, and their voices low while they listened to his briefing.

They had already been on their way when Kyle and Phillip's radios had gone silent, and despite the brusque manner in which the swarm of uniformed officers worked within the cordon, she knew every single one of them was thinking the same as her.

Please let them be alive.

'How close can we get?' asked one of the tactical team, his voice carrying over the heads of his colleagues. 'Has anyone managed to get a visual on them?'

'Kay – what can you tell us about the house?' Disher said, beckoning her closer. 'You've been inside. We need to know everything you can remember.'

'The room Redding uses as a study is here, at the right-hand side of the house as you're facing it,' she said, tracing her finger over the roughly drawn diagram. 'There are French windows leading out to the driveway – that's how Redding says he managed to sneak out to the White Hart to meet with Thorngrove without his wife knowing. The living room is on the other side of the house, and there's an anteroom between the study and the hallway.'

Disher frowned. 'I wonder why Roman didn't access the house through those instead – I mean, if he was looking for Redding...'

'Maybe he didn't know,' Kay suggested. 'If he hadn't been to the house before, he wouldn't have known about that side access.'

'Have you managed to get any more information out of Redding about what went on between him and Roman?'

'Well, he's confirmed he hid the rifle he got from Roman – it's an identical one to that used to kill Thorngrove. He realised after that how dangerous Roman was, and told Gavin and Laura he wanted to make sure he had some sort of protection at home for him and his wife if he turned up unannounced…'

Disher blew out his cheeks. 'Shame he didn't tell us all this sooner…'

'Can't argue with you there. We also think Roman dumped the gun parts in the bin behind the pub to implicate Len Simpson and take the focus away from him, especially after Porter discovered some of his firearms stock was missing.'

'And so Roman's gone after Redding next, not realising we've already got him in custody and then takes the wife hostage instead. Jesus.' Disher ran a hand over his closely-cropped hair, then handed the diagram over to one of his subordinates and pulled on his protective helmet. 'Okay, thanks, detective. We'll take it from here.'

'But…'

'Guv!'

She turned to see Barnes hurrying towards them, his arms laden with stab vests.

He nodded to Disher before thrusting one of the vests at her and handing the rest to Harry Davis.

'Guv – we've got Porter MacFarlane in custody, and Gavin and Laura are speaking to him now,' he said, out of breath. 'What's the latest here?'

'Not good.' She led him away from Disher's vehicle until they were standing at the far edge of the lay-by, then exhaled.

'Kyle and Phillip are in there, so is Patricia Redding. Roman's got control of both men's radios and there's no mobile signal near the house.' Her hands trembled as she buttoned up the bulky stab vest. 'I couldn't reach them in time, Ian. I tried to warn them…'

'Guv… Kay…' Barnes reached out and clasped her hands, his warm skin rough. 'Disher and his team will do everything they can to bring them out alive. It's not your fault they're in this situation. Roman—'

'—is a madman, and selling black market weapons, and his bloody father should've realised that and told us, and…'

'I know. But we're here now, and we're going to work with Disher to rescue them. Okay?'

'Okay.' She gave him a wan smile. 'Good pep talk. Thanks.'

His hands moved to her shoulders, and he gave her a light squeeze. 'You can do this.'

Kay nodded, biting her lip.

'Hunter?'

She turned at the shout, to see Sharp striding towards her, his face grim.

'I got here as fast as I could. Heard anything since the radios went silent?'

'No.'

He lowered his voice. 'As gold commander of this investigation, I'll be taking over as SIO once Disher cedes control.'

She nodded, accepting that the chain of command was fluid in such situations, and relieved that someone with Sharp's experience was at her side.

'Whatever you need, guv,' she said. 'Mark Redding's still in custody in Maidstone, and I've given Paul as much information as I can about the house layout.'

'What about Roman?' said Sharp, watching Barnes return to the cordon. 'Has anyone managed to find out what might've started the illegal firearms dealing?'

'Not yet – Porter's in shock, I think. Laura texted me just before you got here to say he can't understand what his son's been up to. She's found out he got into trouble as a teenager, but there's no juvenile record and Porter assures her it was nothing violent. He got caught pickpocketing.' She shook her head. 'Theirs is a million-pound business, Devon. Why on earth would Roman risk dealing in illegal firearms? I mean, how much money could one person want?'

'I think—'

Sharp's reply was cut short by a shout from Disher.

'Wait.' Kay ran over to where the tactical firearms officer was leading his team towards the Reddings' driveway entrance. 'I need to go with you. I've got two officers in there.'

Disher waved his men onwards before turning to her, his eyes stone cold.

'With respect, detective, you're not going anywhere until my team have assessed the situation and neutralised the threat.' He grimaced. 'And if you're right about this bloke, we haven't got time to bugger about arguing.'

FIFTY-TWO

Kyle slowly raised his hand and slicked away the sweat that was stinging his eyes.

Half an hour had passed since Kay's desperate message, and since then Roman MacFarlane had spent the time mumbling under his breath and pacing the carpet in front of the desk where Patricia Redding sat, terror in her eyes.

Beside him, Phillip had fallen silent while he cradled his broken wrist and glared at their captor.

The dog had stopped barking since Roman's initial outburst, the occasional scratching sound still carrying through to where he sat, accompanied by a whine that made Patricia's frown deepen every time.

'He needs water,' she whispered. 'Please – he'll be thirsty.'

'He'll be dead if you don't shut up.' Roman paused in his pacing and aimed the gun at her. 'I could put one of these through his skull. That would keep him quiet, don't you think?'

The woman whimpered, shook her head and lowered her gaze to the paperwork strewn across the desk.

A built-in cupboard stood open, its contents covering the carpet around her feet and fanning the edges of the ornamental rug in front of the fireplace. Books had been ripped from their shelves, and as Kyle watched Roman tearing the room apart, he held his breath.

The man was trance-like in his movements, but the young constable wasn't prepared to take any chances.

He had no doubt that Roman could use the gun in his hand, and would if either of the two officers made a mistake.

'Why did you come here?' he said, trying to keep his voice calm.

Roman spun on his heel. 'To speak to Mark.'

'What about?'

The other man's top lip curled. 'He has something of mine. I want it back.'

Kyle jerked his chin towards the discarded items littering the room. 'Hence the search.'

He received a grunt in reply.

'Perhaps if you tell us what you're looking for, we could help,' he suggested, rising to his feet.

The gun swung round to face him. 'Stay where you are.'

Holding up his hands, Kyle forced himself to relax back into the armchair. 'No problem. I just thought it might speed things along a bit. Help you on your way.'

'It's none of your business.'

Kyle smiled. 'Unfortunately, you made it our business when you took us hostage.'

Roman suddenly paused in his destruction of Mark Redding's study, and then strode across to the French windows and peered out into the night.

Please, someone, shoot him, Kyle thought, before realising how difficult it would be to get a clean shot through double-glazed glass without killing Patricia in the process.

A need for self-preservation appeared to flit through Roman's mind at the same time.

He stepped back from the windows, then reached out and swished the thick curtains closed, hiding the occupants from anyone taking a keen interest in the house from outside, and turned back to Kyle with a triumphant smile.

Trying to hide his disappointment, the constable glanced across at his colleague, who had grown paler.

'Hang in there, mate,' he murmured. 'I'm sure the cavalry isn't far away.'

'Stop talking,' Roman barked. 'What are you saying to him?'

'Just that my arse is going numb. How're you doing?'

The gunman suddenly moved around the desk and hurried across the rug towards them, his eyes determined.

Kyle shrank away instinctively.

'Give me your vest.'

'What?'

'Your vest. Stand up. Take it off. Slowly.'

The gun waved back and forth, and Kyle found that he couldn't tear his eyes away from the open maw of the barrel.

This wasn't what it was like in the movies.

And this sure as hell wasn't what he'd expected when he clocked in for his shift this morning.

He pushed himself out of the chair and tore away the straps holding the vest in place, eased it over his shoulders and held it out.

'Here.'

'And his. Take his off.'

'Roman… leave him be. He's in pain. He can't do you any harm.'

'Take. It. Off.'

Phillip gritted his teeth while Kyle manoeuvred his arms from the vest and handed it over before slumping back with sweat patches under his arms.

Satisfied, Roman slipped one of the vests over his head and threw the other one on the floor beside the empty hearth, his back turned to the two officers.

Kyle exhaled, taking a moment to search the room for something – anything – he could use to disarm the man.

His gaze passed across the set of brass implements hanging in an arrangement beside the fireplace. Although the poker looked promising, he knew he wouldn't reach it in time.

Roman would fire the gun before he was halfway across the study, and where would that leave Patricia and Phillip?

His thoughts turned to what must be happening beyond the four walls – surely Kay and his colleagues would have realised what was going on, and given the training they all received, he guessed a tactical response unit was now somewhere in the vicinity.

He hoped.

Roman continued to pace the floor, muttering under his breath, and Kyle realised the man was quickly losing what meagre control he might have had.

His eyes flickered to where Patricia sat, terrified, behind her husband's desk, and he realised that it wouldn't matter what plans the tactical team had.

If they didn't do something soon, Roman might panic.

A scratching sound from beyond the anteroom reached him, and he strained his ears.

There it was again.

Was someone at the front door?

Roman spun on his heel, his attention snapping to the open door of the study.

Kyle cleared his throat, clawing at an idea and hoping his hunch was correct.

'What are you looking for in here, Roman? Perhaps I could help you look for it?'

'What?'

He gestured to the open cupboards. 'You were obviously searching for something when we turned up. Did you find it?'

Roman took a step forward, the gun raised once more. 'Shut up. You can't help me. You can't—'

The scrambling of claws on parquet floor tiles echoed through the anteroom and then a black blur shot into the study, a ferocious snarling emanating from within its depths.

Teeth bared, the dog launched itself at Roman, the bulk of the animal knocking the man off balance while his eyes widened in terror.

'Fuck,' he managed.

Kyle curled up in the armchair, trying to make himself as small as possible while the animal sank its teeth into Roman's thigh, part of his brain latching onto the sound of shouts from the direction of the hallway.

Heavy footsteps thumped towards the study, followed by a barrage of shouted commands, and Patricia screamed as she threw herself to the floor at the sound of a single gunshot.

Then all hell broke loose.

FIFTY-THREE

A gunshot, a woman's scream, a yelp...

Kay's mouth dropped open at the sudden barrage of noise exploding from the radio in Sharp's hand, a cold chill clutching at her shoulders and neck.

Before either of them could utter a word, Disher's voice carried across the airwaves.

'Down! Down! Get down!'

She looked across to where Barnes stood beside one of the patrol vehicles, his jaw clenched while he listened to the radio belonging to the sergeant next to him, the blue fleck of the lights casting one side of his face into shadow.

Her heart racing, she wondered if she wore the same horrified expression, and turned to Sharp.

There was a burst of static, jumbled voices, whining and a man crying out in pain, then—

'All clear.'

A strangled sigh of relief filtered through the gathered officers waiting at the cordon, and Sharp turned down his radio.

'Thank Christ for that.'

Then another radio hissed from closer to the patrol cars and Disher's voice carried across from where Barnes was now walking towards her.

Her colleague froze, his radio held aloft.

'We need urgent medical attention. Fast. A vet too, if anyone knows one.'

'What the hell...?'

Kay didn't hear Sharp's next words.

She elbowed her way past two young constables, hearing the ambulances' engines roaring to life as her shoes found the gravel surface of the driveway, and set off at a sprint.

'Kay, wait.'

There was no lighting at the entrance to the driveway, no welcoming lamp above the wooden sign for the Reddings' property, and as she passed the gentle curve that brought the house into view, she uttered a shallow groan.

The downstairs lights poured through the windows, and she realised Disher's team had pulled all the curtains back to reveal the aftermath of their operation and show incoming responders that the situation was now under control.

The French windows leading from Mark Redding's study were wide open, and two of Disher's men stood beside the sports car, rifles lowered while they watched her approach.

Another two men stood sentinel at the front door, one with his chin lowered to his radio.

She slowed, hearing Sharp call her name, but refused to look back.

Kyle and Phillip were part of her team.

She needed to know.

Needed to be with them.

Pulling her warrant card from her pocket, she waved it at the shorter of the two tactical officers as she approached.

'I need to…'

He swung around, blocking access. 'We haven't yet released the room.'

Kay saw Disher halfway across the study with his back turned to her.

'Paul.'

He glanced over his shoulder. 'Let her in. I'll be handing over to DCI Sharp in a second.'

Nodding her thanks to the two men who stood aside to let her pass, Kay crossed the threshold and into a hellish scene.

Roman MacFarlane lay on his stomach, hands handcuffed behind his back while he thrashed under the restraining hands of one of Disher's colleagues despite the blood pooling under his legs.

'He's the one you should be arresting, not me,' he screamed. 'It's all his fault.'

'Stay still,' came the brusque reply. 'You're going to hurt yourself otherwise.'

Kay swept her eyes past him to where Patricia Redding sat dazed in a chair behind her husband's desk, a stunned expression on her face, blood streaming from a deep cut in her forehead while another tactical team member tried to stem the flow with tissues he yanked from a box next to the computer screen.

'Mrs Redding, are you okay?' she said, gulping in deep breaths and trying to calm her own heart rate.

The woman nodded, her gaze drifting to where Disher and his remaining four colleagues gathered around the armchairs next to the fireplace, three of them shielding one of the chairs from view.

Disher turned at the sound of her voice, then beckoned to her, his face grey.

Hurrying over, Kay swallowed at the sight of the dog sprawled across the carpet, a nasty flesh wound gaping in its shoulder while it whined.

One of Disher's men broke away from the group and knelt beside it, stroking its head and murmuring to it.

As she joined the lead tactical officer, the questions in her head tumbled over one another.

What happened?

Whose gun was fired?

Why was the dog injured?

She didn't get a chance to ask them.

Instead, Disher stepped aside, and she saw then what he had been focused on while she'd assessed the damage to the room in the few steps it had taken her to walk from the open doors to where he stood.

A crumpled form sprawled in the soft fabric of the armchair, the russet upholstery doing nothing to hide the pool of blood covering the seat and accentuating the pale features of Phillip Parker.

Kyle crouched next to him, his face stricken as he looked up at her.

'Where's the fucking ambulance?' he cried. 'We need a bloody ambulance.'

Kay turned back to the French windows at a noise, to see the first of the paramedics burst into the room, canvas holdalls in their grip.

'Over here,' Disher said, waving his men out of the way. 'The bullet our suspect fired ricocheted – it caught him in the leg. Doesn't look good.'

Stepping back to let the two ambulance officers take over, Kay pulled Disher to one side. 'What happened, Paul?'

'The dog escaped from the living room just before we came through the front door,' he said in a low voice. 'It went straight for MacFarlane and mauled his leg – he's in a bad way too, but he can fucking wait for the second paramedic team. He fired the gun he was holding but what with the dog attack and the recoil, it went wide, missed your two officers but ricocheted into that coffee table. Walker says the splinters hit the dog at the same time they hit Phillip – we entered the room as Kyle launched himself at Roman while he was lining up a second shot.'

'Shit,' Kay breathed, looking at the chunks missing from the table that were now scattered across the rug.

Despite the two medics, she moved closer to the chair and gently took hold of Kyle's sleeve. 'Kyle, come on. We need to get you out of here.'

'He's dying, guv,' he said hoarsely, his dark eyes reddening as he stood. 'We can't leave him.'

'Dying?'

'There's a substantial amount of blood loss,' the female medic said. 'Looks like a large chunk of splintered wood sliced into his femoral artery. We're trying to stem the flow…'

Kay staggered, then moved in front of Kyle and dropped to her knees, reaching out for Phillip's hand.

'Phil? I'm here. We're doing everything we can, do you hear me? It's going to be all right.' She watched as the medics worked. 'Shouldn't you be taking him to hospital?'

'We can't risk moving him until we've stopped the bleeding,' came the curt response. 'Now if you don't mind…'

A broad hand covered her shoulder and squeezed.

'Kay…'

She shook her head, and wrapped her fingers around Sharp's, seeking strength from her friend and mentor's presence but seeing the desperation in the medics' eyes as they tried to save the man she'd known since his days as a probationer.

Back then, he'd been a skittish skinny individual, partnered with older more experienced colleagues who gradually turned him into the officer she'd grown to rely on, and who had been such an integral part of her investigative team.

'We're losing him…'

Kyle emitted an anguished groan and turned away, his shoulders shaking.

'Phil…' she managed, hoping for a sign the man was going to beat the odds, looking for a flicker of life under his closed eyes.

Phillip's chest gave a last shuddering sigh, and a shocked silence enveloped the small group.

After a moment, Kay rested her hand on Kyle's arm. 'We need to get you to the hospital. That's a nasty cut on your cheek.'

'I'll stay here,' he mumbled, tears shining. 'I'll go when they take him, and then I'll get myself checked out.'

Unable to argue with him, unwilling to rely on her rank to demand he do as he was told in the shocking circumstances, Kay rose to her feet and turned away.

'Kay.' Sharp moved until he was standing in front of her, his grey eyes troubled. 'Kay, listen to me. We've got to go back to the station. We have to re-interview Porter MacFarlane before we deal with Roman.'

She watched, too stunned to reply as Barnes staggered to his feet with the dog in his arms and disappeared through the French windows, bellowing at one of the young constables outside to get him to Adam's vet practice.

'Kay.'

She shook her head to try to counteract the grief that was punching at her heart and turned at Sharp's voice. 'Sorry, what, guv?'

'We need to speak to Porter MacFarlane. I need you. Now.'

'Okay.' Squaring her shoulders, determined to find some answers for her dead colleague and knowing that the rest of her team would be looking to her to guide them through their own grief, she wiped away her tears and gave her mentor a curt nod.

'I'm ready.'

FIFTY-FOUR

Kay took the briefing folder from Gavin with a murmured thanks and paused to read through the additional notes the detective constable had added in her absence.

Both he and Laura had looked up from their desks when she'd walked into the incident room half an hour ago, their faces pale as the news of Phillip's death filtered through from the control room.

She spent the next twenty minutes consoling her team, assuring them that the young constable hadn't been alone when he died, and that Kyle had been checked over by one of the ambulance crew.

She'd drawn the line at his insistence at returning to the station, and after making sure he would follow his doctor's orders and stay in hospital overnight, she made a phone call to one of the appointed psychiatrists used by Kent Police.

Having survived a near-fatal incident herself and ignored the symptoms of severe mental stress on her health in the past, she was determined not to let Kyle deal with the aftermath of his colleague's death alone.

Gavin cleared his throat, and she blinked, concentrating on the blurring words in front of her.

'So, as you can see, guv, the MacFarlanes have been struggling to make ends meet. There's a lot of competition in the marketplace, and they haven't exactly grown with the times.' He moved to her shoulder, then flicked over to the next page in the folder. 'Some of their rivals offer costumes as well as the firearms, and offer to carry out all the Home Office paperwork required for using firearms on productions.'

'Did you find the balance sheets online?' said Kay, her interest piqued.

'Yeah – here.' Laura sniffed, then picked up a sheaf of paperwork and walked over. She wiped her eyes, and sniffed again. 'Okay, this was all on the Companies House website. You can see they were doing all right up until about three years ago, and then two years ago – when those rival companies popped up that Gavin found – they started losing work to competitors. Last year's profit was down by nearly a hundred and eighty thousand pounds.'

Kay gave a low whistle. 'What about the house? Do we know if that's owned outright, or mortgaged?'

'Mortgaged,' said Gavin. 'And re-mortgaged eight months ago.'

'That's not all, guv.' Laura handed her a set of four large photographs. 'These were taken at the MacFarlanes' property an hour ago.'

Kay's eyes widened at the sight of a trapdoor opening

that had been discovered under the workbench in the shed, and then at the cache of weapons concealed under the wooden floorboards. 'Shit. How much was down here?'

'If everything they found was sold on the black market, we think there's about forty thousand pounds' worth,' said Gavin. 'Most of that stock hasn't been proofed.'

'Do you think Porter knew about the illegal firearms sales?' said Kay, sliding the photographs into the briefing folder.

'I'm not sure,' said Laura. 'We've both re-read their previous statements, and nothing they've said suggests that he did.'

'Having said that, it's interesting that it was Roman who suggested the audit,' Gavin added.

'Unless he was covering his tracks and trying to lay the blame on his father.' Kay closed the folder. 'Good work, both of you. Gavin, do you want to join me in the interview? Barnes is still at Adam's surgery.'

He nodded, then dashed back to his desk and picked up his jacket and notebook.

'How's the dog?' Laura said. 'I wondered... I mean, I didn't want to ask because of Phillip and everything, but...'

'I don't know. I haven't heard from either of them.' Kay frowned. 'Listen, if you want to talk any time, just ask, all right? I know you and Phil worked closely together, and...'

Laura wiped away fresh tears. 'Thanks, guv. Might just take you up on that.'

'I'm ready.' Gavin wandered back, his eyes keen despite the late hour.

Kay handed him the folder, and took the notebook from him. 'You're leading this one. You've earned it.'

FIFTY-FIVE

Porter MacFarlane's solicitor rose to his feet as Kay walked into the interview room, pulled himself up to his full height and buttoned his jacket.

'Detective Hunter, my client would like to see his son.'

'Sit down.'

She ignored MacFarlane's large sweating form on the other side of the table, his face covered in an ugly yellowing bruise on one side, and several cuts to his cheek.

Instead, she crossed to the recording equipment, nodded her thanks to Gavin as he pulled out a chair for her, and recited the formal caution.

Gavin settled into his own seat, and she took a moment to glance across while he arranged the folder contents to his liking and ignored the impatient huff the solicitor gave as he waited for the interview to begin.

Her protégé emanated a growing confidence, one that she had nurtured and encouraged since they had lost a team member to another police force, and pride surged through her.

It was dashed away a split second later at the memory of Phillip dying in the line of duty, and that she'd had to leave him in order to interview the man who now mopped his brow with a cotton handkerchief and squirmed under Gavin's scrutiny.

Casting her gaze to the table, she opened the notebook and readied her pen.

'Mr MacFarlane, how long have you and your son been trading illegal firearms?' Gavin began.

Porter's already ashen features paled further, and he raised a shaking hand to his forehead. 'I had no idea... I'm so sorry...'

'Answer the question, please.'

'I don't know.' Porter dropped his hand. 'I never knew.'

'Mr MacFarlane, you own that business. You have firearms licenses in your name. It's your responsibility to know.'

'He... lately, I...'

Gavin waited, and Kay silently congratulated him on the tactic.

Silence was often a suspect's enemy.

The man in front of them took a deep breath. 'I haven't been well, these past two years. I knew I should've listened to my doctor, but that's easier said than done, isn't it?'

Both Kay and Gavin remained impassive.

'I'm overweight, I like a drink... It started with type 2 diabetes, and now it's my heart. I suffer from stress, and... well, I suppose Roman was taking over more and more of the workload from me.' Porter shuffled in his seat as if to accentuate his words, his shirt and jacket straining over his belly. 'I was a fool. We were losing money but I was kidding myself that things would improve, that things would go back to how it was before. Before those two competitors started undercutting our fees in order to win work. We couldn't afford to do the same. I owe too much...'

'The illegal firearms dealing?' Gavin prompted.

Porter shook his head. 'I had no idea. I've left Roman to run the business since the end of last year. I've lost interest, to be honest.'

'You seemed pretty interested when you were showing me around last week,' Kay said.

The man gave a thin smile. 'I've never lost the love to show off. I suppose, at heart, I'm a frustrated performer. Besides, that part of the business is fun.'

'Why did you keep delaying the stock audit?' said Gavin.

'I-I...'

'You see, Porter, that makes me think you knew about the illegal sales and turned a blind eye. As long as money was trickling into the business and keeping you afloat, you didn't care where it came from.'

'That's not true. I told you – I had no idea.'

Gavin placed each of the photographs taken that afternoon in front of the man, whose mouth wobbled at the sight of the trapdoor. 'Are you sure?'

A shuddering sigh emanated from the man, his stale breath wafting across the table to where Kay sat. 'I... I hoped I was wrong.'

'But...?'

'I wondered what was going on...' Porter looked to his solicitor, who gave an almost imperceptible nod, then back to the two detectives. 'We started getting late appointments to view firearms. I get too tired in the afternoons these days so I'd always let Roman deal with them. Except none of them ever turned into firm orders, and Roman was never asked to attend production sets to assist with any armourer responsibilities afterwards either. I asked him, perhaps a couple of months ago, why he wasted his time with these people but he said it was to show willing. He said he was trying to coerce people away from our competitors, so I let him get on with it.'

'We're going to need names.'

'I can't. That's the thing, you see. He... Roman never put them in the appointments diary. He just wrote their initials on a sticky note next to his computer to remind himself when they were due to turn up.'

'Did you see any of these people?'

'No.' Porter blushed. 'I usually have an afternoon siesta.'

Gavin paused, checking the documents in front of him, then met Porter's gaze. 'A witness informs us that he saw a handgun with the proof markings missing, and that Roman threatened him if he told anyone. Is that what happened to you this afternoon? Did you find out what he was really up to?'

The man instinctively reached up and touched the sticking plaster that covered one of the deeper cuts to his face. 'I wanted to know what was going on. I overheard him on the phone on Monday night, arguing.'

'Who with?'

'I don't know. It got ugly, though. I heard him tell whoever it was that if he didn't give back whatever Roman had sold him then he'd be next.'

Kay's attention snapped up from her notes. 'Were those his exact words?'

'Yes. I remember it clearly because I was so shocked. I've never heard him sound like that.' Tears rolled over the man's cheeks. 'I was too troubled by what I'd heard to confront him straight away but I couldn't sleep that night worrying about it. I wondered then what he had got into. I walked down to the shed early on Tuesday morning before Roman got up, and that's when I found out we were missing the two rifles. I ran back to the house to report it, and Roman came downstairs as the police turned up.'

'You didn't say anything about his phone call on Monday night when we interviewed you that day,' said Kay.

'I wanted to give him a chance to explain himself.' Porter exhaled. 'I suppose I still refused to believe that what I heard him say had anything to do with the missing rifles, let alone that poor man's death.'

'Two men's deaths,' Kay snapped. 'One of our officers was killed tonight thanks to your son's actions. Thanks to your negligence.'

'He only did it because he cared about me.'

Gavin slapped the folder shut and pushed back his chair, glaring at the man who cowered before him.

'Tell that to the victims' families, Porter.'

FIFTY-SIX

Sharp was waiting for Kay when she walked out of the interview room, his arms crossed while he leaned against the wall and stared at the low ceiling.

He looked exhausted and after she sent Gavin back to the incident room with a murmur of thanks, she wondered if her eyes held the same fatigued shock.

'How did it go?' he asked, stretching his back and cricking his neck.

'Well, I'll award him ten out of ten for stupidity.'

'Where's Roman?'

'He should be here any minute. According to the treating doctor at Maidstone Hospital, he needed stitches in his leg but it's all dressed and he's only going to need some painkillers and antibiotics for the next week.'

'More's the pity.'

They turned at the sound of the security door opening at the end of the corridor to see Roman MacFarlane being led towards them by Harry Davis.

The constable's grip on the man's arm was none too gentle, and Kay recalled how Phillip had been under the older officer's tutelage for his first shifts at the station.

Seeing the pain in Harry's face as he guided Roman into the next interview room, she vowed to speak with him before the roster changed at daybreak to offer her condolences.

Sharp ran a hand over his face as the door swung closed behind them. 'Are you going to be all right to run this one, or do you want me to?'

'I'll do it.' Kay looked at the stack of folders on the floor beside his feet, then crouched to pick them up. 'Is this everything?'

'Including CCTV footage from a farm on the junction with the main road and the lane leading to the MacFarlanes' place.' Sharp grimaced. 'I pulled in Aaron Stewart and Dave Morrison to go through it earlier. They've already identified two cars that travelled in the direction of Porter's place since June that are registered to known criminals – one with an armed robbery conviction from fifteen years ago.'

'Christ.' Kay fluffed her hair with her fingers, then buttoned her jacket and turned towards the interview room as Harry emerged.

When she entered, she glared at the two men who sat side-by-side on one side of the table, her gaze falling to the bandages that swathed Roman MacFarlane's thigh.

Despite the mild painkillers administered at the hospital, he still appeared to be in a lot of discomfort, and she fought back the urge to kick him as she took her seat.

The solicitor, who Kay recognised as a hardened duty

solicitor from Tonbridge, kept a poker face while she and Sharp arranged their files and started the recording with the formal caution.

'When did you start dealing illegal firearms, Roman?'

Kay watched the man opposite her, dark shadows under his eyes and a taut line across his brow, while he nibbled at a thumbnail and kept his gaze lowered.

'I asked you a question,' she snapped.

He jumped in his seat as her hand slapped the table.

'When did you start selling the guns?'

'A while back.'

His voice was low, and she leaned closer to hear him.

'When?'

He shrugged, then dropped his fingers from his mouth before spitting the remnant nail to the floor. 'July last year, maybe.'

'Why?'

'Because the business is fucked.' Now he looked up, his gaze holding hers. 'I'm the only one doing anything to make sure it survives. You've seen the state of Porter?'

'Your father?'

He snorted. 'Whatever. He's as bad at that as he is trying to run a fucking business. Pissed all the profit away years ago. Some inheritance I'm going to have.'

'Is your father dying?' Kay couldn't keep the surprise from her voice.

Porter had looked overweight, yes, but—

'It's only a matter of time,' said Roman. 'And if he goes before the mortgage is paid off, I lose everything. I can't even sell the business, the state it's in at the moment.'

'If you were selling illegal firearms, why were you urging your father to audit the stock?'

'Because I could add the new stuff without raising suspicion, of course.' He smirked. 'Hide it in plain sight.'

'Tell us about Dale Thorngrove.'

'All Mark Redding's fault. Ask him.'

'I'm asking you.'

Roman scowled. 'I didn't know him personally. Thorngrove, I mean. Redding bought a rifle from me a while back – said he'd lost his licence after a drink driving ban and was only going to use it on private land. I don't usually sell to people like him, but a sale's a sale, ain't it? And we needed the money. Then he comes to me and says he's got a mate, wants to buy a gun too and I'm like, who the fuck are you telling about my business?'

'But you sold it anyway.'

'No. I didn't. I told him to get stuffed. And I told him he needed to stop talking about where he got his bloody rifle from. I told him to tell his mate to go to one of the local licensed dealers. Do it properly. That's when he said he couldn't – his ex-wife was making up stuff about him so he'd never get approved.'

'So, what happened?'

'Redding tells this Thorngrove bloke I've said no, and that's when he starts trying to blackmail us both.'

'Redding told Thorngrove your name?'

'Yeah.' Roman choked out an incredulous snort. 'Just shows what sort of a dickhead he is, right?'

'Right,' said Kay, sensing a chance to side with the man opposite her. She bit back her disgust. 'What happened then?'

'Redding arranged to meet with him to try and talk some sense into him. I told him he'd better, 'cause otherwise I'd deal with them both. That's why I went, see? I didn't trust him to sort it out.'

'When we last spoke to you, you told us you were cleaning a carriage that was being hired out.'

'That only took a couple of hours.'

'So you went to the White Hart?'

'Yeah. Parked a mile or so away and walked there. Waited until they came out.' Roman sneered. 'I was right. They were arguing walking back to Redding's car.'

'Which one?'

'That shit heap of a four-by-four his wife drives.' He smirked. 'I figured he didn't want to be recognised. Rest of the time, he's driving around in that sports car of his.'

'What were they arguing about?'

'I really thought Thorngrove would have more sense and back off once Redding spoke to him, but it was pretty evident that wasn't going to happen. So I dealt with him.'

Kay sat back, shocked at the matter of fact way in which the man spoke of cold-blooded murder.

Roman gave a malicious grin. 'What's the saying? Killing two birds with one stone, isn't it? I figured Redding wouldn't be telling anyone else where he got that rifle from after he saw that.'

'Which rifle did you use to kill Thorngrove?' Kay asked, recovering. 'The one you sold to Redding?'

'No – that was another problem. I took an identical one from our stock. Figured if you lot thought two were stolen, it'd slow you down a bit.'

'Which is why you destroyed it and chucked the parts in the bin outside the White Hart?'

'Yeah, well. That Len was starting to poke about as well on the sly. I heard he was asking his regulars whether they knew what was going on. I reckoned if I made it look like he was involved then he'd lose some customers and keep his mouth shut.'

'Why did you take Patricia Redding hostage?'

Roman paused, turning to his solicitor.

'My client would like it noted on the record that he didn't intend for the young police officer to die,' said the man. 'It was an accident.'

Kay's heart punched her chest, and she slid her hands to the edge of the table, gripping it until her fingers whitened.

'Carry on,' said Sharp. 'What happened?'

'I went there to speak to Redding.'

'Speak to him, or kill him?'

'Detective!' The solicitor leaned forward.

Sharp ignored him and glared at Roman. 'Answer the question.'

'To speak to him. I wanted the other rifle back, and I was prepared to pay him for it.'

'Why?'

'I didn't want him trying to blackmail me next. He'd already phoned me in a state because you lot were asking him all them questions, and I knew it was only a matter of time before he let slip my name.' Roman paused, chewed at his nail for a moment, then dropped his hand. 'Too late by then, wasn't it? Your two boys turned up five minutes after I'd arrived. I panicked, I s'pose.'

He gave another shrug. 'Sorry.'

'You got one thing right,' said Kay, her voice little more than a croak. 'They were both just boys. And one of them is dead because of you.'

FIFTY-SEVEN

A feeble afternoon light attempted to break through the blinds across the incident room windows when Kay and Sharp traipsed through the door, accentuating the sombre mood that permeated the air.

Most of her team had gone home after Barnes had debriefed them, leaving a few stragglers behind who sat at desks with stunned expressions while they tried to finish their work.

Kay edged past Laura's desk, giving the young detective constable's shoulder a squeeze and murmuring that she should go home, before moving to the whiteboard at the far end of the room.

Her gaze wandered blindly over the notes, photographs and sticky notes that covered the surface while she hugged the briefing folder for Roman's interview to her chest.

Soft footsteps padded over the carpet tiles to where she stood, and she acknowledged her mentor's presence at her side with a slight nod towards the board.

'Where did we go wrong?'

'You've got to stop worrying that you missed something,' Sharp murmured.

'But we did, Devon.' She turned to him, her throat constricting. 'We spoke to him and Porter, even before the break-in. Porter lied about the state of the business, and he lied to himself about what his son was up to.'

'You don't believe his story that he had no idea then?'

'Do you?'

He didn't answer, and instead turned his attention to the tall figure who'd entered the room and was now walking towards them, his bulky protective clothing replaced with jeans and a sweatshirt.

Paul Disher nodded to them both in greeting. 'Thought I'd drop by after filing my report. You'll get a copy by email.'

'How're you doing, Paul?' said Kay.

'I'll be okay, as soon as I'm back on active duty. I got a call from my DI to say I'm stood down pending the official enquiry.'

'Nothing to worry about, Paul,' said Sharp. 'It'll only be a formality.'

'I know. It isn't the first time, guv – and unfortunately in my line of work, it won't be the last,' came the stoical reply. 'I just wanted to catch you before you left to let you know if you need anything, you can phone me.'

'Thanks,' said Kay, shaking his hand. As he left, she saw Gavin heading towards them. 'You're going the wrong way. You should be heading home, Piper.'

'In a minute, honest. I just wanted to give you a quick update,' he said. 'I sent a copy of the MacFarlanes' inventory files over to Andy Grey at HQ with a request to fast-track the data. I thought I'd head back to their place in the morning and do a proper stocktake with Laura's help, if that's all right? I was rostered to work this weekend anyway.'

Kay smiled. 'I think that's a great plan.'

'Thanks, guv.'

'Actually, Piper, we wanted a quiet word with you,' said Sharp, the corners of his eyes crinkling at the sight of Gavin's worried frown.

'Oh?'

'Yes, in fact you've already pre-empted part of what we had in mind. Given the illegal firearms found under the shed, and the information we'll hopefully get from Andy in due course, we'd like you to head up a new investigation to trace the weapons Roman MacFarlane has sold since he started his black market enterprise. It'd certainly add some weight to our case against him. Think you can handle it?'

The detective constable nodded, unable to speak.

'What we're thinking is that you've got two suspects – the men Aaron and Dave found on the CCTV footage,' Kay added. 'You could start with those and see where it leads you.'

'Right. Yes,' said Gavin, recovering from his shock. 'I've already traced current address details for both of those through the DVLA while you were speaking to Roman.'

'Hopefully once it hits Roman how deep the shit is that he's in, he'll offer some more names as well,' said Sharp. 'Because without proof marks on those weapons, it's not going to be easy.'

'That should keep you out of trouble for a while anyway,' said Kay, 'and it'll give you a taste of running your own major investigation.'

'Guv, that's great.' Gavin tried, then failed to prevent a grin spreading. 'I won't let you down.'

'I know. Just be careful, okay? You know the sort of people we're dealing with.'

'Got it.'

Sharp turned to her as Gavin walked back to his desk, and gave her a rueful smile. 'Do you think that'll stop him from being poached by headquarters?'

'For a while, maybe.' She watched while the detective constable spoke to Laura, his hands animated while he told her the news, and despite her sadness she gave him a congratulatory punch on the arm. Kay smiled. 'It'll set him up well for a DS promotion, in any event.'

'Reckon you've got room for two on the team?'

Her attention snapped back to the DCI. 'I'm not letting either of them go. Not that easily. I made that mistake once before.'

'Noted.' He gathered up his jacket and bit back a yawn. 'Right, I'll catch up with you tomorrow at Northfleet so we can brief the chief super and the deputy ACC. My advice – stay away from the news tonight. You know what it's going to be like. Turn off your phone when you get home too. You're not due back on duty until Monday.'

'Thanks, guv. For everything,' she said, following him towards her desk.

He turned for the door, then paused. 'Are you sure you don't want me to come over to Cranbrook with you?'

'You've already had to be the bearer of the news. Get yourself home. I'll be fine.'

She dropped the folder next to her keyboard, her gaze travelling to Phillip's empty seat, his workspace cluttered with sticky notes and empty soft drink cans.

Behind his chair, the wall was festooned with memes he'd printed out and pinned up, jostling for space amongst cartoons and photographs of him larking around with friends.

All of it jarred with the grief that ached in her chest and stung her eyes.

Barnes looked over as he pushed back his chair, car key in hand.

'That's me done, guv. I think I'm going to need a stiff drink when I get home. Are you heading off too?'

'No, not yet.' She gave a weary sigh. 'There's one more thing I have to do first.'

FIFTY-EIGHT

Kay swore under her breath, glared at the tiny paper cut on her finger, daring it to bleed, and then turned her attention back to the contents of the filing cabinet's deep drawer.

Inside were half-opened boxes of black pens, the black notebooks she and her colleagues favoured, and – for some inexplicable reason – two stainless steel forks.

Her search was hindered by the fact that the light sockets in Sharp's old office had been ransacked in the years since he'd left for Northfleet, with the LED bulbs being taken by her team to replace broken ones out in the incident room rather than fight their way through the procurement process.

'I know you're in here,' she muttered, rummaging through a decade's worth of forgotten stationery and leftover party supplies.

She'd already removed five crushed paper cups, a half-used reel of blue and white crime scene tape, and a broken stapler that she suspected had once belonged to Barnes, but had yet to find what she sought.

She didn't really want it, if she were honest.

She simply needed something to do.

Something to drag her thoughts away from the broken, grief-stricken faces of Phillip Parker's parents when they'd opened their front door to her two hours ago.

She knew she should've gone straight home afterwards, but as she'd passed through Maidstone, she'd automatically turned into the driveway of the police station and headed up to the incident room.

It was empty, of course.

Even the cleaners had passed by and were already working their way along the floor above, the sound of the vacuum cleaners roaring through the building and any surfaces not covered in the detritus of an investigation at its end emanating a lemony scent that carried through to Sharp's old office.

After spending an hour at Phillip's desk, slowly placing his personal belongings into a storage box she'd taken from another DI's office farther along the corridor, a terrible exhaustion had seized her and she'd sunk into his chair, spinning back and forth for a moment, lost in thought before returning to Sharp's office.

'Got you.'

Triumphant, she pulled the half-empty bottle of bourbon towards her, wrinkling her nose at the sticky residue around the neck.

She was sure the last time she'd seen it was at a Christmas party two years ago.

Certainly before Sharp had moved to Northfleet.

Scrambling to her feet and dusting off her trousers, she unscrewed the lid and poured a decent measure into a clean coffee mug before placing the bottle back in the drawer.

Wandering over to the window, her silhouette framed by the lights in the incident room behind her, she took a sip and grimaced.

'God, that's rough.'

There were no blinds in here, but she hoped the darkened glass gave her some privacy while she contemplated the town skyline and tried to gather her thoughts.

A shadow fell across the door behind her, and she inhaled a familiar scent.

'Hughes said I'd probably find you up here.' Adam walked over to the window and wrapped his arms around her, resting his chin on her shoulder. 'How're you holding up?'

'Not too good.' She took another sip of the bourbon. 'Sorry, I meant to phone you... time got away from me.'

'I thought it might.'

'How's the dog? Is he...?'

'Resting. He's a lucky one, I'll give him that. He should heal fine.'

'That's good.'

He kissed her hair. 'Thinking about Phillip?'

'Mm-hmm. He wasn't just a good officer, Adam. He was someone's son. I went to see his mum and dad earlier, and I...'

She broke off, unable to finish the sentence as tears rolled over her cheeks. 'I had to tell them we... I... I couldn't save him. Now Sharp and I have tasked Gavin with locating the rest of the illegal firearms.' She tore her fingers through her hair and turned away from the window. 'I've willingly endangered another member of my team.'

'No, you haven't.' Adam wagged his finger, his eyes stern. 'He's got support, he's got experience, and he's got you. Gavin's learned not to go rushing off into a dangerous situation without back-up.'

'Kyle and Phillip did.'

'They didn't know Roman was holding Patricia hostage, did they? And you didn't know that when you asked them to go there. Sharp told me. Roman already had a gun pointing at them by the time you found out and tried to reach them on the radio.' He gently tilted up her chin. 'You've told your team enough times not to do this to themselves, so why are you?'

'Why am I what?'

'Playing "what if?" and questioning every decision you've made this past week.' He didn't wait for an answer, and kissed her nose instead. 'Stop it.'

Her lip wobbled, and she sniffed in reply.

'Come on. Let's get you out of here.' Adam gently prised the glass from her fingers. 'Can't have you turning into a trope, can we?'

She snorted. 'I've had two small sips.'

'And I've got a decent Tempranillo open at home. Much better for the soul.'

'Is that right?' Despite her sadness, she smiled.

'Yes.' He looped his arm through hers, leading her out of the office and over to her desk before plucking her jacket from the back of her chair while she collected her bag. 'And besides, I'm sure Phillip wouldn't want you moping around here. He'd want you to take a moment to reflect on the fact you got your man, and that he'll be going away for a long time.'

Kay's throat constricted. 'He would, yeah.'

They walked towards the door, and she reached out for the light switch, her gaze resting on Phillip's empty chair once more.

There would be an enquiry in the coming weeks, and time for further reflection, but for now, she knew Adam was right.

'I'm going to miss you, Phillip,' she whispered, then leaned into Adam's embrace and closed the door.

THE END

THE END

ABOUT THE AUTHOR

Rachel Amphlett is a USA Today bestselling author of crime fiction and spy thrillers, many of which have been translated worldwide.

Her novels are available in eBook, print, and audiobook formats from libraries and retailers as well as her website shop.

A keen traveller and accidental private investigator, Rachel has both Australian and British citizenship.

Find out more about Rachel's books at: www.rachelamphlett.com.

Lightning Source UK Ltd.
Milton Keynes UK
UKHW041710150223
416956UK00007B/186